PRAISE FOR LINDSEY J. PALMER

Salt Sisters

"A masterpiece. Deeply emotional, tautly written, and completely believable, *Salt Sisters* is the best book I've read in a long time."
—Kristan Higgins, *New York Times* bestselling author

"Palmer perfectly captures the beauty and pain of a fraught relationship between twin sisters, both longing for the other's love and understanding, both finding it so hard to give."
—Susan Rieger, author of *Like Mother, Like Mother*

"Lindsey J. Palmer's *Salt Sisters* captures the beauty and complexity of family and motherhood. When Jocelyn and Maddy Marx reunite on idyllic Cape Cod, they must confront their painful past and shattered bond. Told in Palmer's emotionally layered prose, the characters wade through the slow tide of grief, forgiveness, and eventual healing. A heartfelt testament to the endurance and extraordinary power of sisterhood."
—Rochelle Weinstein, bestselling author of *We Are Made of Stars*

"I was immediately drawn into the story of Jocelyn and Maddy—twin sisters whose journeys through motherhood drive them apart and, ultimately, bring them back together with grace and understanding. Authentic, heartfelt, and deeply relatable, *Salt Sisters* is book club fiction at its best."
—Christine Nolfi, bestselling author of *The Museum of Lost Dreams*

"It's often said that it's impossible to know what's really going on in someone else's marriage, but you can get deliciously close in *Reservations for Six*, Lindsey Palmer's smart, compelling, and completely believable novel. Palmer portrays these marriages with great wisdom and empathy—and well-placed shots of anger and humor. I thoroughly enjoyed spending time with this ensemble of intelligent, well-meaning, and often confused friends as they struggled to know when to compromise and when to dare change."

—Karen Dukess, bestselling author of *Welcome to Murder Week*

Otherwise Engaged

"Palmer sustains a heady level of emotional tension throughout her novel of love and ex-lovers . . . Love, jealousy, and friendship are explored in well-crafted prose . . . This novel is fun and consistently satisfying."

—*Publishers Weekly*

"Combining relationship woes and female friendship, Palmer creates a humorous take on what happens when a woman is scorned. Secondary characters, including Molly's best friends and her sister-in-law, are well developed, and their own storylines give the novel even more depth. Molly's relationship with her type A mother will have readers laughing, as will her inner monologues as she's reading Gabe's novel. An excellent read, best enjoyed with a good glass of wine."

—*Booklist*

"Palmer hits the right tone that is both funny and poignant as she documents Molly's downturn from together fiancée to crazy ex-girlfriend. Perfect for fans of Emily Giffin and Elin Hilderbrand."

—*Library Journal*

"In her fun, zippy new novel, Palmer riffs on fact versus fiction, the strange allure of certain exes, and—compassionately and humorously—the mixed feelings a young woman today may have about marriage."
—Ada Calhoun, bestselling author of *Crush*

"A winning novel about the powerful sway of an ex, reminding us, as Faulkner wrote, 'The past is never dead. It's not even past.' Poignant and funny, with an endearing heroine who thinks of herself as steady and predictable but who is really a mash of churning emotions about almost everyone and everything in her life."
—Susan Rieger, author of *Like Mother, Like Mother*

If We Lived Here

"*If We Lived Here* is the sweet, surprising story of a couple forced to weather all sorts of storms as they try to build a life together. The trials faced by Emma and Nick will be relatable to anyone who has ever taken a chance on love—with all its complications."
—Sarah Pekkanen, #1 bestselling coauthor of *The Golden Couple*

"*If We Lived Here* is a vivid depiction of both the claustrophobia and the potential of love and real estate. It's a heartfelt exploration of what makes a home, and a funny, engaging chronicle of the growing pains of adult life."
—Jen Doll, author of *Save the Date*

Pretty in Ink

"Filled with juicy gossip and outrageous office politics . . . a dishy, catty book that's . . . an indulgent roll in the mud. Palmer writes this side of womanhood brilliantly."
—*Publishers Weekly*

"A lighthearted gambol through the ever-changing world of women's magazine publishing, former magazine editor Palmer's debut contains the authenticity of experience and the salacious story snippets fans of *The Devil Wears Prada* will appreciate . . . With different chapters devoted to different POVs, the politics of the magazine industry find full display in this deliciously delectable read."

—*Booklist*

"*Pretty in Ink* is a lively romp through the halls of a spot-on, believable contemporary women's magazine. Lindsey J. Palmer's hilarious observations are grounded by an inside-baseball understanding of this antic universe. The novel offers sharp commentary on the importance of balancing work and real life. Bottom line: It ain't easy."

—Sally Koslow, former editor-in-chief of *McCall's* magazine and author of *The Real Mrs. Tobias*

SALT
SISTERS

OTHER TITLES BY LINDSEY J. PALMER

Pretty in Ink

If We Lived Here

Otherwise Engaged

Reservations for Six

SALT SISTERS

A Novel

Lindsey J. Palmer

LAKE UNION PUBLISHING

Published by Lake Union Publishing, Seattle

www.apub.com

Amazon, the Amazon logo, and Lake Union Publishing are trademarks of Amazon.com, Inc., or its affiliates.

EU product safety contact:
Amazon Media EU S. à r.l.
38, avenue John F. Kennedy, L-1855 Luxembourg
amazonpublishing-gpsr@amazon.com

ISBN-13: 9781662540257 (paperback)
ISBN-13: 9781662540264 (digital)

Cover design by Emily Mahon
Cover image: © Raymond Forbes LLC / Stocksy; © Taiga / Shutterstock

Printed in the United States of America

To Juli Breines, whose love of the Cape inspired my own

PROLOGUE

Jocelyn didn't kidnap her sister's baby, although later, people would say that she had. It was her own foot pressing the gas, her own two hands on the steering wheel, no matter that it didn't feel that way. There was the lighthouse, wide swaths of red and white flashing through the fog, growing larger and larger until it was right in front of her. The car swerved around the turn and followed the lip of the land by the sea. The road was abandoned at this time of night. The sliver of moon looked lonely through the mist.

In the rearview mirror, Jocelyn saw that Rose was asleep in the car seat, strapped in and secure. She counted the girl's breaths, shallow and even. She studied her pink cheeks, her button nose, her rosebud mouth. She was a beautiful baby. And she looked so peaceful now that she was safe, here, with Jocelyn.

A peek of beach came into view over the dune. The whoosh of waves sounded gentle—harmless, even—but the ocean was a dark void, swallowed by the night. Jocelyn shuddered at the sight of it.

Again, voice raw, she started up the song about the blackbird and broken wings and learning to fly. How long had she been singing to soothe her niece—an hour, maybe two? It was hard to say.

No one knew where they were. Everyone was probably out searching, panicking, their imaginations running wild about what

Jocelyn was capable of. She pictured her sister's face twisted up in anguish as she called out her daughter's name, in vain. Well, good. This was all Maddy's fault. She'd driven her to this.

Jocelyn felt a twinge in her belly, then glanced to the back seat for reassurance: There was the baby, okay, here, with her, fine.

PART 1

Chapter 1

JOCELYN

Jocelyn was replenishing the bowl of chocolates when she saw her phone screen light up with her sister's name. It was the second time Maddy had called that morning, and for the second time, Jocelyn ignored it, a little guiltily. Why her sister had planned her baby shower here in the hometown she hated was a mystery to Jocelyn.

She turned her attention back to the open house, passing out information folders to the new arrivals. Along with glossy photos of the custom-built house and its two-acre property, she'd included a map of the peninsula, shaped like a flexed arm jutting off the coast of Massachusetts; a star was stamped on what would be the tip of the elbow, as if to signal to potential buyers: *Your future vacation here*. She spent a moment touching up the arrangement of white roses and ivy on the console table. Everyone knew the trick of cinnamon simmering on the stove—they'd be sniffing at the air trying to detect mice rotting in the walls—but flowers could be transformative.

Not that Jocelyn had to work much magic today. These waterfront behemoths pretty much sold themselves. The second-home buyers would present their all-cash offers the moment they glimpsed ocean through floor-to-ceiling windows, already workshopping the name they'd have carved on a placard in an old-timey font: Little Slice of Heaven or Shore Thing.

The total fixer-uppers were easy sells, too, as long as they had good bones. The DIY types would burst in, salivating at the thought of tearing out all that laminate countertop, then revealing the dramatic before-and-after photos on their socials.

The in-between houses were tougher, since they were just regular life, slightly beat-up edges and all. Naturally, Jocelyn had a soft spot for them.

The foyer was bustling now. Jocelyn smiled at a family of four, long and lean like egrets. She welcomed a couple around her age, arms wound around each other, telegraphing sex. They were probably here on a whim, another story to tack on to their beach-and-lobster-roll vacation recap to friends back home in Boston or New York.

Jocelyn wasn't the type to follow people around, pointing out closets and light fixtures, as if they'd never been inside a house before. She answered questions when asked, and otherwise idled. She liked observing the retirees, who always seemed so at ease, their children raised and careers complete, all expectations in the past. She avoided the young families: the moms overloaded with babies and their accessories, the dads reprimanding toddlers to stay off the furniture. If Jocelyn got too close, with the moms especially, she was liable to make eye contact, and then she'd feel a connection, and that would put her in the danger zone—and she was at work, after all.

Just last week at a showing, she'd been stationed at a window watching hummingbirds flit up to the feeders when a gummy arm encircled her leg. She'd looked down to find a small child latched on to her shin. "Sorry," a woman called out, jogging over, her expression more amused than apologetic. "He's such a lovebug. He probably wants to tell you he adores the house." Jocelyn had pasted on a polite smile and simultaneously drifted up and out of her body. It was a deft, well-practiced move. Then the moment passed, and she returned to herself, mother and child gone.

◆ ◆ ◆

Peeling off the rotary to Eastham in her Subaru Forester, Jocelyn eyed the voicemail icon on her phone. She didn't have to play the message to know it would be Maddy scolding her in a chipper tone for not yet being in touch. Jocelyn fluttered her lips, then dictated a text: Hey, I had a showing. What's up? Anticipating Maddy's question, she added, I'm picking up the balloons on my way.

The reply came in an instant: I was hoping we could hang out before. I'm at Mom and Dad's.

Jocelyn dictated back, Sorry, I still have to get ready. I'll see you there. She considered adding that she was looking forward to it—she knew she should. Instead, she dictated, I hope you're excited! It was the best she could do.

Back home, in her two-bedroom cottage by the bay, Jocelyn swiped away Maddy's kissy-face emoji and dashed off a note to her clients that the morning had gone well. By the time she exited the shower, her fingers were prunes and she had just five minutes before she had to leave. The dress code was "festive chic" or "smart casual"—Jocelyn couldn't remember exactly. She put on the first thing she pulled from her closet, a batik maxi dress, then slipped on espadrille wedges, gathered her damp hair into a French twist, and scrutinized herself in the mirror. She hoped her nerves wouldn't be noticeable.

The baby shower was at the Wagansett, the premier country club in Chatham, a town Maddy had always favored over their own; Chatham was upscale and preppy, Eastham salt of the earth. The club's entrance was an arch wrapped in climbing roses and clematis, and after making it safely through with her bunch of pink balloons, Jocelyn steeled herself against a Corinthian column. She craved a cigarette, though she'd quit years ago.

"Phew, you're not even inside yet. I thought I was late." It was Betsy, thank god.

Betsy's family had moved in next door to the Marxes the summer before the girls all started kindergarten, and she and Jocelyn had been best friends ever since. These days Betsy and her wife ran the Blushing

Buoy, a fried-fish joint up by Marconi Beach in Wellfleet. They lived in a classic Cape behind the restaurant, along with their two golden retrievers and three fat guinea pigs.

"I didn't know you were coming today," Jocelyn said, squeezing her friend hello.

"Believe me, I'm surprised Madam Maddy deigned to extend me an invite." Betsy's eyes twinkled mischievously. "Of course, I'm very happy for her."

"Of course." Jocelyn attempted a smile.

"Well, let's get this over with, shall we?" Betsy hooked an arm through Jocelyn's. "You'll be fine, I promise."

Inside, Betsy went in search of the bar, while Jocelyn spotted her sister and observed her from across the room. Maddy was teetering in stilettos, in a little black dress she might've worn to any number of Manhattan cocktail parties, only with ruched siding to accommodate her new figure. Her dark hair fell in her signature bob, straight-ironed into compliance. Maddy couldn't be described as beautiful, but she was always well put together. Jocelyn had lighter hair, and she was softer and rounder, too. No one had ever mistaken the two of them as identical. Even now Maddy was the kind of pregnant woman who looked like she'd swallowed a basketball, limbs slender as ever. According to old wives' tales, that meant she'd be having a boy. Jocelyn wished Maddy were having a boy.

When she approached, belly first, exclaiming, "Hey, twin!" Jocelyn told herself she could do this; she could be there for her sister.

"Hi, Mad. It's good to see you. You look good."

Maddy narrowed her eyes. "I'm bloated, and my ass is the size of Nantucket. Fourteen more weeks, then someone's getting evicted." She wagged a finger at her stomach.

"Um, where should I put the balloons?"

"Just add them to the others." Maddy pointed to a lavish array in the corner, each of the dozens of lilac orbs stamped with cursive lettering: "Mama Maddy, est. 9.8.18."

"Cool, will do." Jocelyn unloaded her own inferior bunch, then loitered along the wall, observing the clusters of women in shades of pastel, hair styled into beachy waves.

"Hiding already?" It was Betsy, holding out two beverages. "Pick your poison: Mama Spritzer or Baby Girl Greyhound."

Jocelyn grabbed the less neon one and took a sip. It was too sweet and, disappointingly, a mocktail. Without missing a beat, Betsy produced a flask and topped it off. They clinked glasses. "Cheers to . . ." Jocelyn trailed off.

"Getting through the afternoon," Betsy finished.

"Amen."

Jocelyn caught a whiff of jasmine shampoo, the most comforting of scents, as her mother appeared at her side. "There you girls are." Claire handed them each a stack of bingo cards. "I need your help handing these out." Jocelyn's mother was a firm believer in the virtue of keeping busy.

Betsy saluted Claire, then jumped right in, explaining to a group of women, "If you hear someone say a phrase on your card, mark off the box. Get a whole row and you win."

Jocelyn tagged along, mumbling, "I feel like people know how to play bingo."

"Adorable!" a woman exclaimed, then dictated the contents of her card: "Sleep training, birth plan, push present."

"What's a push present?" Betsy asked.

"A gift you get for giving birth," the woman replied.

"As in, the baby?" Jocelyn asked.

"You're funny," the woman said, in lieu of laughing. "Maddy asked Justin for diamond studs—nothing dangly, so the baby won't paw at them. They're exquisite."

Betsy nodded. "I bet."

Jocelyn remembered the earrings she'd brought for her mother. "Excuse me."

Claire was chatting with her colleague from the school: "She's already interviewing nannies for after her maternity leave. Apparently they'll do laundry and make dinner, too."

"Where can I get myself one of these nannies?"

"Mom, here." Jocelyn affixed the earrings to her mother's lobes, then stepped back to admire them; the emeralds brought out the flecks of green in her eyes. "Perfect."

"Thanks, Cricket," Claire said.

"So how much longer is this thing?"

Claire tilted her head in pity—they'd been there only half an hour. "Why don't you stand over by the advice book and ask guests to sign? Or go mingle with Maddy's friends, if you prefer." She waggled her eyebrows teasingly.

Jocelyn sighed. Fine, she would go check out the advice book. It was an oversize pink Moleskine, cover customized with "tips for raising our sweet baby girl" in gold calligraphy. Jocelyn picked up the pen and held it suspended until it grew heavy in her hand. She put it back down.

She spotted Betsy striding toward the exit with her phone pressed to her ear, gesturing wildly. It was probably the restaurant.

Jocelyn meandered to the buffet. She was spearing a cube of Gouda when her sister's voice rose above the din: "September eighth. Given my luck, it'll be a terrible heat wave." Jocelyn happened to know that Maddy loved the heat, but Maddy often said things just to say them; she considered herself a conversationalist.

"Your mother must be beside herself," someone said. "Her first grandchild!"

Jocelyn felt like she'd been punched in the gut. She stood very still, waiting, she realized, to hear how Maddy would respond.

"She's very excited," Maddy said.

Jocelyn could feel her sister's eyes on her; she probably wore a pleading expression—because, really, what was she supposed to have said? But Jocelyn couldn't bring herself to return her gaze.

She knew she couldn't leave. But she could give herself a little break, pressing up against the picture window and peering out at the water. The beach was empty. This club was the kind of place where guests liked the idea of the ocean but didn't actually want to encounter seaweed or sea creatures, preferring the heated pools with swim-up bars. It looked like the ocean was having a tantrum—the waves wild, whipping hard against the shore before exploding into spray. Jocelyn empathized.

Her mother sidled up beside her. "Maddy's opening gifts, and then you're home free. And listen, I'll tell her no if you want, but she asked if you'd collect the ribbons to make the bouquet."

"The bouquet?"

"Think of it like found art." Claire squeezed her hand. "You can do really creative stuff with ribbons."

"Mom, must you always find the bright side?"

"Alas, 'tis my fate," Claire said with a simper.

Maddy sat on a veritable throne at the front of the room, surrounded by shiny packages. After ripping open each one, she cooed or gasped, as if she hadn't painstakingly picked it all out herself for the registry. There were receptacles to transport and soothe the baby, trinkets to stimulate and entertain her, and a panoply of products to return Maddy to her prepregnancy self. Jocelyn hadn't realized until this morning that her only wrapping paper was Hanukkah themed, and Maddy seemed to know that she was grabbing her sister's present.

Her flicker of disappointment would've registered only to someone who knew her well, the way her lip curled up to reveal half a dimple. It happened when she realized the gift was a wipe warmer, the only item left on the registry aside from a thousand-dollar stroller by the time Jocelyn had logged on.

"Thanks, Joss," Maddy said, not quite making eye contact. Jocelyn's gift wrap hadn't included a ribbon, so she stood there with nothing to do with her hands. She remembered how Maddy had made a big stink back at her wedding shower about guests who dared to gift off registry. You just couldn't win with her. And look how she couldn't hide her snicker when she opened Betsy's gift, a hand-knit baby sweater, bright fuchsia with big yellow flowers. In fact, she made eyes at Jocelyn, who widened her own eyes back, because the sweater really was ugly. Luckily Betsy was still outside. Maddy dropped the sweater among the wrapping detritus, and Jocelyn chortled; her sister was such a bitch.

Maddy saved her parents' gift for last: a shoebox wrapped in Claire's signature butcher paper printed with star fruit and cucumber rounds. Jocelyn braced herself for what she knew was inside.

"Of course," squealed Maddy, handling the white muslin dress with the Peter Pan collar, edged with embroidered forsythia. "It's so precious."

Every baby girl in the family got one, hand-stitched by Claire. There was a whole album of Jocelyn and Maddy as chubby infants in theirs—and a different set of photos that Jocelyn couldn't bear to look at. The sight of the dress flooded her with sense memories: the texture of the flowers under her thumbs, the intermingling scents of milk and talcum powder. Only when one of Maddy's friends gently took the ribbon bouquet from her clutch did Jocelyn realize she'd been crushing it.

"It's so much stuff for such a little person, right?" the woman remarked. "It seems ridiculous, but every new mom gives in and gets it all. I know I did. We're all just so scared, we figure if there's some magic something we can buy to help keep our baby alive, we have to have it, you know?"

Jocelyn didn't respond. She was watching Maddy pose with the stupid ribbon bouquet, feeling her own reserves of keep-it-together-ness running out, when the woman added, "So, do you have kids?"

It always happened this way. The air turned solid, impossible to ingest. Jocelyn nearly stumbled under the weight of it. Then she was sinking, no floor beneath her feet, the near decade since that time erased, and she was back there, back in it. When the loss bloomed big in her chest, she didn't fight it; in a way, she welcomed it. She felt ashamed that she didn't live like this always. Because she had, for a time, and it was painful to realize how it had faded. Sometimes she felt like doing anything besides steeping herself in grief was a betrayal to her daughter. She closed her eyes and pictured Juniper skittering down the shore, chasing plovers. She'd just learned to walk and was already running, that wide-eyed look on her face like, *Can you believe this, Mama?* No, Jocelyn couldn't believe it—not then, not now.

The clink of a fork against a glass jolted her back to the room. The woman was gone.

Maddy was calling for everyone's attention and beckoning for Justin, who must've just arrived. "My hubby and I have some news," she announced. She was totally in her element, beaming in the spotlight, surrounded by presents and fanfare all in her honor, supportive husband at her side. "We're moving to the Cape! I'm coming back home!"

There were cheers and claps and gasps. Jocelyn had to remind herself to breathe. When she saw her mother perform a little skip as she raced to embrace Maddy, Jocelyn decided she'd had enough. She'd tried—she really had. She eyed the mountain of gifts, swiped a fuzzy sheep, and chucked it in the trash on her way out. The last she heard of the event was the stuffed animal's low, whining "Baaah."

Chapter 2

MADDY

"Your announcement surprised me." Justin was rubbing lavender oil into Maddy's feet, which she appreciated, technically, but his touch felt too much like a tickle.

"It just seemed like the right moment," she said.

"You know I'm game," he added, "but I didn't think you'd decided yet."

"Well, I decided today." Maddy was antsy. "Should we go down to the beach for sunset?"

"It's been a big day. Let's just take it easy, okay?" Justin gave her *that look*—the furrowed-brow one implying she was fragile, which she'd become all too familiar with through two years of doctors' appointments about her dysfunctional uterus.

Still, she wasn't in the mood to fight. "Fine."

Justin squeezed her foot—finally, enough pressure. "How about room service?"

They were treating themselves to a night at the Wagansett—a suite, although one that faced the garden rather than the ocean—and tomorrow they'd drive up to Truro for a babymoon in one of those adorable seaside cottages.

"Order me everything," Maddy said, suddenly ravenous.

As they ate, Maddy shared moments from the shower: how when someone mentioned Kegels, Audrey, mother of three, had declared "Bingo!" and then announced that she'd just peed a little because, duh, not enough Kegels; how Claire's kooky friends had cornered Maddy to share their archaic beliefs about child-rearing; and how Maddy's sister had left without saying goodbye.

"I get that today was hard for her," Maddy said. "I just wish she could at least pretend to be happy for me."

"Babe," Justin said gently, "even setting aside her history, Jocelyn isn't exactly a baby shower kind of person."

"No shit. Do you know what she gave me? The freaking wipe warmer. Could she send a clearer message about how ridiculous she found the whole event?"

"To be fair, I've told you I think wipe warmers are kind of ridiculous, too."

Maddy felt her voice rising. "An infant's skin is warm, and the wipes are cold. It's as simple as that."

"You're right," Justin said. "The wipe warmer is essential. So it's a good thing Jocelyn got it for you. What a thoughtful sister." He was smirking—her very handsome husband—and it calmed Maddy down a notch.

"The bottom line is, I've been making every effort to spend time with her this weekend, and she's completely blown me off."

"Oh, babe, try to cut her some slack." Justin worked his fingers on his phone. "There. I invited your family to breakfast tomorrow." Not a moment later, his phone pinged. "Jocelyn's in. Great."

Maddy rolled her eyes. "I guess *you* have to be the one asking. God forbid she give her own sister the satisfaction."

"That's part of the idea of moving out here, to repair all this, right?" Justin waved his arms around to signify all the years of Maddy's troubled relationship with her twin.

"Sure, yeah."

At least, that was how Justin had pitched it to her: the importance of family now that they were starting one of their own. Which Maddy believed, she really did. But she'd always had so little in common with her sister: Maddy was practical and ambitious, whereas Jocelyn was a dreamer and a little lazy. Things had first really gone off the rails in high school. There was that awful incident with the guy Maddy had such a crush on, and even after he spread a humiliating rumor about her, Jocelyn had stayed friends with him. Maddy remembered seeing the two of them joking around in the cafeteria a few days later; she'd dumped her tray, fled the building, and sprinted down to the beach, where she barfed up her sandwich onto the sand. After that, she declared herself done with her sister. She swore off boys and doubled down on academics and extracurriculars (debate team and varsity tennis), while Jocelyn kept floating through school, more focused on what happened after class than during it.

Ironically, both sisters had ended up in the same college town. Maddy had worked her ass off to secure early admission to Amherst College, and then Jocelyn mentioned almost as an aside that she'd be attending UMass Amherst, the only school she'd applied to. The sisters' freshman dorms were less than two miles apart, and they ran into each other far more frequently than Maddy would've liked. Until Jocelyn returned home halfway through their junior year—and then, well . . . the thought of that was a dark pit, and Maddy backed away quickly.

But that was all so long ago, and now Maddy was having a baby. Everyone said it took a village, and like it or not, her village was here. Plus, Maddy did occasionally pine for the sand between her toes as she pounded the Manhattan pavement. There were some half-decent reasons to move back to the Cape.

Including the main one: money. She and Justin couldn't afford their life in the city anymore, not since Maddy had been fired from her job, and she felt physically ill at the prospect of finding new work in her field. Still, there were plenty of other places to live, almost all of them cheaper than New York, but Maddy admitted the Cape had a pull on her.

"So we're really doing this?" Justin asked.

"I guess so." Maddy's heartbeat quickened.

"I'm sort of nervous." Justin had grown up in Westchester, attended Columbia and NYU Law, and lived in the city ever since—a quintessential New Yorker. But Maddy knew he dreamed of learning to surf and fish, and of outfitting a camper to spend weekends on the Outer Beach. "If there's anyone I'd upend my life with, it's you, babe."

"Same." Maddy leaned in for a kiss.

As they settled into bed, she thought about how Justin always had a way of grounding her when she started to spin out. In many ways he was her opposite, so relaxed and go with the flow, and the irony didn't escape her that she'd married a guy a lot like her sister. But unlike with Jocelyn, Justin's contrasting qualities complemented Maddy's own. She snuggled up to him and, within a minute, felt the rise and fall of his steady breaths.

But sleep wouldn't find Maddy. Her dinner now seemed to expand inside her, and heartburn raged. Maddy was normally hyper-attuned to her body; she'd spent years toning it to peak athletic performance. But now it was like a foreign object. It was hard to believe that some women loved being pregnant—Jocelyn had felt that way, of course. Maddy, however, couldn't wait to give birth so she could bounce back to her old self and find her freaking abs again.

She was trying to get comfortable in a new position when she felt a kick to the rib cage. Justin marveled whenever he caught her stomach bumping up from a fetus foot or hand, but it made Maddy feel like a freak show. The jolts were painful and provided yet another reminder that her body was no longer her own.

Again, Maddy felt the urge to move. She couldn't take off on a head-clearing sprint—she'd been banned from running since week eighteen, when her obstetrician demanded she take it easy—but she could walk down to the water, like she'd wanted to do earlier.

The night air was humid, but at least there was a breeze, and the cool sand soothed Maddy's swollen feet. You couldn't buy the pleasure of a midnight walk on the beach, not even in a high-end Manhattan spa.

Manhattan. Maddy thought of her home city of the last nine years with deep ambivalence. Everything she'd once loved about it—the people, the hustle, the towering stories of chrome and steel—now pissed her off. It had begun around her first miscarriage, nearly two years ago, which was when Justin first floated the idea of leaving. One more commute spent shoved into some hipster's rank armpit on a packed train; one more attempt to wrest an item out of her closet without sending everything else toppling out; one more of a thousand little indignities that made up a typical day in the city, and Maddy thought she might lose it.

And then, of course, she did. She'd been an account director at Becker-McKay Creative for the past four years and had worked her way up to the position for another five years before that. Everything she'd built—all the companies she'd coaxed to a deal, all the results of her work she'd seen splashed across Times Square billboards and in Super Bowl ads—had fallen away in the course of a single afternoon six weeks ago.

◆ ◆ ◆

The air was dry when Maddy stepped out of the Wagansett the next morning, all yesterday's humidity burned off. She pictured eggs Benedict under a canopied table by the pool, a cabana boy serving them iced lattes. But her mom texted to say they were already on the beach with bagels.

It was low tide, and Maddy spotted her family on blankets a ways down the shore. As they trekked across the sand, Justin shouldering their chairs, Maddy gave herself a silent pep talk to try to keep things breezy.

"What a day," she announced when she reached them, then immediately stepped on a shard of shell and winced.

Jocelyn squinted up at her. "You okay, Mad?"

The nickname had the effect it always did—it made Maddy mad. "I'm fine," she said, shaking out her foot.

Her father stood to hug her, awkwardly accommodating her girth. "So you're moving back home," Jed said. "The whole gang together again, wow. I'm curious. To what do we owe the pleasure?"

"We're all dying to know," Claire added.

Her parents eyed her, waiting, making Maddy feel as if she were under interrogation. What happened to easing into the morning with pleasantries? Jocelyn, meanwhile, was peering up at the sky, and Maddy felt momentarily thankful for her sister's indifference.

"It just felt like time," she said. "Now that we're having a kid and all."

"But what about your jobs?" Jed asked. He patted Justin on the back. "Are you planning on taking up landscaping, son?"

Maddy bristled at the joke—it was common knowledge that Justin wasn't the handy type. "Justin will keep his job, just work remotely," she said. Her husband was a lawyer for a nonprofit. He'd left a prestigious law firm job around the time they'd started trying to get pregnant. The drastic salary cut was supposed to have been mitigated by better hours, but Justin still often worked around the clock.

"I'll go back to the city now and then for meetings," he added.

"And you, dear?" Claire asked Maddy.

Maddy lowered herself clumsily into a beach chair. "Well, with the baby coming, I figured it was time to take a break."

"A break?" Her mother's voice spiked in pitch. "As in, you're quitting?"

Maddy didn't deny the point.

"You, the world's top go-getter," Jed added, "leaving your job?"

"Yes," she said, teeth clenched.

This got Jocelyn's attention. All three of them stared at her slack-jawed, like, could she possibly be the Maddy Marx they knew? It made her furious, a familiar feeling.

"I'm looking forward to being a full-time mom," she said.

Jocelyn laughed. "Forgive me, Mad, but I just don't see it."

Maddy shot Justin a look, like, *Please back me up here.*

"Maddy has always been very successful in her career," he said diplomatically, "but she's ready for something new. I, for one, am excited for the change, and I hope all of you will support her, too." He took Maddy's hand.

"Of course we'll support you," Claire said. "We're just surprised, is all."

Jed piped up: "Hey, Joss can find you a house."

Claire added quickly, "I'm sure there's still a lot to be figured out."

"Right," Maddy said. She addressed Jocelyn: "I wouldn't want to put you in an awkward position, the two of us driving you up the wall with our picky preferences."

"That makes sense." Jocelyn's tone was unreadable. "I can recommend a colleague, if you want."

"Excellent," said Justin. "Someone who won't resent the invasion of us washashores."

"Washashore" was the disparaging term the locals used for out-of-town transplants. Maddy found it odd how no one pointed out that *she* actually wasn't a washashore.

"Well, this'll be great," said Jed. "Jocelyn and Madelyn, together again."

Being called her given name annoyed Maddy almost as much as being called Mad. She'd always been embarrassed by her and her sister's matchy-matchy names; by kindergarten, she'd ditched Madelyn for "Maddy." Her dad's wistful tone irked her, too. Throughout their lives, Jed had suggested that if only the sisters spent more time together, they'd be the best of friends. It was a nice fantasy, Maddy supposed.

She didn't register the greenhead fly until the sting exploded from her right calf. "Fuck!"

"Maddy!" Claire chided.

"Isn't it too early in the season for goddamn greenheads?" she barked.

Jocelyn coughed out a laugh, and Claire rolled her eyes.

"Can I help?" Justin asked, but Maddy waved him off. After a greenhead bite, there was nothing to do but wait out the pain.

"Look, they have cornhole," Jocelyn said, pointing near the tennis court. "Wanna play?"

"Why not?" Maddy said. "It'll be fun to kick your ass."

"I mean, you're a little out of practice."

"Excuse me, you're talking to the Cornhole Champion of Windmill Weekend."

"From like 2003."

"Whatever," Maddy said. Talking shit with her sister had brightened her mood.

The weight of the beanbag in her hand brought back a rush of teenage memories: parties on the beach, summer evenings yawning into night, and Maddy's own cornhole skills sharpening with practice as the steady stream of beers made everyone else's game suffer. She'd never been much of a drinker, especially in high school. She'd made a point to stay vigilant, keeping a nervous eye on her twin, who was liable to end up over by the dunes with whatever guy, always so reckless. Even the thought of sand near her private parts made Maddy squirm.

This time she spotted the fly before it bit. "Sadist prick," she spat, smacking at her thigh with the beanbag. "You know, in all those breathless write-ups about the wonders of Cape Cod, no one ever mentions these little fuckers."

"People don't usually talk about the bad stuff," Jocelyn said.

"I guess not."

Maddy's next toss landed right in the hole. "Ha, beat that."

Her sister's lob limped toward its target, but made it in, too. "Ta-da!"

The two of them scored shot after shot.

"This kind of isn't even fun," Maddy said, the closest she'd come to admitting that Jocelyn's game was as strong as her own. But then she missed one, and her sister sank hers.

"Victory!" Jocelyn declared, taking a bow. Maddy congratulated her through gritted teeth.

"It's just a game, Mad," Jocelyn said. "You know it's okay not to win all the time."

Maddy's laugh came out sounding funny; even she couldn't tell if it was sarcastic or sincere. Then the men wanted a turn, so the sisters ceded the court.

Jocelyn indicated Maddy's shoulder. "You're burning." She tossed her a tube of sunscreen.

"Apparently I'm out of practice with beach bumming, too."

Jocelyn shrugged. "It's like riding a bike."

Maddy felt a modicum of warmth toward her sister. "By the way, thanks for coming yesterday." She hoped Jocelyn would intuit the empathy beneath her words—that she understood this wasn't easy for her. "I invited Betsy for you, you know."

"Thanks, I guess," Jocelyn said. "I thought it was nice that you'd invited her, for you—that you'd reached out to at least one of your old friends." The comment rankled Maddy; why did Jocelyn care who she kept in touch with? "I've gotta say, Mad, I thought you couldn't stand it here. You certainly act that way when you visit, like you can't wait to get the hell off Cape and back to your real life."

"My real life," Maddy mumbled. "What's that?"

"What?"

"Nothing, never mind." Maddy studied her sister. "You've never felt defined by your job, have you?"

"Nope," Jocelyn said, "which I realize you don't get."

"Well, I'm starting to wish I did." She hesitated, then said, "Look, I know you're wary of me moving back." Maddy wanted to confess that she, too, was wary—and more than that, that she hoped Jocelyn would help her with the transition, and that the two of them might have a do-over. But a blockage formed in her throat. "Anyway, now we can compete again at Windmill Weekend. It's time for a Marx-sister comeback, right?"

"Sure, Mad," Jocelyn said, but her tone was unconvincing.

Chapter 3

JOCELYN

Everything had been all mixed up since Maddy's baby shower, including this house, a custom architect job with trapezoidal windows and a narrow spiral staircase that Jocelyn now discovered led to a closet, because of course it did. She called down to her clients that it wasn't worth the climb.

"Funky, right?" quipped the seller's Realtor, a slick wheeler-dealer type named Chad.

"That's one word for it," Jocelyn muttered, undertaking the descent.

Chad tapped his pinkie ring against the mantel. "By the way, my new client is someone you know." He paused long enough for sweat to collect at Jocelyn's hairline. "Your sister."

"Oh. I think she might've mentioned that." She had not.

"She's a spitfire. Her and her husband, real city mice."

"Uh-huh." Jocelyn wasn't interested in Chad's commentary about Maddy. She ushered her clients out and wished Chad the best of luck with this gem. He just laughed.

Back in her car, Jocelyn texted Betsy: Meet me at the secret beach?

As she waited for a reply, she turned over the property's listing papers so she wouldn't have to see Chad's fluorescent smile. Hopefully she wouldn't cross paths with him again during Maddy's house hunt. She guessed her sister would be drawn to those total renos that all looked blandly the same. Like her apartment in New York, where everything was ivory and greige—"clean design," she'd called it while touring Jocelyn and her parents around when they were in town for her wedding. The apartment was on the fortieth floor of a luxury building on the Upper East Side; Jocelyn's ears had popped on the elevator ride up. Jed got woozy looking out the window, and when Claire asked for a glass of water, Maddy interpreted that to mean Perrier, which Claire politely set down on a coaster and left untouched.

Jocelyn's phone buzzed with a text: SUP girlie! Meet you in an hour. Already her sour mood was dissipating. She swung home to load her stand-up paddleboard onto her roof rack, then continued on to Cod Coffee, the town's best source of caffeine.

Francisco greeted her from behind the register, filling a cup with dark roast before Jocelyn said a word. "How's my girl?"

"Busy busy."

"'Tis the season." Francisco had a line out the door June through September. Today Jocelyn got lucky, snagging one of the three stools at the counter. The next customer ordered a matcha latte and a cold brew with oat milk. Watching her former boss bustle around by the espresso machine, Jocelyn fought the urge to pitch in, even though she knew she wouldn't be much help. Back when she'd worked here, the menu was drip coffee, blueberry muffins, and glazed doughnuts, period.

Although her memory from that time was admittedly hazy. Her head had been clouded by the euphoria of new motherhood, that strange mix of sleeplessness and bliss. She'd started frequenting the little café when Juniper was only a couple of weeks old, just to get out of the house. She'd order a large dark roast, then sit at the counter playing with Junie's tiny toes and basking in the compliments of other customers. She hadn't been thinking of a job—she was living with her parents, who were covering her expenses—but as summer approached, Francisco asked whether she wanted to pick up a few shifts. He knew by then that Junie was an easygoing baby. Jocelyn could stash her in a bouncer and take breaks for feedings. Sold.

She'd loved the job. It kept her busy and made her feel useful; plus, she didn't have to give up time with her baby. Except occasionally one of her old classmates would drop in, home from college, and they'd look startled to find Jocelyn at the register, sometimes with Junie strapped to her chest. It knocked her off kilter, seeing what an oddity she was to her peers. Still, she didn't acknowledge their pity. If anything, she pitied them their ordinary lives and savored her own luck at having Junie, the perfect little companion. Working at Cod Coffee had been an ideal arrangement.

Jocelyn waved bye to Francisco, who was serving gluten-free scones to a pair in biking spandex. Getting to the secret beach required a dizzying number of turns through the backwoods of Wellfleet, throwing off even the savviest of summer people. Unlike so many locals, Jocelyn didn't mind the annual influx of tourists—they made up so much of her business, after all—but she also sought out quieter spots to stay sane through peak season. She pulled into the little lot, unloaded her paddleboard, and then followed the snaking path through the marsh grass to the beach. The day was balmy, the sky cornflower blue. She paddled out to Betsy, who greeted her with a booming rendition of the *Jaws* theme song, jabbing Jocelyn's board with her paddle.

"Help, shark attack," Jocelyn said half-heartedly.

"Just keeping you on your toes." Betsy nodded to a nearby seal. A colony of them could mean a shark was close. But even with the uptick of great whites in recent years, and their periodic encounters with humans, Jocelyn wasn't worried. In her experience, the scary stuff in life rarely turned out to be the things people were conditioned to fear. She thought sharks were beautiful creatures.

It was pleasantly hypnotic to slice the paddle again and again through the rippling water. They hit a calm spot and lay back on their boards. The sun shone strong on Jocelyn's cheeks. She slathered on SPF like everyone else these days but still believed sunshine was the best medicine. Betsy, on the other hand, had her wide-brimmed hat pulled low; she remained pasty all summer, and not just because she practically lived at the restaurant.

"If only we could fast-forward to fall," said Betsy, "when I'll finally get some peace and quiet."

"Speak for yourself. Maddy plans to move here in September."

Betsy sat up. "That's actually happening?"

"Supposedly," said Jocelyn. "She hired this slimy Realtor named Chad." She didn't admit that she was a little hurt Maddy hadn't let her refer someone, as she'd said she would.

"Well," Betsy said, "you could always come to Costa Rica with Jewel and me." After running the Blushing Buoy through shoulder season, Betsy and her wife always skipped off to some warm-weather destination for an extended vacation.

"I wish."

"Why do you think she's doing it?" Betsy asked.

Jocelyn shrugged. "The pregnancy's freaking her out. She's used to being in control of everything, and now she's staring down the great unknown. So, naturally, she's upending her whole life." Despite her flippancy, Jocelyn felt a pang of sympathy for her sister.

"Well, wherever you go, there you are."

"Try telling Maddy that—she's won medals for running as fast as she can."

"And how are you doing with the pregnancy?" Betsy asked.

"Oh, I don't know," Jocelyn said. "I'm trying to focus on all the differences. Like, with mine, I wasn't scared. Even though it was a surprise, it was the best kind."

"Do you remember when you called me?"

Jocelyn beamed. "Of course. You were the first person I told."

"I was in my catering and special events class." Betsy had attended the hotel management school at Cornell. "Talk about a special event! I thought you were bonkers to want to have a baby, but you were so giddy, it was contagious."

Jocelyn had also been in class when she felt the shift in her body, like the floor beneath her had tilted a few degrees. The suspicion had been building for several days, and at that moment she knew. She bought a test, then called Betsy. Unlike Luke, who would go ghostly pale when she told him, then offer to pay to take care of it, Betsy shared in Jocelyn's excitement, happy to listen to all her fantasies of what it would be like to have a child.

"I just can't see Maddy as a mom," Jocelyn said. "I mean, what'll she do when spit-up ruins her outfit? Or when she plans some detailed agenda and her baby's like, nope, no sirree, not happening?" She was going for laughs, but Betsy just gave a pensive nod. Jocelyn knew it was easier to make digs at Maddy than admit the truth: It wasn't that she couldn't see her sister as a mom; it was that she worried she couldn't bear to.

They'd drifted to the next beach, and the current had turned, so paddling back required muscular strokes. By the time they spotted their towels, Jocelyn had sweated through her shirt.

"I know all this Maddy stuff brings up a lot for you," Betsy said. "But I hope you remember you deserve to be happy."

Betsy said a version of this to Jocelyn so often that the words had basically lost their meaning—except to reassure her that her friend had her back. "Thanks, Bets."

Chapter 4

MADDY

"Here's to our little pineapples!" Maddy said, and the women clinked their seltzers, toasting to the size of their thirty-five-week fetuses.

Maddy loved everything about her pregnancy group. She loved debating the merits of different strollers and cribs. She loved how their bellies attracted so much attention. She loved the narrative arc of their weekly meetings, how they were all building to the same finale: all six of them due in early September. She especially loved the juice bar's acai bowls—today's was granola with pineapple, coconut, and honey; heavenly—even though she knew she shouldn't be spending fifteen dollars on a glorified bowl of fruit.

They were talking maternity leave. "People say taking care of an infant is a full-time job," said Callie, an attorney, "but when I try to picture what I'll be doing all day, my mind draws a blank."

"And what'll happen to our brains?" Ava was an immunology researcher. "I'm planning to do crosswords to keep myself sharp."

"Google gives us six months," said Trish, a data scientist, "but I bet I'll return early. I think I'll start losing it at home; plus, I worry about what I'll miss at the office."

Maddy considered chiming in. She'd thought all these same things, back before her career imploded. But she hadn't shared that here. This was her sacred space, where she could still act like the optimal version of herself. Justin had asked her that morning why she kept attending these meetings, given their impending move, since wasn't the point to make friends for when you all had babies together? She'd replied that she still needed support now. But really, the group let Maddy pretend that things weren't changing—that come fall, she'd join this pack of new moms on maternity leave, everyone in transitional athleisure out for stroller walks in Central Park.

"I don't know, guys," said Caroline, a creative director. "Am I the only one who's looking forward to a break from the grind? I'm excited for the change."

Maddy felt grateful for the sentiment. She'd been willing herself to feel this way, too, to embrace her new circumstances. When Caroline smiled at Maddy, it gave her a burst of courage to speak up: "Speaking of change, my husband and I are leaving the city. We're moving to Cape Cod, where I grew up."

Everyone exclaimed: saying it was amazing, calling her brave, expressing envy over her future yard and storage space. Maddy basked in the validation.

It was Callie, the attorney, who cut through the positive feedback to ask, "And what about work?" The question was posed gently, but Maddy still felt the sting.

"Oh yeah, is your firm letting you go remote?" added Trish.

"No, um, I've decided to leave my job."

They all waited, these successful professional women, because surely there was a part two. If she was leaving her job, then what would she be doing instead? The silence probably lasted only a few seconds, but it felt like minutes. Maddy's underarms went damp.

"Well," she said, "there's this start-up that helps small businesses with branding, launched by a couple old friends of mine. They're bringing me on to run their accounts."

"So cool!" said Trish. The others nodded; then the conversation moved on to doulas and night nurses. Maddy shrank in her seat. Where had all that come from? Why had she lied?

When the hour was up, Maddy felt herself saying goodbye for good.

Back home, a text came in from her best friend, Krista, an invite to dinner at an omakase bar at 10:00 p.m. Maddy sighed. Krista was single and childless, and simply didn't get it. Ever since this pregnancy stuck, things had gotten weird between them, and the strain had only worsened after Maddy told Krista she was moving. She'd wanted Krista to be happy for her and to say how much she'd miss her, but her main reaction had been to ask if Maddy was joking. It made Maddy think of that famous John Updike quote: how the true New Yorker believed that anyone living anywhere else had to be, in some sense, kidding. She'd felt a door close on the friendship then, although Krista continued to send passive-aggressive texts disguised as friendly invites.

Maddy was considering how to respond when the daily MLS listings hit her inbox. She clicked the email, and the first house made her breath catch. It was a three-bedroom bungalow in her hometown, in pristine shape and, incredibly, within their price range. Maddy had gotten over the fact that they couldn't afford anything close to the seaside mansions she'd admired as a kid, but this place was just a ten-minute walk to the beach. It looked chic and modern, with chrome appliances and custom window treatments, and the open floor plan made it appear bigger than its fifteen hundred square feet, at least in the photos.

"Did you see Chad's email?" Justin called from the other room. "Should we make an appointment for tomorrow?"

"And battle traffic on a summer Sunday? It'll be at least a six-hour drive."

Justin appeared in the doorway. "Plus, you'll have to stop to pee every hour. But so what? It'll be fun."

Maddy smiled. She adored her husband.

◆ ◆ ◆

The day felt charged with possibility. After the chore of getting out of the city, they flew down the highway, and Maddy's shoulders relaxed; leaving Manhattan always made her realize just how tense she'd been. Justin fiddled with the radio, landing on the Velvet Underground's "Sunday Morning." Maddy sang along, pleased to remember the chorus, and Justin whistled, nailing all the notes.

Maddy had slept fitfully the night before, waking frequently to replay the pregnancy meeting in her mind, and the looks of the other women when she'd said she'd left her job (before she'd invented the phony gig). But here in the car, she directed her attention forward. She and Justin high-fived when they reached the Massachusetts border, and as they crossed the Sagamore Bridge, the unofficial entry to the Cape, Maddy rolled down her window to breathe in the brackish air.

The house was as beautiful as it appeared in the slideshow that she'd scrolled through on repeat during the drive. The lot was nestled at the end of a cul-de-sac, and the property was lush with birch trees and pitch pines—what the listing called "mature plantings." Stretching her legs, Maddy took in the details: the wood facade and shingle siding, tall windows flanked by royal-blue shutters and quaint dormer windows above, a pair of chimneys, and a sweet little front porch. There was even a detached garage with a bonus room upstairs that could be Justin's office. Justin took her hand as they strode up the path—toward their future.

Walking from room to room, Maddy ignored the Realtor's chatter about the boiler and the septic system; she was busy envisioning her life here. Maybe she'd reinvent herself as a woman who woke up not from an alarm with her mind already racing, but naturally at dawn; who drank her coffee—no, green tea—on the porch; a woman who gardened and knew all the varieties of flora; a *mother*. This was a home for a fresh start.

"Give it to me straight, what do you think?" Chad asked. They were huddled out front, canopied by oak trees.

"It's perfect," Justin said.

Maddy squeezed his arm. "It really is."

"Babe, should we do this?"

"We should," Maddy declared. She'd never felt closer to her husband.

"That's what I like to hear," said Chad, pumping a fist.

They settled on a number, 5 percent above asking so their offer would be competitive. Chad insisted on good-luck fist bumps. Then they decided to drive around town, past the old windmill and town hall with its stately columns, and soon they were around the corner from Maddy's childhood home. Feeling upbeat, she suggested they pop by.

Jed answered the door in a UMass sweatshirt, making Maddy wonder if he ever wore apparel from *her* alma mater. His eyebrows shot up. "Did I know you two were coming by? Am I going senile?"

"No, Dad. We were in town to see a house. We're putting in a bid."

"That's great news! Come on in."

They followed the aroma of bacon inside. Jed was fixing himself a BLT—he said he'd make them some, too. Maddy plopped onto the couch. Rusty, her parents' elderly cocker spaniel, settled at her feet, and she rubbed his ears. She asked where her mom was.

"Off setting up her classroom," Jed called from the kitchen.

"Ah." Maddy was privately relieved it was just the three of them. She could picture the slightly baffled expression her mother wore whenever Maddy described something she was excited about—a work win or a sweet bargain she'd scored on a designer dress—which always put a damper on Maddy's enthusiasm; she was glad not to have to deal with that now.

"So let's hear about this dream house," Jed said, carrying a platter of sandwiches to the table. "Does it have walls and floors and support beams?"

"A roof, too, if you can believe it," Justin said.

"Ha ha," Maddy said, appeasing her dad, who she knew didn't care about details like walk-in closets or vaulted ceilings. "It's really lovely," she added, and left it at that.

"And it's just a couple miles away, on Blueberry Lane," Justin said, feeding bits of bacon to Rusty.

Jed's eyes lit up. "That's even closer to Jocelyn. Well, good luck on the offer."

As they ate, Jed cataloged which birds he'd spotted lately, and Maddy let it wash over her like white noise. Throughout her childhood, her dad had worked long hours as an accountant. And when Claire and Jocelyn had buddied up on their latest mother-daughter venture—marring the basement walls with garish murals, belting out show tunes while baking brownies, even getting high together (Maddy suspected though never proved) and knitting scraggly, useless scarves—Maddy would slip into Jed's office to do her homework. It was peaceful in there, and Jed was so focused that an hour might pass before he noticed her. He'd look up from some spreadsheet, startled to see her sprawled out on the daybed, and ask whether she wanted a Coke, even though she never drank soda. Still, Maddy kept coming back, hoping that eventually they'd forge a bond half as strong as her mother and her sister's.

On their way out, Jed finally asked after the baby.

"All's well, Dad. Five more weeks."

"Are you scared?"

Justin looked taken aback—most people asked if they were excited—but Maddy replied, "Obviously."

"Well, you should be. Parenthood is a high-stakes venture. Also, a joy. Especially when you get a two-for-one deal." Jed winked. "Hey, why don't you swing by the school? Jocelyn's there helping Mom."

"We've got a long drive—"

"We'd love to," Justin said, cutting her off.

"Fantastic," Jed said, beaming. Maddy shook her head with a smile, then reached out for a hug.

"Bye, kids." Jed waved them off, adding a little wave to Maddy's belly.

Maddy could imagine Jed as a grandfather, sitting cross-legged on the floor to join in on silly games and pretend play. He hadn't been that kind of dad—he was usually working, a little oblivious to domestic life—but it was how he'd been the first time around as a grandfather, the little she'd seen of it. Maddy was certain she'd excel at certain aspects of motherhood: the teaching of skills and the meal planning, the doctors' appointments and the camp sign-ups, all the work of it. But the part where you got down on your kid's level and entered their world, where you just hung out together, Maddy was nervous about that. Would her daughter even like her? Well, it was good she would have Jed in her life. It was good they were returning home—or so Maddy kept telling herself.

Chapter 5

JOCELYN

When Jocelyn had offered to help her mother set up her classroom, she hadn't realized she'd be assembling bizarro IKEA furniture. Claire told her to follow about half the instructions, then to go rogue, to get kids thinking about form and space. So here was a three-legged table with its fourth leg stuck out sideways, and there a bookshelf with its shelves crowded toward the top. "Excellent," Claire said, examining her work.

Jocelyn went to take a break in the texture nook, nuzzling against a faux-bearskin rug. "Don't you ever get tired of teenagers?" she asked.

"Nope. They're in this swirling state of becoming, perfect for making art. Come help me spray-paint."

In the color corner, Claire arranged plaster animals on a tarp, then started spraying, turning an alligator hot pink, a pig royal blue, a turtle pale yellow. Jocelyn picked neon orange for the pug. The project was so very Claire, who was constantly questioning conventions, searching for a slant. That quality had made her a great mom, Jocelyn thought, although less so for Maddy, who'd always hewed so dutifully to the norm.

"Yoo-hoo, anyone here?"

Speak of the devil—the familiar voice startled Jocelyn. She and Claire swiveled to the doorway, spray cans in hand.

"Don't shoot," Maddy said, hands up, Justin at her side.

"What a nice surprise," Claire said. "We could use some extra help."

"What are you guys doing here?" Jocelyn asked.

"We just saw the most perfect house," Maddy said. "A bungalow on Blueberry Lane."

Jocelyn had seen the listing—she made a mental note to study it more closely later. As her sister gushed, Jocelyn moseyed to the wall of lines, took a Sharpie, and added one line per sentence spoken by Maddy, like an inmate marking her time.

"I can't quite believe we're putting in an offer." Justin's laughter conveyed his nerves.

"It's a big step," Claire said.

"Well, don't get your hopes up," Jocelyn said. "They're probably getting other bids."

Maddy nudged the table with the wonky leg. "What's with all the junk?"

Claire explained about the elements of art—line, shape, space, value, form, texture, and color—and how she was going back to basics for her final year of teaching. Justin asked about value, and Maddy asked about the sanitariness of the texture nook. "You know," she added, "I don't think I've set foot in this building since graduation."

This didn't surprise Jocelyn. "I come to visit Mom here, so it's not really a trip down memory lane for me."

"Show me around, then."

Reluctantly, Jocelyn obliged. In the hallway, Maddy peeked into classrooms and hunted for her old locker.

"Jocelyn, hi." It was Ms. Goodman, the college counselor. She always invited Jocelyn to Career Day, probably to demonstrate how you could get a decent job even after dropping out of college, but Jocelyn didn't mind. "And—holy cow!—is that Maddy Marx?"

"Hey, Ms. Goodman. How's the college advising life?"

"Oh, fine, although none of the students are quite like you. Amherst couldn't resist that perfect GPA! I still hold you up as the exemplar of what can be achieved if you work your tail off."

Jocelyn waited out the lovefest—Ms. Goodman marveling at Maddy's impressive job (which, interestingly, Maddy didn't mention she was leaving).

"What a doll," Maddy said, after they'd parted ways. "This place is frozen in time, huh?"

"Well, they updated the science labs," Jocelyn said, feeling strangely defensive of the school, "and added a pool."

"You really know your stuff. It's like you tour people around buildings for a living." Maddy chuckled at her own joke. "Let's check out the auditorium."

That was somewhere Jocelyn had had no reason to visit since graduating. As the double doors swung open, the scent of sawdust zapped her back in time.

Maddy was already halfway down the center aisle, then climbing onto the stage, where she cleared her throat and seemed to grow six inches. "It's an undeniable truth that the issue of genetically modified foods is of paramount importance to the student body."

Jocelyn laughed a little. Maddy had been the star of their high school debate team, delivering countless speeches from that very spot. For four long years, the family had endured Maddy's practice orations at the dinner table, except when something kept her late at school and the rest of them could eat in peace.

"Get up here, Joss." Bidding on a house had apparently put Maddy in a funny mood.

Jocelyn hesitated, but once she was onstage, the memories hit. Her senior year, she'd auditioned on a dare for the musical *Anything Goes*, and landed the role of Hope. Slipping into character and belting out songs had been transformative, making Jocelyn feel both steady and light as air. She'd only ever recaptured that feeling with Junie. Now the musical's lyrics came rushing back to her, along with the choreography. Performing shuffles and ball changes, she sang about life being delightful and delicious and de-lovely.

Maddy whistled in appreciation. "You were such a star."

Jocelyn stopped, self-conscious. "Not really. But I had fun."

"I bet you did. Didn't you and the male lead enjoy some de-lovely time backstage?"

Jocelyn sighed. "Aidan Sharp, what a dreamboat. We'd sneak back to the props room after practice."

"Until he caught you with someone else, if I recall."

Jocelyn snorted at the memory. "Ezra Woodman—no, Wood*son*. He did the lights. Aidan was outraged, like how could I possibly two-time him with a lowly crew member?" The twins' laughs were indistinguishable.

"You had half the guys in school wrapped around your finger," said Maddy.

"I don't know about that." It was such ancient history, but Jocelyn remembered: those heady afternoons backstage, she and Aidan peeling off each other's costumes, sometimes singing snippets of the show as they fumbled around, their bodies so similar in size and pliability. Then it was something else with Ezra, who was a full head taller than Jocelyn and already had muscles like a man; the way he handled her a little roughly, silent except for an occasional grunt. They would go to his empty house after school—Jocelyn recalled his bedsheets, gritty with sand. Back then, every day felt like an exploration.

"I was just having fun," she said.

"Duh," Maddy said, scrutinizing her. "The other girls were all boy crazy, dreaming of getting married and having their crushes' babies. But you'd get with a guy, then send him off, with zero emotional attachment. It made all of them want you."

Jocelyn hadn't really experienced it that way. She'd found it thrilling to glimpse a boy at his most vulnerable, and she'd been curious about the different ways different boys could be with her, and how she could be different with each of them, too. But she didn't know how to explain that to her sister, so she responded to the other part: "I don't think all the girls were like that, Mad. Maybe your friends."

The two of them had traveled in such different circles: Maddy's clique was so serious, always studying and signing up for all the résumé-boosting activities, while Jocelyn's friends were more serious about socializing than schoolwork (except Betsy, who managed to hang out and still pull straight A's). "You dated that guy Ryan for a minute, didn't you?"

Maddy stiffened. "Ryan Parker was an asshole." Jocelyn waited for more, but Maddy moved on. "Anyway, I was too busy gunning for valedictorian to focus on dating. Plus, I couldn't compete with my sister, who was bedding every boy in sight."

"Whoa. Easy, Mad."

"I just mean, your shadow was long. Speaking of which, how's your love life these days? I haven't heard of any new prospects recently. In years, actually."

It was always like this, whether they were seventeen or thirty-one: Their conversation would be coasting along just fine, until a sudden dig from Maddy soured it. It made Jocelyn regret when she didn't stay vigilant. Part of her wanted to spar with her sister, but she knew the wiser course was to defuse things: "If you must know, Aidan Sharp and I still screw around sometimes in the props room."

Maddy cackled. "So that's why you never left home. You couldn't get enough of Aidan's baby blues." She was bantering, sure, but the edge hadn't left her voice.

Now Jocelyn couldn't resist striking back. "And is this why you're coming back, Mad, to relive your days as a debate champ? Maybe you could start coaching the team, return to your roots, become colleagues with Mom."

Maddy went pale, and Jocelyn felt a bit bad—maybe she'd gone too far.

They were interrupted by the creak of the double doors. "There you are," Justin called out.

"Hey, babe," Maddy replied, back to breezy. "We were just waxing nostalgic about our glory days."

"Nice. Well, your mom's trying to rope me into some papier-mâché project, but we better hit the road if we want to get back home before dark."

"Coming!"

Jocelyn accepted her sister's perfunctory hug, then watched her stride up the aisle and leave with her husband. Left alone, she sighed in relief. She imagined the couple's conversation on the drive home: Maddy raising doubts about the house, Justin suggesting that maybe they keep looking, or that they reconsider the move altogether, then their joint decision to pull the bid. As if the conversation had really happened, Jocelyn felt the bubbling up of a good mood. She performed a pirouette while belting out the chorus to "It's De-Lovely," then curtsied dramatically to the empty theater.

Chapter 6

It always took Maddy a moment upon waking to remember she was pregnant (in her dreams, her stomach was washboard flat), so when she woke up in a puddle, she was mortified, thinking she'd peed herself. Only when Justin rolled into the wet and said, "Oh shit, it's happening," did Maddy realize that, at thirty-eight weeks, her water had just broken.

No contractions, not yet. But still the hospital wanted her there pronto. Maddy felt utterly normal as she showered, repacked her go bag, and then debated whether to flat-iron or curl her hair. It was not the profound experience she thought she should be having in her final hours pre-motherhood. It made her worry, for the millionth time, that maybe she wasn't cut out for this.

They decided to walk the ten blocks to the hospital. It was the special brand of late-summer day when the city was bathed in sunshine, the air just the slightest bit crisp. They stopped at Starbucks, and when Maddy ordered a grande cappuccino and mentioned she was in labor, the barista nodded distractedly and said, "Five fifteen, please." It was such a New York moment, its residents so unshockable, and a wave of grief overtook Maddy. Saying goodbye to her childless self was too big to fathom, but bidding farewell to her city felt specific and real.

"Is it a contraction?" Justin asked, spreading a hand against her lower back.

"No, just a moment of panic about the move."

"Got it. Shall I regale you with the charms of our dream house?" It was their recent version of pillow talk: Justin soothing Maddy to sleep by describing the house that—despite Jocelyn's warning that they might get outbid—they were currently under contract for. The closing was in three weeks, moving day in four.

"Tell me a New York story instead." They were strolling down First Avenue at what Maddy thought of as third-trimester pace.

"Once upon a time, there was this Laundromat on Thirty-Second and Lex."

"Oh, I love this one!" Maddy never tired of recounting their meet-cute.

"I'd waited till the last possible minute to do my laundry, which meant I was wearing my middle-school basketball shirt from 1997."

"And going commando," Maddy added.

"Don't jump ahead—you didn't find out about that until at least five hours later."

"Apologies. Continue." Her smile felt tattooed onto her face.

"I was washing my whites, minding my own business, when I noticed this striking girl by the dryers."

"Woman."

"Sorry, this striking *woman* by the dryers. She had a laptop, and was typing furiously, until she got distracted by a lady folding sheets."

"'Folding' is quite the euphemism," Maddy quipped.

"Hey, who's telling this, you or me?" Justin said. Maddy made the lips-zipped gesture. She was having fun. "So, the striking woman approached the lady and pretty much took over."

"Everyone should know how to fold a fitted sheet," Maddy said.

"Anyway, it took me through the spin cycle to get up the nerve to talk to her. Her reaction? Annoyed."

"I was in the zone. I had to finish a pitch deck."

"So I backed off. Until my own sheets came out of the dryer, at which point I angled myself so she'd have a view. I'd picked up some pointers from her demo, and she had no choice but to compliment my artistry. We started talking. When her load was done, I watched her move colorful, lacy things to the dryer. She noticed and gave me a withering look."

"I wasn't going to let some creep ogle my underwear."

"Well, at least not until a few hours later. I asked if she wanted to get a drink. Her reaction? Another withering look."

"It was eleven a.m."

"I revised my invitation to coffee."

"I indicated my travel mug."

"Hence, we stayed put. When she finished folding, I offered to carry her laundry home."

"But I didn't allow strangers to my residence."

"So I proposed we bring our laundry to our respective residences, then reconvene for a meal."

"You suggested Penelope, my favorite brunch spot. How could I refuse?"

"We ate blueberry pancakes and French toast. You said you were from Cape Cod, but rarely left Manhattan."

Maddy could hear herself reciting the words; it was a line, but also basically true. For years she'd returned to her hometown only for Thanksgiving and the occasional summer weekend.

Justin grasped Maddy's hand. "I told you I'd stay in Manhattan forever if it meant staying with you."

"I don't know why I didn't kick you to the curb for such cheese." But actually Maddy had found it sweet. She swore she'd known right then and there that they'd end up together.

"Au contraire. You followed me home like a puppy dog."

"Well, I knew you had clean sheets."

Maddy was smiling moonily at her husband when a powerful cramp sent her doubling over at the curb. She'd half forgotten where they were headed. Now it felt utterly real.

Justin knelt beside her, rubbing circles onto her back. Between gasps, she managed, "I know we've tried so hard for this, but I don't think I'm up for having a baby."

"No problem," Justin said. "We'll just nix the whole thing and head home."

Maddy looked at him with pleading eyes, suddenly mourning this chapter of just the two of them.

"Oh, babe," he said. "We'll take it moment by moment, and soon we'll meet our daughter."

Our daughter, Maddy mouthed, the words like a foreign language.

◆ ◆ ◆

The contraction tore through Maddy's torso. A sound of prehistoric horror blasted from what felt like her bowels. She saw white. She was certain she wouldn't survive this. "Epidural," she yowled, "now!" When the pain passed, she shoved her frizzed-up hair behind her ears and felt like a failure.

Like everything else she attempted, Maddy had planned on winning pregnancy and childbirth. She was unfazed by the statistics—that it took most women four to six months to conceive, that 70 percent of labors included epidurals. Maddy wasn't most women. She'd always risen to the top, always been the exception to the rule. Plus, when they'd started trying, she'd only been twenty-eight.

Maddy made the mistake of glancing at the needle—the longest she'd ever seen—just before it stabbed her in the spine. She grew woozy, petrified that it would land a few millimeters off and paralyze her. The fear subsided when the numbing set in—what a relief to feel nothing.

As it turned out, Maddy *had* been the exception to the rule, the one about most women getting pregnant within a year of trying. The only upside of confronting her period in her panties each month was that it made Maddy push herself harder in other areas of her life, to make up for her failed fertility. She went all in at the office, landing several big accounts and getting a promotion around the one-year mark of their trying (and failing) to get pregnant. She became a beast on her daily runs, shaving a full minute off her mile. When Justin gently suggested that maybe all that exercise was hindering the process, she defensively quoted Dr. Feldman, her OB, who'd encouraged her to keep active, for stress relief. But it wasn't really about stress for Maddy; it was about outrunning her disappointment in herself.

Now the contractions were muted, like they were happening to some other version of her across the room. Maddy ached; she felt itchy. A nurse who looked like a teenager suggested she get some rest until things picked up; there was still a long road ahead.

At month fifteen, just as they'd been starting to explore other options, Maddy got pregnant. She took four tests in a row, and the two faint pink lines appeared on every last one. But shortly after her first visit with Dr. Feldman, there was bleeding, and when she returned, no heartbeat. The pregnancy had come and gone almost as if it had never happened—Maddy felt half crazy, like she'd invented the whole thing. Especially since Justin never wanted to talk about it.

Maddy drifted in and out of sleep, having little sense of time or place. The young nurse popped by periodically to check her vitals. Justin was there, too, reading in a chair or pacing by the window; when she begged him not to leave, he replied, "Where else would I be?"

They'd started trying again as soon as they could. The next pregnancy came just a few months later, and Maddy was so scared of what might happen that she committed to not thinking about it. She took on a client whose massive success had disrupted the e-commerce sector, and another promotion came soon after. It hadn't been the two celebratory glasses of champagne, Dr. Feldman assured her, or the appointment she'd missed because of a meeting in San Francisco. But those things hung over Maddy like a shadow when the bleeding began again.

That time she'd been further along, edging up to her second trimester. Maybe she'd been hoping for some compassion when she disclosed her situation to her manager, Susan, or maybe she'd just been too exhausted to hide it. Susan, a mother of three, responded, "I'm very sorry to hear that," before launching into the day's agenda. Maddy blocked off three hours in her calendar for the D&C, then packed a wad of thick pads in her purse and returned to the office. Dr. Feldman called to check on her, demanding she go home. Maddy said she would, but then couldn't bring herself to cancel the rest of her day.

The nurse nudged Maddy awake. "The contractions are coming closer now. Soon it'll be time to push." Justin squeezed Maddy's hand, but it didn't have any effect on her. For all their talk of "our" pregnancy, for all the joint prenatal visits and birthing classes, Maddy was on her own now, just her and this baby fighting its way out of her.

Something had shifted in Maddy after the second miscarriage. Where once her internal dialogue was all problem-solving and decision-making, she began second-guessing herself, and—even more debilitating—questioning the value of making all those decisions in the first place. She was still killing it at work, but so what? Doing everything it took to close an account started to seem pointless to Maddy. Where, she wondered, had she gotten the idea that this was the best way to be? What was she striving for, and at what cost?

Dr. Feldman appeared in the delivery room, asking how everyone was and whether they had any fun plans for the weekend, ha ha. She was a few years older than Maddy, and Maddy thought of her like a big sister. She'd seen Maddy through years of effort and heartbreak, and had always been kind but direct with her. Maddy felt tears on her cheeks. "Don't cry," Dr. Feldman said, handing her a towel. "You're so close to the good part."

At the office, Maddy had remained a loyal soldier, but slightly less so. She no longer stayed late or canceled plans to put out work fires. She stopped talking about her job, too. When Justin asked about her day, she mumbled an answer. She'd catch him watching her while she zoned out to sitcom reruns on TV, like he was trying to solve a puzzle. Maddy thought of her sister, who'd gotten pregnant so easily, literally by accident, and she couldn't help feeling resentful. Ironically, she also half dreaded getting pregnant again, fearing that she'd only be put through more pain.

From between Maddy's knees, Dr. Feldman coached her to hold her breath and push as hard as she could. Maddy pushed away the collapse of her career. She pushed because she was told to do so and she was a rule follower and a people pleaser; she pushed because she didn't want to be that way anymore. She pushed until she thought her body would tear in two—and maybe after all that exertion, she could finally rest.

Maddy and Justin hadn't been tracking her cycle when she got pregnant the third time. They'd barely been having sex. But one night they went to one of those two-drinks-minimum comedy shows, which led to a romp on the couch, and an epic hangover a couple of weeks later turned out to be morning sickness. That was the first difference—Maddy's other pregnancies hadn't made her sick. The first time she'd chalked it up to her fortitude, but later she learned a lack of nausea could be a sign of an unviable pregnancy. This time she could barely take the subway without bolting through the doors at the next stop to hurl into a trash can; she took to bringing barf bags on her commute.

Dr. Feldman kept issuing commands: *Push, hold your breath, now push.* The baby was moving too slowly through the birth canal. If there was any time for Maddy to draw on her inner reserves and prove her strength, it was now. This was her moment. She could do it; she could do anything. Were these sentences coming from Dr. Feldman, or were they in Maddy's head? She heard other snippets: talk of an episiotomy and forceps. She'd been taught to avoid such interventions, but who cared now? Bring in every intervention, gather all the tools, just let this child make its way out of her.

Maddy had started missing the occasional deadline and drifting to sleep at her desk in the afternoons. At twelve weeks, she told her manager, who responded, "So that's why you've been so off your game. Don't worry, things improve after the first trimester." After that, it became almost easy to leave early or call in sick, to show up unprepared for client meetings, or in a few cases to space on them altogether, even when she was *this close* to signing Glossier.

At eighteen weeks, Dr. Feldman related the many ways that the pregnancy was high risk. No air travel, she told Maddy; no exercise. At nineteen weeks, Maddy was put on probation at work. Susan had once been a mentor and a mother figure; now Maddy pitied her, a woman who'd leaned in and drunk the corporate Kool-Aid, and who, at age fifty, was still wearing stilettos and working twelve-hour days, and probably never saw her kids. Maddy called her actual mother and confessed how lost she felt. Claire told her to put the phone to her belly, and she sang the baby a lullaby, loud enough for Maddy to hear, too.

Maddy squeezed her eyes shut and told herself she was strong and capable, even if she didn't quite believe it. A baby was trying with all its might to move through her, and she would do everything in her power to help. When she opened her eyes, she saw that Dr. Feldman had multiplied into half a dozen bodies in scrubs, all huddled around. She turned inward, urging herself, *Maddy, let's do this.*

On the fateful day of her meltdown, Maddy had been meeting new clients, the C-team of an Instagram-famous aromatherapy brand, and Susan insisted they get their makeup done before the lunch. Leaving Sephora, face contoured to the hilt, Maddy didn't recognize her own reflection. The restaurant was a white-tablecloth establishment with trendy forty-dollar entrées that everyone took three bites of, then spent the rest of the meal pushing around on their plates. It was all such a prodigious waste.

Their pitch was classic empty empowerment garbage, about how the company's unique blend of essential oils could unlock users' true selves and set them up for success on their own terms. It was the kind of faux-feminist nonsense that Becker-McKay Creative was famous for in the wellness sector. No matter how media savvy and sophisticated modern women claimed to be, Maddy's team could still convince a huge swath of them that its clients' products were the key to an elevated life—the solution to problems that the team itself had invented or at least amplified to potential customers. The underlying message was always the same: The easiest way to fix yourself (your body, your personality, your mental health) was to *spend, buy, consume*. And ta-da, Becker-McKay raked in the profits.

In the conference room, Maddy smiled her way through her spiel, trying not to be sick. Then the baby started kicking—jab, jab, jab, as if pleading with her to pay attention. The words of the presentation turned ugly in Maddy's mind, the images on the slide deck grotesque. She had to get out. She excused herself, beelined it to her office, and then endured the rest of the panic attack on the rug: body trembling, heart racing, breath struggling to escape her throat.

Eventually she was startled from her stupor by a forceful knock on the door. "What the actual fuck, Maddy?" Susan barked. "The clients lost all confidence after their account lead up and vanished. We lost the account."

Maddy blinked, still hazy, muscles like lead. "I'm sorry," she said. And she *was* sorry—it was awful to see Susan so angry, her skin blotchy through her makeup. But regarding the account, Maddy found she didn't give a single shit.

Susan scrutinized her, lips pursed. "You know, Maddy, for years I considered you my protégé. You were going to take over the world. But you're no longer who I thought you were. I'm sorry it has to be this way. HR is expecting you."

An hour later, Maddy left the building for the last time, her boss's words playing on a loop in her head: "You're no longer who I thought you were." This continued for days. No longer account director for one of Manhattan's top branding agencies, who was she? A vessel, it seemed, a message reinforced by her husband, who was constantly reminding her to take it easy since she was with child. Maddy tried pregnancy yoga but grew impatient at the slow, willowy movements. She took a magazine to a café but ended up staring forlornly out the window at all the professionals who had places to be. Between binges of reality TV, Maddy listened to Justin dream about leaving the city. Before, she'd tuned out this kind of talk. But now her days of fat paychecks were over, and come month's end, their exorbitant rent would still be due. Maybe it was time for a change.

"Focus now," Dr. Feldman said. "We're in the final stretch." At the doctor's urging, Maddy filled her lungs, then pushed like she'd never pushed before. She'd been preparing her whole life for this, all that running, all that hard work, all her stamina stored up for this very moment. "One more big push over the finish line."

Maddy released a groaning, moaning roar. She felt a righteous euphoria, a oneness with every single woman who'd been through this—with her sister, even—and an understanding that every last human had come into the world through such heroic efforts.

A modest heft was deposited onto her chest, and Maddy took her in: dark hair, mottled skin, puffy slitted eyes. It wasn't like a reunion, and Maddy didn't fall instantly in love. But she was curious. "Who are you?" she asked. The baby began wailing. "I know. Really, I know."

◆ ◆ ◆

They named her Rose, and several weeks passed in a muddle. The first schlep to the pediatrician's office. Maddy scarfing down mixing bowls of cereal in the dead of night as Rose suckled her greedily. The whole ordeal of going to the bathroom. A visit from Justin's mother, who rocked Rose, giving Maddy a break, but only at the price of listening to her rant about how only fools would leave the center of civilization for the boonies, not that anyone ever asked her opinion. Rose crying, sobbing, shrieking, until Maddy couldn't distinguish her daughter's tears from her own. Her friend Krista showing up with champagne, nodding politely through Maddy's birth story, saying how cute Rose was, but never once asking to hold her. The old friends hugging goodbye in the awkward-armed way of acquaintances, Krista saying, "I guess I'll see you," then Maddy bawling through Rose's entire nap.

The day before their departure, Maddy left Rose with Justin to run to the bodega, where she bumped into Caroline from her pregnancy group, pushing a stroller. Maddy peeked at the napping infant, so tiny in his little red cap, and her emotions surged. She apologized, wiping away tears.

"My hormones are wacko, too," Caroline said. "Plus, aren't you about to move?"

Maddy nodded. She couldn't bring herself to say it was tomorrow.

"The city will miss you, and it'll be great."

Maddy surprised both of them by pulling Caroline into a tight hug. "Thank you."

She bought the baby wipes, the bodega cat purring against her ankle, and then she returned to the apartment that was hers for one last night.

Chapter 7

JOCELYN

The day Maddy and her family were moving to town, Jocelyn made sure to fill her schedule: yoga with Betsy, then an afternoon of showings with a new client. His name was Kyle Taylor, and he'd been polite on the phone as Jocelyn collected basic info: He had a Boston address and was looking for a three-bedroom or a two-bedroom with an office. He'd vacationed once in Truro but didn't know the Cape well. No mention of a partner or family, and Jocelyn didn't pry.

The three houses they were seeing were in three different towns and varied across Kyle's price range. Jocelyn was early to the first one, a classic colonial down the road from Little Pleasant Bay, but her client had beaten her there. He was leaning against a silver BMW SUV—tall and lanky, with a swoop of auburn hair. He wore a soft-looking blue Henley, chino shorts, and those trendy wool sneakers. As Jocelyn went to greet him, she wished she'd touched up her lip gloss.

"You must be Jocelyn," he said, the corners of his eyes crinkling as he smiled. Jocelyn placed him at around forty. He shook her hand with a strong grip. "I'm Kyle."

"So nice to meet you, Kyle. Shall we head inside?"

"You lead the way, boss." She appreciated the sentiment, though, really, she was the one working for him.

Jocelyn liked getting to know her clients' tastes. As Kyle toured the house, attentive to the chatty seller's Realtor, she noticed that his reactions matched her own: interest in the wainscoting in the hall, puzzlement at the floating shelves in the kitchen, bemusement at the paintings of neon-colored cats in various states of alarm (the sellers were artists). Kyle stood close to Jocelyn in the small rooms; he smelled fresh, like Ivory soap.

"Well?" she asked as they conferred afterward at the curb.

"It's a nice house," he said. "I bet that couple's been very happy here."

"You don't have to be polite," Jocelyn said, charmed. "It's not *my* house."

"I know, but I mean it, even if it's not right for me," he said. "Maybe I'll commission one of those cat paintings for my haunted house on Halloween."

"You have a haunted house on Halloween?"

"No, Jocelyn, I do not." The glint in his eyes sent a flutter through her belly, which she tried to ignore.

"Well, it's all an education. To see what's out there, cat portraits and all."

They caravanned to the next property, in East Harwich. At a red light, Jocelyn checked her rearview mirror, and Kyle waved. It was a mild, clear-skied afternoon, and she imagined bailing on the appointment and heading to the beach instead, new client in tow.

On the sidewalk, Kyle examined his surroundings: a cul-de-sac of new homes abutting a golf course. "Very suburban." He said it like he had a bad taste in his mouth.

"This part of town is a bit different," Jocelyn said. Privately she liked that Kyle was not into the development aesthetic.

"I used to live in the burbs," he said. "Needham."

"Sure, I know it." Jocelyn was familiar with most of the Boston suburbs from previous clients—she associated Needham with an Irish couple and their three freckle-faced sons.

"Not that I spent much time there," Kyle said. "I was at a corporate firm then, working seventy-hour weeks. Two years ago, we moved to the Back Bay"—Jocelyn's ears perked up; *who was "we"?*—"and I took a job as general counsel at a textbook publisher. Endless contracts, a little mind-numbing. But now I actually see Nina. That's my daughter." *Oh.* "It's been hard for her, though. She doesn't love the city. Plus, she just started middle school." He sighed, like, could there be a worse fate? "I thought it would be good for us to have a getaway out here, near nature and the ocean and . . . I guess I don't have to sell *you* on Cape Cod."

His laugh was hearty, and contagious. Jocelyn was still processing this onslaught of information: Kyle was a lawyer. Kyle had relocated from the suburbs to the city. Kyle had a daughter. And where was the girl's mother?

"All ready for you!" the agent hollered from the entryway. Jocelyn greeted her warmly—Millie Johnson was a flighty older woman who practiced real estate as a hobby because she liked to schmooze; her husband ran a tech company out of their waterfront Osterville estate, which Jocelyn knew because Millie was always blathering on about the headache of flood insurance.

The house was just what Jocelyn had expected: cavernous, with vaulted ceilings and a great room that was more like a ballroom. And cheaply built. Millie had no qualms about hanging on Kyle's arm as she led him from the primary bedroom to the en suite bathroom and peppered him with questions: "Double vanities, one for you and one for . . . ?"

"Just me," Kyle said, not betraying annoyance, as Jocelyn would have in his place. "Well, me and my daughter. We're looking for a little place to get away to." The "little" sounded deliberate.

Outside, Kyle exhaled audibly, and Jocelyn didn't even bother to solicit his summary. "This next house might be more your speed," she said.

"It's all an education," he replied cheerfully. "So this is Harwich, and now we're heading back north?"

"Exactly, up to Eastham. Here, hold out your arm."

Kyle complied, bending at the elbow; he clearly knew where she was going with this. He flexed, flashing a wry smile. "Okay, this is the

Outer Cape," Jocelyn said, indicating his forearm. "I'm partial to it since it's got the national seashore all along the coast, the most beautiful beaches in the world." She pointed to Kyle's fist. "The northernmost tip is Provincetown, which is super lively, with shops and galleries and nightclubs; plus, there's the harbor. It's big with artists and the gay community."

"P-town's where the *Mayflower* first landed, right?"

"Sure is, and there's a giant monument there commemorating it."

"I bet most of your clients think it was Plymouth." Kyle looked proud of himself, which made Jocelyn laugh.

"A-plus for your knowledge of the Pilgrims. Moving on." She touched his wrist. "Here's Truro, very upscale. The beaches are spectacular, with huge dramatic cliffs, and the homes are gorgeous. The Highland Lighthouse is the oldest and tallest on the Cape." She touched a bit lower. "Next is Wellfleet. Stunning beaches and kettle ponds, rambling pitch pine woods, a pretty harbor, and the cutest downtown of funky little shops. If you like oysters, Wellfleet is the place to eat 'em." She moved to the meat of his forearm. "This is Eastham."

"Let me guess: breathtaking beaches?" Kyle said. Jocelyn matched his smirk.

"The *most* breathtaking, in my opinion. Plus, ponds and hiking trails and the rail trail for biking. Eastham's a little under the radar, more affordable than the rest of the Outer Cape. It also has good access to the Lower Cape, which is here." Her fingers graced his elbow. "Am I boring you yet?"

"No, but my arm's getting a little tired."

"I'll speed it up. The Lower Cape is more bustling, especially in the offseason, with more of a year-round crowd. You've got Orleans, Brewster, Harwich, and Chatham, with the Nantucket Sound down here. Farther inland"—Jocelyn pointed to but didn't touch his bicep—"is the Mid Cape, then the Upper Cape, which confusingly is south of the Lower Cape." She indicated his armpit. "And that's the Sagamore Bridge, which runs over the Cape Cod

Canal. It's famous for its charming arch and epic traffic jams. And that's Cape Cod!"

"Bravo!" Kyle said, shaking out his arm. Jocelyn curtsied.

Her phone pinged with a text from Maddy to the family group chat: ETA 4 hours. Cape Cod, here we come! Jocelyn swiped it away.

They were early for their next appointment, so Jocelyn proposed showing Kyle around the town. She led him to First Encounter, the most dramatic bay beach, an oil painting of striped sand and sea at low tide. Next, they drove past the 350-year-old windmill, then across Route 6 to Ocean View Drive, where they pulled over and trudged out to the dune. Kyle gasped at the view of winking waves below. After that, they wound around the town center, busy for September, with people in and out of the post office, the general store, and Sam's Deli. They still had a few minutes to spare, and they were just around the corner from a road Jocelyn had been avoiding all month. She took a sharp inhale, turned onto Blueberry Lane, and for the first time laid eyes on her sister's new house.

Jocelyn was surprised and—she wasn't above admitting it—slightly disappointed at how lovely it looked: solidly built and expansive, but not obscenely large. A screened-in porch on one side, charming dormers, and well-maintained garden beds. Through oversize windows, she spotted wide-planked wood floors and high ceilings. The only visible grandiosity was a crystal chandelier. It would be the perfect setting for one of Maddy's dinner parties, everyone eating fussy hors d'oeuvres and ha-ha-ing at each other's witticisms; *but wait*—the guests Jocelyn was imagining would've had to drive three hundred miles to attend such a party. It was truly unreal that Maddy was moving back.

Kyle's SUV pulled up beside Jocelyn's Subaru, his passenger-side window rolled down. "Is this the house? It's cute."

"Oh no, sorry. We had extra time, so I decided to . . . I didn't even realize I'd parked." Flustered, she began again: "My twin sister bought this house. We grew up in Eastham, I don't think I mentioned that— my parents live nearby, and so do I. Maddy and her husband live, or I guess *lived*, in New York City. They just had a baby, and now she's moving back—today, actually." Jocelyn heard how all over the place she sounded. "Anyway, it's a pretty street, so I thought I'd add it to the tour." She chuckled unconvincingly.

"It's nice," Kyle said. "But I can't tell if you think it's a good thing or not, your sister moving back."

It sounded like an invitation, which made Jocelyn feel comfortable telling the truth. "Honestly, I'm mostly confused. Maddy left at age eighteen and never looked back. She hardly even visits. She set up her whole life to be the opposite of what it would be here. So I don't get why she's coming back."

"I see," Kyle said. Jocelyn appreciated that he didn't say the obvious thing: that having a baby changes you. Especially since, as far as she was concerned, having a baby just made you more yourself; it was losing a baby that changed you. "Maybe she misses you."

"Ha! You don't know Maddy." Now she was anxious to change the subject. "Ready for the next house?"

This one was a key-in-a-lockbox situation. As Jocelyn let them in through the kitchen, she explained about the iconic Cape Cod style: simple but charming, offering the option of single-floor living, with bonus lofted rooms. "You'll see variations—some with three-season porches, or finished basements. This one's a little dated."

They wandered from den to bathroom to a bedroom with a nameplate on the door—"Quinn" in bubble letters. Noting the hockey skates and the same scuzzy fleece blanket she'd seen in a hundred boys' bedrooms, Jocelyn followed Kyle in. He perused the shelves like he was at a toy store.

"This one was my favorite," he said, pulling out the game of Life. Jocelyn didn't point out that you weren't really supposed to riffle through the owners' stuff. She flipped through the cards, all of life's dramas on fast-forward: Get into college, pick a career, move, retire. Kyle handed her the orange-car game piece, taking the yellow one for himself. She watched as he populated his car with peg people—a blue and a pink in the front seat, another pink in the back—then he removed the pink from the front. In her car, Jocelyn placed a pink in the driver's seat and cupped a second pink in her palm.

"Do you remember the goal of the game?" Kyle asked.

"Of course," she said. Life had been a go-to for her and Betsy growing up. "Whoever ends up with the most money wins. Then you retire in style and become a philosopher." They both burst out laughing.

Kyle checked his watch. "I'd love to stay and play, but I've got to grab Nina. I sent her on a bird-watching tour, and she's been texting me nonstop about all the weirdos there. I promised her ice cream after."

"Take her to Bob's Sub and Cone," Jocelyn said. "It's the best."

"Noted, thanks."

Unlocking his SUV, Kyle said, "Well, I can already tell we've got a good thing going here. I'll text you when I'm coming back to town, probably next weekend."

"Sure. I'll set up more showings."

"In the meantime, good luck with Maddy." Jocelyn was touched that he remembered her sister's name. "And don't forget"—he cleared his throat, then broke into the jingle—"you can be a winner at the game of Life!" He winked and drove off.

Jocelyn stood there, all keyed up. She'd just met Kyle, but she felt as if she'd known him for years. She couldn't remember the last time she'd felt this way. No wonder she'd opened up about Maddy.

Another text arrived in the family chat, this one from Justin: the words road trip! above a snapshot of Rose asleep in her car seat, pink and plump, with wisps of dark hair hovering over her head like a halo.

Jocelyn had forced herself to look at every photo they'd sent of Rose, since the first one that accompanied the birth announcement a month ago: "Welcome, Rose Jay Wells. 8 lb., 6 oz., born August 24, 2018, at 5:02 a.m., healthy and perfect." That text had woken Jocelyn up, and she'd held her breath as she took in the image from bed: the tiny head with slits for eyes and a button nose. This person hadn't existed a few hours earlier, and now she did, and she was Maddy's daughter. By the time Jocelyn managed to set down her phone, her hand had a cramp.

Jocelyn was relieved that Rose looked nothing like Juniper, who'd been born with a full head of white-blond hair, big marble eyes, and pouty lips. Still, she dreaded meeting her niece. She feared her throat would close up, or she'd start crying and be unable to stop. Or she'd be bowled over by the intensity of her love. Or she'd feel nothing at all. Every option seemed equally unbearable, and the uncertainty made her wild with nerves.

As Jocelyn got undressed that night, something dropped from her pocket: the little pink peg. She picked it up, and the melody to "Blackbird" floated up into her head. She'd sung it on a loop to Juniper as an infant, the only lyrics her sleep-deprived brain could conjure up. She squeezed the peg in her palm, then tucked it away in her jewelry box.

Chapter 8

Maddy's expectations had been high. She'd expected a welcome committee and regular check-ins, and now that they were far from the frenetic city, she'd expected Rose to get with the program and calm the F down. Maddy had expected herself to calm down, too.

Her parents had plans the night they arrived, so they stopped by the following evening, bearing symbolic housewarming gifts of bread and salt (though Maddy would've also appreciated some nonsymbolic actual food to make a meal with). Jed marveled at his new granddaughter, and Claire bounced her around a bit, handing her back when she grew fussy. Before long they were standing to go. They were apologetic: September was always so busy for Claire at school, and Jed was leaving in the morning for a bird-ers' trip, planned months ago. Meanwhile, for the past week Jocelyn had been inventing excuses to not come over. The more her sister avoided her, the more determined Maddy was to get her to visit.

When Maddy complained to Justin that she felt abandoned, he urged her to give it time, saying transitions were always tough. But he already seemed perfectly adjusted, retreating to his office all day, not emerging until five or sometimes six at night.

Maddy tried to set up a schedule for her and Rose: breakfast, tummy time, walk by the bay. But by the time she polished off a bowl of leftover pasta and endured ten minutes of Rose screaming bloody murder as she whispered encouragement for her to stay on her stomach, Maddy was spent, and bagged the rest of the plan. The one afternoon they made it to the beach, the wind whipped wildly, and a speck of sand must've gotten into Rose's eye the way she started howling. A pair of twentysomethings gaped at Maddy like she was abusive to have brought an infant there.

So Maddy stayed home and tried not to think about how in New York all she'd had to do was step outside to be among people, and how she'd often walked around the block just to revel in strangers' admiring glances at her newborn. If she was going to be a shut-in, she told herself, she could at least be productive. She made to-do lists for Rose's naps: Organize the linens, marinate the chicken, write thank-you notes for the baby gifts. But she didn't do any of it, and when the gray of evening descended and all she had to show for her day was a milk-stained nursing shirt, Maddy felt like a tiny speck of dirt.

She almost texted her sister to ask how on earth she'd done this. But Jocelyn clearly didn't want to hear from her. She thought about texting Krista but then imagined her friend's response: something encouraging on its face, but with an I-told-you-so undertone. She sent her parents a cute pic of Rose and was dismayed when it took Claire an hour to mark it with a heart-eyes emoji and no reply at all came from Jed. It was the middle of the school day, and her dad probably didn't have cell service on his trip, but still.

Maddy had initially scoffed at the advice to sleep when your baby slept. But after a morning of bouncing a cranky Rose on the yoga ball until she felt her thighs might snap, Maddy passed out shortly after her daughter did, too tired to even shrug on a quilt. Which was how Justin found her an hour later, sprawled across their bed in her maternity sweatsuit. His presence woke her, and she was instantly annoyed. His clean-shaven face, his crisp button-down, his gentle murmur of "I'm so glad you're letting yourself rest"—it all annoyed her. It took restraint for her not to growl, "Well, I *was* resting." Moments later, Rose began wailing, and Justin said, "She sounds hungry." *No shit, Sherlock. If only you had the tits heavy with milk.*

Justin said he could stick around for another ten before his next call, and he did all he could to be useful, which was to say, absolutely zilch. Oh, he tried, gazing at Maddy adoringly as she breastfed their daughter, but it just made her feel insane to consider that he found her even remotely appealing in her current state, when she herself felt like a husk of a person. If she'd requested a glass of water or a magazine, he would've jumped to fetch it. But Maddy couldn't ask for what she really needed, which was an escape: from this tiny creature so frighteningly dependent on her, from the mud of exhaustion collecting inside her, from this strange new world she'd found herself in, from all of it.

The worst part was, Justin seemed happier than ever. He'd bounce out of bed and sing in the shower; he'd coo over Rose, eyes wide with awe; and every time he heard a trill outside, he'd grab his binoculars to marvel at the birds—*the friggin' birds!* Plus, he got to leave: Every weekday morning he went to his office above the garage, where he used his brain and conversed with adults, staying there for eight or nine or sometimes ten hours, despite Maddy's pleas for him to sign off right at five. At the end of his workday, he'd take Rose from Maddy's arms, and the baby would calm, like magic. He'd encourage Maddy to do something restorative, like take a bath. *A goddamn bath!* It was all just so infuriating.

So, on the eighth day in her new house, in her new life, with her five-week-old baby and her own future a blurry smudge, Maddy lowered her expectations. She was craving peanut butter, so she would get a jar of peanut butter. It was bright and fair out, and although there wasn't a twenty-four-hour bodega on the corner, the Superette was just a mile away. She would take the stroller, lack of sidewalks be damned.

Maddy didn't consult her phone to see how long it had taken her to get out the door; she wasn't going to beat herself up over inefficiency, not today. Once outside, she spotted four small beings in the next yard, running around with water guns. In the city, Maddy had been trained to tune out the people around her, to avoid sensory overload; only weirdos talked to their neighbors. But here on their dead-end street (she no longer thought of it as a cul-de-sac), the presence of other humans was like flashing neon. Marching to the property line to get a closer look, Maddy was nailed in the neck by a stream of cold water.

"Ashton, you little shit!" a woman shouted.

It was Kelsey, the mother, a fleshy woman in a sweatsuit whose blond-streaked hair was pulled back by one of those accordion headbands popular two decades ago. Maddy had met Kelsey once before: She'd dropped off a piss-yellow Jell-O mold the day they moved in, and visibly grimaced when Maddy said they'd come from New York. Maddy had waited nervously to be asked what she did for a living, but the question never came. Instead, Kelsey asked which exterminator they planned to use, since mice ran rampant around here; she suggested Prime One. The moment she was gone, Maddy dumped the Jell-O into the garbage and watched it jiggle revoltingly among the trash. Justin looked disappointed, saying he thought it was a nice gesture.

She decided to make an effort now, despite the water dripping down her back. She steered the stroller next door, and when Kelsey waved, Maddy was shocked to see a cigarette between her knuckles. "Sorry for my sons," Kelsey said. "They're basically feral."

"That's okay," Maddy said. "We're just headed to the store. Need anything?"

Kelsey gaped. "You're walking?"

"Sure. It's a beautiful day."

"Whatever floats your boat." Kelsey whipped her head in the other direction. "Jayden, let go of your brother's hair this instant. Don't make me come over there."

Maddy slipped away. She'd walked about a hundred feet when a man appeared in the other yard adjoining Maddy's. He was hunched with age and wore a USS *Forrest Royal* hat.

"I'm Marshall," he called out, eyeing Maddy's yoga pants. "Did you just wake up?"

"Actually, I've got an infant who wakes me up at five." Maddy didn't intend to sound so hostile, but what kind of way was that to greet your new neighbor? And had he not seen what Kelsey was wearing two houses down?

Marshall hobbled down his walkway, and before Maddy knew it, he was clutching Rose's arm. She lurched to swat him away. "That's a little close."

"She's a princess," Marshall said. "But where's her hat on such a sunny day?" Maddy went from beaming to bristling. "You know, I couldn't believe what you folks forked over for your house. We came in 1976, and paid thirty-eight grand, not a penny more. They were just putting in the street."

Maddy kept looking for an opportunity to extract herself from the conversation, in the meantime learning how Marshall had gone to war on the GI bill, how he'd been a postal worker and had an excellent pension, and how he'd been meaning to come over and show her husband how to work the generator. Maddy was miffed at his assumption that she wouldn't also want to learn how to work the generator, never mind that she actually had no interest. Finally, she broke in with "It was nice meeting you," then strode off.

The walk started off pleasant enough, Rose babbling in long vowels as Maddy chanted, "Peanut, peanut butter, and jelly." She wasn't running a marathon, or even jogging a mile, but putting one foot in front of the other was a small reminder of her body's former strength. They reached the pond, where a flock of ducks was cutting a vee across its surface. "A duck says quack," Maddy told Rose. "Quack, quack, quack," she continued, feeling only slightly unhinged.

She started salivating as the Superette came into view. She'd request a spoon and eat the peanut butter by the spoonful on the way home. The parking lot was empty, which didn't strike her as odd—there was so much space here, and only so many people to fill it—until she saw the handwritten sign on the door: Closed today, see you tomorrow!

Rage churned in Maddy. Was this not a place of business, with set hours of operation? A handwritten sign! With no explanation! What if she needed something urgently, like baby formula? Maddy wanted to report the store to the Better Business Bureau. She wanted to kick through the window to take her peanut butter. She wanted to throw a goddamn tantrum.

Rose took her cue and began crying.

"Oh no, no, no."

Defeated, Maddy started the walk home, but the movement didn't soothe her baby—if anything, Rose wailed even more forcefully. Maddy tried drowning out the sound with a podcast, but after the fourth long-winded ad, she ripped out her earbuds in frustration. The heat beat down, and Rose's cheeks were pink. She thought of Marshall's scolding about the hat and felt dismayed to realize he'd been right. Rose's screams grew so shrill that Maddy pictured her as a baby opera singer, shattering her mother's nerves instead of glass. She considered surrendering to the pavement, lying there until someone competent showed up to soothe her baby. To squash the idea, she scooped Rose up and shush-bounced her with one arm while pushing the stroller with the other. A car slowed as it passed, and the driver's stare seemed to stain Maddy with judgment.

She heard the roiling before she felt its consequences, a tornado in Rose's stomach that exploded through her diaper and onesie and all across Maddy's shirt. No wonder she'd been so mad. Maddy deposited her soiled baby into the stroller, where she fell instantly asleep. Attacking her shirt with baby wipes only made it worse. It looked like peanut butter, she observed with horror. She prayed Marshall wouldn't still be out when they got home.

Instead, sitting on her front porch was Jocelyn. Maddy blinked to confirm it: her sister, in the flesh. She had an impulse to hide until Jocelyn gave up and left, but Jocelyn had already spotted her. As she stood up and waved, her tank top rode up from her peasant skirt, revealing a flat, tan stomach, the sight of which made Maddy murderous.

"I was in the neighborhood," Jocelyn said, smirking, because when was she not? Not that that had stopped her from waiting more than a week to come by. "Gorgeous day, huh?"

Maddy swiped beads of sweat from her brow. "Yeah, gorgeous day to walk to the Superette, only to find out it's closed, only to trudge home cradling a screaming infant who decides to shit all over me." It felt good to blurt it all out.

"Tough break, Mad," Jocelyn said, "though it is kind of your color." Maddy smiled in spite of herself. "Here, I brought you some things."

She handed Maddy a canvas tote filled with stoned wheat crackers, a tub of Boursin, lavender honey straws, and—a lump formed in Maddy's throat—a jar of peanut butter. "All my favorites," she said.

Jocelyn plucked out a honey straw. "Mine, too. Why don't you go change, and I'll stay here and get acquainted with my niece. Take as long as you need."

Maddy didn't tear up until she was inside. This was her nicest nursing top, ninety-two dollars from a Park Avenue boutique. She tossed it in the trash and pulled on one of Justin's old T-shirts, dismayed at how snugly it fit around her belly.

No longer in the mood for peanut butter, Maddy carried the cheese and crackers outside. But the porch was deserted, the stroller empty. Panic sliced through her. She couldn't catch her breath. She knew she should've been worried about her sister meeting Rose. *What had Jocelyn done?*

A minute passed, two tops, before she heard her voice. "Mad, are you all right?"

She wheeled around to see Jocelyn in the side yard, rocking Rose like the picture of maternity. Rose was content, cradled in the crook of her aunt's arm, belly down and chin tucked over her elbow. It had never occurred to Maddy to hold her that way. "She woke up, so I cleaned her up and we took a stroll around the property. Those hydrangea bushes are going to be gorgeous in bloom."

Maddy sat hunched over on the steps, sore after her surge of panic, her terror now replaced with bewilderment: *What was wrong with her?*

Jocelyn joined her on the porch and handed over Rose, who immediately went for Maddy's breast. Maddy couldn't help feeling a flicker of triumph—Jocelyn might've had the magic baby hold, but only Maddy could nourish her child.

"Can I get you anything?" Jocelyn asked.

"Cracker with cheese, please."

The three of them sat and ate. And then: *Boom!*

"Whoa," said Jocelyn. Rose unlatched and began howling, and both sisters rubbed circles onto her back.

"What on earth was that?" asked Maddy, her eardrums ringing from the sound.

Jocelyn gestured to the next yard, where Marshall stood with a rifle. "Finally nailed that darn coyote!" he hollered. "He's been terrorizing my cat for months."

"Mazel tov," Jocelyn called back. Marshall tipped his hat.

"Fuckin' A," said Maddy. "What redneck hovel have I landed in?"

"Oh, come on, Mad," Jocelyn said. "Remember Mr. Barnes growing up?"

"Sure," said Maddy. The mean old man on their road—he'd had a penchant for shooting animals in his backyard, too. "Pity the turkey who dared cross his path."

"He'd make such a fuss about shooting his own Thanksgiving meal—"

"Straight from my deck!" Maddy declared in an old-man voice, finishing her sister's sentence. "That guy was such a bigot. He taught me the word 'homo' when Gordon and Marc moved in across the street."

"Yeah, he wasn't thrilled about that," Jocelyn said. "But he always plowed their driveway during snowstorms."

"Because he said no real men lived there," Maddy recalled with a grimace.

"True," Jocelyn said. "At least their driveway got cleared. We were always breaking our backs shoveling."

"Seriously. I can't believe I'm going to have to shovel again," Maddy said. She groaned, but was thinking, *This is actually nice.* "What ever happened to batty old Mr. Barnes?"

"Heart attack," said Jocelyn. "It was a week before he was found."

"Jeez, that's dark."

"I know." Jocelyn stood up. "Well, I've got a showing in Brewster. Sorry to skip out."

"Thanks for coming by, and for the snacks," Maddy said. "Hey, are you going to Mom and Dad's for Sunday dinner?"

"As always," Jocelyn said. She kissed the top of Rose's head. "She's beautiful, Mad. Congrats. And give my love to Justin."

Maddy felt an acute longing as she watched her sister drive away. Of course she had somewhere else to be—everyone always had plans, everyone but Maddy.

◆ ◆ ◆

It was only midafternoon, and the hours until the end of Justin's workday yawned before her. It got worse when the sun started fading—the room's shadows grew longer, illuminating dust motes and making time stand still in a way that Maddy remembered from being a teenager. She'd felt so desperate to climb out of life's slowness and have anything at all happen. She'd counted down the days until college. Now she didn't know what to count down to.

When Justin finally showed up—at six thirty, a full hour after he said he would—Rose was on her play mat, tracking the spin of plastic farm animals overhead, and Maddy lay in a lump on the couch, eyes sandy with fatigue.

"Sorry, my meeting ran over. I'm so glad to finally be home with my girls." He sighed with satisfaction. Maddy wanted to meet his eyes, but it was as if he stood behind smudged glass.

"I'm gonna get some air," she said, because it sounded like something someone might do to feel better. She grabbed the box of crackers on her way out.

Maddy looked up and saw stars. She urged herself to experience wonder—it had never gotten dark enough in the city to see stars. But when wonder proved to be too tall an order, she tried to look for constellations. But it turned out she only knew the Big Dipper. So she settled for breathing in the night air and eating crackers, and quickly devoured half a sleeve.

"Hey!" she heard someone call—Kelsey from next door.

Maddy replied with a half-hearted "Hi."

"Can I interest you in a beer?"

Yes, thought Maddy. Kelsey waved her over. She was still in her sweatsuit, now topped with a Patriots windbreaker.

"Cheers." They clinked cans of Coors Light, a brand Maddy hadn't drunk since college. One gulp and she felt the alcohol slide down her throat and settle in her belly.

"I saw you with Marshall earlier," Kelsey said. "You gotta keep it moving with that guy. Stop to chat and he'll suck you in."

"Did you hear him shoot that coyote?"

"Why do you think my hellion sons are so obsessed with guns?" Kelsey said. "The other day I couldn't find Otis, and Marshall had him over there teaching him how to hold a rifle. You should've heard my husband go off on him. The dude's off his rocker."

Maddy laughed. It was nice to be gossiping with another adult.

"Oh, here." Kelsey held out a tissue. Maddy looked down to see two wet coins leaked through her shirt. She was overdue to nurse.

"Sorry, I'm gross," she said. The tears flowed fast, and Kelsey passed her another tissue.

"Hey, I've been there, four times over. Once was more than enough for me, but I just kept getting knocked up. I thought at least I'd eventually get a girl, but nope."

Maddy dabbed at her eyes as a new wave of emotion welled up. "It took me two years to get pregnant. I wanted it so bad. But now . . ."

She trailed off, shaking her head. She hadn't admitted it to herself until this moment, how guilt-ridden she felt to have worked so hard to get here, only now to yearn to be anywhere else. She couldn't believe she'd said this much to a near stranger.

"Oh, honey. It gets better. Of course, then it gets worse." Kelsey gestured to the water guns in her yard. "And then it gets better again. But the shit you're in now? That's the absolute pits, swear to god."

Maddy wasn't sure whether to believe her, this life coach in the form of her schlumpy neighbor, but she didn't outright dismiss her, either.

"I'm going to light up, if you don't mind." Kelsey held up a pack of cigarettes. "Want one?"

"Um, I shouldn't. Maybe just one puff." Maddy hadn't smoked since college. Kelsey passed her the cigarette, and the hit of nicotine made her feel lightheaded, and a tad less agitated. "I better get home to feed the baby."

"I'm out here every night," Kelsey said. "You're always welcome."

"Thanks." Maddy couldn't help imagining what her friends from the city would think if they saw her here now. But also, she thought maybe she *would* come back tomorrow. It would be something to look forward to.

Chapter 9

Jocelyn knew people who could fix the things Maddy was complaining about—a musty smell by her bulkhead, a leaky faucet in her bathroom—but she assumed her sister was enjoying her rant, so she didn't bother chiming in. Instead, she babbled at her niece, who squirmed on Justin's lap, and she passed bits of Moroccan chicken to Rusty, panting under the table. How quickly they'd slipped back into their old dynamic: Maddy setting the conversational agenda, taking up all the air in the room.

It was their first Sunday family dinner since the move, and Jocelyn felt nostalgic for the before times, when Maddy would be a five-minute presence on FaceTime, until the screen darkened and disappeared her again from Jocelyn's world.

But now Maddy was here at the table, griping about how *she'd* recruited some big client to her company, and now *someone else* was getting all the credit for their success. Claire asked about the client; apparently it was a lifestyle weight-loss tea.

"What?" Maddy snapped at Jocelyn.

"Nothing," Jocelyn said, not realizing she'd made a face.

"Weight-loss tea, eh?" Jed said. "English breakfast, hold the breakfast." Everyone but Maddy groaned at the corny joke.

"Think what you want," Maddy said, "but I cared about my job. And I worked with nonprofits, too—we set up that partnership with Neiman Marcus and those crocheters in Rwanda."

Jocelyn held up her hands in defense and caught her parents exchanging a look.

"Those scarfs were great," Justin said, a hand on Maddy's shoulder. "Remember, I gave one to my mom?" Maddy didn't look appeased.

"Who wants ice cream?" Claire asked brightly. Every week, Jocelyn brought over two pints from the Ice Cream Café: mocha fudge to share, and mint chip to stash in her parents' freezer. This time she'd swapped out mocha fudge for cookie dough, Maddy's favorite flavor as a kid.

"Not me—I'm off dairy." Maddy sighed. "Rose has been so gassy."

"Ah, I hope that helps," Claire said. "Next week we'll get sorbet."

And that was pretty much all Maddy had to say about her daughter. When Claire asked how she and Rose were faring, Maddy replied, "Oh, fine," and then went quiet for the first time that evening. Jocelyn noticed how her eyes shone, and how she blinked rapidly, working hard, it seemed, not to cry. Maddy wouldn't want to be scrutinized, so Jocelyn looked away.

Rose was hiccuping, her little features scrunching up with each spasm. She was a fussy one, never quite content, which didn't surprise Jocelyn, given that she was Maddy's child. But even so surly, Rose was a dear. Being around her reminded Jocelyn how much she loved babies.

"Hey, Cricket," said Jed, "I hear you sold that little white cottage on Duck Pond."

"Ah, remember our picnics there?" Claire said.

"Of course," Jocelyn said. Nestled in the Wellfleet woods, Duck Pond was her favorite spot to go to tune out the world. She liked to imagine its formation: During the Ice Age, when the glacier covering what was now Cape Cod retreated, blocks of ice got stranded and buried, then melted to form kettle ponds; that was the water they swam in, twenty thousand years later—amazing. When Jocelyn had heard that the owner of the cottage wanted to sell, she dropped by that very day to introduce herself.

"That place is so special, it feels almost sacrilegious for you to do business there," Maddy said. They all ignored the rude comment.

Claire leaned in to Jocelyn. "And tell us about this new client of yours, the cute single guy."

"I don't know that Kyle's single," said Jocelyn, feeling herself blush. "He's nice, and funny." She'd mentioned Kyle to her mom in a flush of excitement, the way she'd once divulged details about guys back in high school. To Claire's credit, she didn't make a thing out of the fact that it'd been ages since Jocelyn had mentioned that kind of interest in anyone.

"You have a crush on your client?" Maddy asked, voice sharp. "Sounds messy. I'd never fraternize with someone I work with."

"Then it's a good thing you don't work anymore." The retort flew out of Jocelyn's mouth, and she instantly regretted it. Everyone seemed to be holding their breath, until Rose started fussing. Jocelyn saw the tremor in her sister's hand as she patted Rose's back. "Anyway, all I said, Mad, is that he's nice."

Again, Justin tried to defuse the tension: "Well, I look forward to hearing more about Kyle the gentleman suitor."

"Gentleman suitor, oh my god." Jocelyn giggled in spite of herself. "I'll keep you posted—like, about which house he buys."

"You do that," Justin said, chuckling.

Maddy stood up abruptly, announcing, "Rose needs a diaper change."

They all gave her space. But when five minutes passed and she still hadn't returned to the table, Jocelyn excused herself.

In their old shared bedroom, she found Maddy on the bottom bunk, face cast down. Rose was idling on the rug, her bulging diaper as yet unchanged. Jocelyn sat down beside her sister.

"I'm such a disaster," Maddy said.

"No, you're not," Jocelyn replied. "You're a new mom. You're figuring it out."

"Figuring what out? How to wait out the clock until bedtime, and be miserable in the meantime? This shit sucks."

The declaration struck Jocelyn like a slap. She'd been keeping it together all night—keeping it together since Maddy moved back—but now anger reared up inside her. *Ungrateful bitch.*

Maddy glanced at her, cheeks tearstained, and rolled her eyes. "I'm sorry, okay? I know I can't say that shit to you. I wasn't trying to, but you busted in on my private moment."

"You're right," Jocelyn said. "I'm sorry. I was worried about you."

"Let me ask you something," Maddy said, sniffling. "I know how much you loved being a mother, how you were such a natural, et cetera, et cetera, but did you love it right away? Did you cherish *every moment,* like people are always demanding I do? Or do you think that's just how it came to seem in retrospect?"

Jocelyn's whole body went tense, and she looked to the door. It turned out she wasn't up for this.

Maddy groaned. "Fuck, sorry. I'm so tired. I know you were the best mother to grace god's green earth."

Her tone was sad, not sarcastic, and it gave Jocelyn a stab of sympathy, recognizing the millionth way she and her sister were different: Maddy didn't like having a baby. Jocelyn still couldn't face her head-on, but she could be helpful. She hoisted Rose up on the dresser and pulled a pack of wipes from the diaper bag.

Yes, Jocelyn had loved being a mother right from the start. The role had suited her perfectly, opening up her world to this tiny being and seeing everything through new, cerulean eyes. Most people spent their lives looking backward or planning ahead, but Jocelyn had always been best in the present, just like her baby—and their present together was everything. She'd liked it all, even changing diapers, the way Junie had gazed up at her all moony-eyed, just like Rose was doing now.

But Jocelyn would be generous. "No one likes changing diapers, Mad."

"And she poops around the clock," Maddy complained. "It can't be normal."

"She's a baby," Jocelyn said, then added gently, "She's extraordinary."

"It's just . . . I'm feeding or cleaning or changing her around the clock, and meanwhile you're running around town making deals and wooing sexy clients. You have everything, and—"

"Stop," Jocelyn said, wheeling around. She handed Rose off to Maddy, feeling suddenly dangerous. "*You* have everything, and don't you forget it."

She fled the room, heart pounding. She leashed Rusty and led him outside. Claire called after her, but she didn't turn back.

◆ ◆ ◆

Jocelyn couldn't sleep. It was too quiet, too empty, and she kept thinking of Maddy a couple of miles away, probably nursing her daughter. Jocelyn had worked so hard over the years to feel okay on her own, solid and whole, and all it took was one heated encounter with her sister to unravel it all. She hated that Maddy still had that hold over her.

It was nearly midnight when she shrugged on a sweater and drove to Nauset Light. She plodded down the pathway that had finally been cleared to replace the wooden stairs that got destroyed every winter and had to be rebuilt again by summer. She slipped off her shoes. The sand was cool under her soles, the shore dotted with clumps of black seaweed. It was high tide, and Jocelyn peered out at the water, inky and tumultuous. She only ever came here at night. She set out due north, knowing she could walk and walk, probably to the tip of P-town, and likely not encounter a soul along the way. She thought back to when she'd discovered she was pregnant, on that beautiful May day of her sophomore year. She remembered every detail.

Seeing the two pink lines, she knew she was supposed to panic. To run to the nearest clinic or, barring that, to freak out about how now her whole life would change. But although she hadn't known she wanted a baby, and certainly hadn't planned it, Jocelyn felt sublime. School, money—she'd figure out the practical stuff. The important thing was, this was the start of something amazing.

She'd called Betsy to share the news (she wouldn't tell Luke until that evening), then skipped to the computer lab, where she'd pored over medical websites to learn all about the feats her body was achieving: her heart rate accelerated to pump surges of blood, her cells forming into an embryo that already had a nervous system, the starts of a brain, a spinal cord. *Incredible.*

She'd spent the afternoon babysitting a kindergartner named Grace. At the playground she studied the clusters of mothers, thinking how soon she'd belong to their crowd. When Grace got hungry, they shared a tub of apple slices.

Jocelyn had been majoring in early childhood education. But the ed classes she'd taken so far had bored her—the dense blocks of text about pedagogical theories and the dry lectures about "the child" from professors who seemed to have never actually met one. Jocelyn wondered then whether her interest was not in teaching kids but in having one of her own—sitting on a playground bench eating snacks and brushing the slippery hair off the face of a small human. It seemed crazy—she knew other people would say it was crazy to take this wild leap. But she'd never felt so certain about anything.

Jocelyn turned and locked eyes with her sister, running toward them on the other side of the chain-link fence. The encounter wasn't that surprising. The playground abutted Amherst's campus, and Maddy's daily runs spanned many miles. Grace called out to ask her what she was running from, which made Jocelyn laugh. They waved, and Maddy waved back with a frown, not breaking her stride, her lean muscles accentuated by slick spandex. Jocelyn was curvier, and soon she'd grow even more so—the thought made her giddy. For once, a run-in with her sister hadn't rankled her; how could she be bothered when she was so full of joy, when new life was blooming inside her?

Jocelyn could still conjure up that feeling more than a decade later, walking down the beach under a sliver of moon. As hurt as she'd felt months later at Maddy's disinterest in her niece, becoming a mother had made Jocelyn mellower with her sister; she'd had something—some*one*—so much more significant to care about. Jocelyn ached, thinking of Junie. She kicked at a piece of driftwood and chucked the shell of a hermit crab downshore. If Maddy were to run by right now, Jocelyn thought she might trip her.

Ascending the pathway, she spotted the familiar Volvo station wagon next to her Subaru. She opened the passenger-side door and slumped into her mom's car, the seat heater already going.

"I thought I'd find you here," Claire said.

"Yeah, well." Years earlier, this had been a nightly ritual: Jocelyn and her mom sitting side by side, staring out at the sea where she'd strewn her daughter's ashes. Now they watched the flash of the lighthouse, blinding them for a second before whipping past.

"Remember when you girls were teenagers and I used to take you to open houses?" Claire asked.

"Of course," Jocelyn said. "We'd go just for fun. Maddy hated it, wondering what was the point, but I loved seeing all the different ways people lived. Fast-forward, and now I'm a Realtor." She wasn't trying to be snotty—she appreciated this origin story—but tonight she felt on edge.

"Well, it wasn't just for fun, actually," Claire said. "You and Maddy had always butted heads, but it really ramped up in high school. I thought it would help if we had a bigger house, so you could each have your own room."

"Huh." Jocelyn hadn't known that part. But it didn't surprise her. Their teenage years had brought out Maddy's bitchiness in full force—she'd honed a casual cruelty that could cut Jocelyn, and in response Jocelyn became an expert at acting like her sister's words had no effect on her. Their terrible tug-of-war.

"Anyway," said Claire, "your father claimed we couldn't afford it, and maybe that was true. He always believed in the two of you working things out."

Jocelyn scoffed. "We should've gotten the bigger house."

"Come on, you adore our house," Claire said.

Jocelyn didn't deny it. She'd loved growing up there, and raising Junie there, too.

The car grew thick with silence before Claire spoke again: "I know this is hard for you. It's hard for Maddy, too. Both things are true, okay?"

A thin layer of Jocelyn's anger melted away. "Okay."

"All right, out you go. It's way past my bedtime."

"Thanks, Mom."

In her own car, Jocelyn followed the beam of the lighthouse as the landscape was illuminated in strips: beach grass, dune, shore, her face, and back to beach grass. Jocelyn sent good thoughts out to sea, then headed home.

◆ ◆ ◆

As Kyle came into view, Jocelyn felt a shiver up her spine. It had been two weeks since their first meetup, and Jocelyn wasn't sure whether she'd built him up too much in her head—she hadn't.

"I got an insider tip on the best local coffee," he said, winking. "I hope you like milk." He held out a sky-blue paper cup from Cod Coffee, which Jocelyn had told him about. What a dork.

"Thank you," she said. "Shall we?"

They were at an open house for a ranch-style home set on a pond in West Brewster, but a walk around its path revealed a rank odor from the transfer station two properties over. "Imagine this on a hot summer day," Jocelyn said with a shudder. "Total gag-fest."

"At least you wouldn't have to go far to dump your trash," said Kyle, always with the silver lining.

He'd suggested touring the next house, a historic building in Orleans built in 1890. Jocelyn was charmed by his enthusiasm.

The house was all dark wood and sloping floors, and Jocelyn felt transported back in time, like she should hunker down with her knitting by the fireplace and wait for a man to bring home the hunt (she had a particular one in mind). The upstairs ceilings were three-quarter height, so Kyle had to duck.

"It's like a museum," he said, marveling as they wound their way through the railroad setup, until it dead-ended in a bathroom with a claw-foot tub. "Can you imagine if I had to walk through Nina's bedroom every time I had to relieve myself? An eleven-year-old's worst nightmare."

An eleven-year-old. Jocelyn was thrown by this information. She *could* imagine it, sort of, because it stayed with her like a shadow, what it would've been like to have a daughter who was two, then three, then four, and so on. And, now, nearly eleven. Like Nina.

Kyle beckoned Jocelyn to join him in a pair of rocking chairs by the bedroom window. The caning was surprisingly sturdy, their rocking smooth. Given a few minutes, Jocelyn might've been lulled to sleep.

Vibrations sounded from Kyle's pocket. He pulled out his phone. "Speaking of Nina, she's asking how much longer I'll be."

"Where is she?"

"At the beach, wearing not nearly enough layers." It was a crisp fall day. "I insisted on bayside so she'd have cell service. That earned me a big eye roll. But now look, she already misses me. She can be so desperate for independence, and then an hour later she's like a toddler clinging to my leg." Kyle's thumbs were flying across his phone screen. "I didn't ask, do you have kids?"

Jocelyn noticed she wasn't having her usual reaction. She inhaled deeply. "I had a daughter. She would've been almost eleven now."

Kyle looked up from his phone. "Oh, I'm so sorry. What was her name?"

"Juniper." When was the last time she'd said it aloud? "We called her Junie."

"That's pretty."

"I only had fifteen months with her. She drowned."

They kept rocking. The window looked out on a giant oak tree, its leaves rustling in the wind.

Kyle broke the silence: "A couple years ago, there was a car accident. My wife died. Olivia—I called her Liv. It was a hit-and-run. They never caught the driver."

"How awful." Strangely, Jocelyn wasn't shocked to hear this. It was like she'd intuited the grief in Kyle's eyes, recognizing something they had in common. "You must have fantasies about what you'd like to do to that driver."

"Sometimes," Kyle said. "For a while I felt nothing. I was in such a haze that first year, barely functioning. And Nina was just a kid when it happened. I didn't notice her changing, growing up. Now it's like I'm living with a stranger." He shook his head at the enigma of tween girls. "I just feel clueless as a father."

"I'm sure you're doing better than you think."

"I appreciate you saying that, but I don't think so." He dropped his head into his hands, and a choking sob escaped him. "Sorry. I think I need some air." He was out the door before Jocelyn could insist it was fine.

She would give him a minute. She kept rocking, thinking about how Kyle was a widower, while there wasn't a word for what she was. Eventually she retraced her steps through the old house. Outside was a shock: the fresh air, the bright sky, the return to present day. It was like they'd opened up about their losses in another century.

She found Kyle by his car. "Hey, are you all right?"

"Yeah, thanks. I'm sorry, I didn't mean to unload on you back there."

"No worries." Jocelyn smiled up at him, squinting at the sun. He smiled back. "So what's she into, your daughter?"

"Begging for a smartphone, mostly. What else? Um, nail art?" His intonation seemed to question whether this was really a thing.

"Take her to Nailed It on Ocean Road. Ask for Lorraine." Jocelyn had sold Lorraine an Acorn Deck House in West Harwich after her business first took off.

"Thanks."

"Meanwhile, we'll keep at it."

Kyle held out his hands. "Next time you see me, I'll probably have flowers all over my nails."

"Hm, I picture you as more of a butterfly guy."

"What can I say, I'm a man of mystery." Kyle raised an eyebrow. But Jocelyn was thinking she already knew everything she needed to know about him.

Chapter 10

MADDY

Maddy looked down and laughed at herself. She was standing in the stinky muck of low tide, in rubber overalls that extended into boots and must've weighed twenty pounds—waders, Kelsey had called them when Maddy pulled them on in her neighbor's basement.

Maddy hadn't planned to spend Saturday morning clamming with Kelsey. But there she'd been on the road, in her own pair of waders, when Maddy stepped outside, feeling at a loss. Rose was down for a nap, and Maddy was going to suggest that she and Justin play cards, or watch a movie, or do anything at all together, since he'd been working so much and their only interactions lately were about baby logistics. But Justin preempted her by saying he had to work on a brief and suggesting she take some "me" time, when the last thing Maddy wanted was more time in her own head.

Kelsey had caught her staring. "Hey, I'm off to catch my next meal," she hollered, holding up a wire basket with kickboards stuck to its sides. "Want to come?"

Maddy couldn't think of anything better to do. So she borrowed Kelsey's husband's waders and clam rake, and off they went to the salt marsh, Kelsey's Ram truck towering over the other vehicles on the road.

As they stepped gingerly through slippery grass out to the flats, Kelsey explained how each type of quahog corresponded to its size, littlenecks versus cherrystones and chowder clams. The littlest ones were the tastiest, but they had to be at least a certain size to take, or you could get busted by the town—that was why they carried clam gauges. The point was to give the little guys time to grow, to keep the shellfish population healthy. "You can spend a boatload on these babies in a restaurant," Kelsey said, "or you can dig up a bucket of 'em yourself basically for free. Plus, coming out here is the only time I get away from my goddamn kids."

Clamming was dirty, difficult work, and Maddy was an instant fan. She liked the labor of it, grunting and sweating as she dug through the mud until her rake hit on something hard, then reaching in and pulling out a slate-gray treasure. She didn't even mind the ache in her lower back because her mind cleared of noise and her senses sharpened. As she and Kelsey worked quietly, Maddy breathed in the algae smell and listened to the distant susurrations of the sea. When one of them unearthed a clam, they'd air-high-five, and Maddy would puff up with satisfaction. It took an hour to fill up the bucket.

On the drive home, Maddy was spent. Not like she felt after a day with Rose, but a good, satisfied kind of spent; she knew she'd sleep well tonight (at least until Rose's first feeding).

Stepping out of the borrowed waders, she thanked Kelsey. "That was way more fun than I expected."

"I know, right?" Kelsey said. "It's kind of addictive."

Maddy indicated the bucket. "Now what?"

"House rule is, I dig 'em, Larry cooks 'em. He makes a mean clam chowder. Why don't you guys come over for supper?"

"We'd love to."

But it was a hard sell to Justin, who just wanted to relax that evening, since his brief had taken much longer than expected. He relented after Maddy pleaded. So, at six o'clock, they walked next door, Justin in a chambray button-down and chinos, Maddy in a linen jumpsuit, and Rose in a paisley onesie and matching sweater. Maddy's mood was peppy: It was their first social engagement since the move.

Kelsey's backyard was littered with toy trucks and sports equipment, and the boys ran around with baseball bats that looked to be real aluminum. Maddy tried not to picture knocked-out teeth and streaming blood. But Kelsey's husband, Larry, seemed perfectly relaxed as he carried out a cooler. "Hey, guys," he said. "Bud Light, Coors, or White Claw?" He wore track pants and a T-shirt, and Kelsey came out in her usual evening sweatsuit. Maddy felt overdressed on behalf of her family.

"Thanks, I'll stick with one of these," Justin said, indicating the four-pack of Outermost IPAs he'd carried over. Maddy accepted a White Claw.

"I'm so glad we're doing this," Kelsey said. She popped open two Bud Lights and handed one to Larry. "To Blueberry Lane."

"To Blueberry Lane," Justin and Maddy echoed, and the couples clinked cans.

They sat around the firepit. It was too chaotic for any awkwardness, with the boys wrestling all around them, pausing only to chug from plastic cups of Sprite. "Don't mind our pack of animals," Larry said, more laid back than Maddy thought she'd ever been. She was grateful that Rose was staying calm in Justin's lap.

"Can I hold this cutie?" Kelsey asked, and Maddy hoped she didn't notice Justin's brief hesitation before handing Rose over. It turned out Kelsey was a baby whisperer. She propped Rose on her lap and sang "Five Little Ducks" until Rose gurgled with glee.

The boys had already eaten ("Two large pizzas," Kelsey grumbled) and went inside to play video games. The chowder was heavenly—creamy with hits of smoky bacon and tender potatoes, plus the clams, briny and fresh. "I can't believe we caught these ourselves!" Maddy exclaimed more than once, full of pride.

"Marsh to table," Larry said. "The best kind of meal."

He told them about his work as a general contractor—he and his buddy had come up together and now were business partners. They'd actually built that extension over there after Kelsey couldn't quit getting pregnant—big belly laugh. Maddy applauded the workmanship, confiding that she and Justin could barely hang a picture frame. Larry asked about Justin's job, and Justin delivered the spiel Maddy had heard many times, about how he'd left his big, soulless law firm to join a nonprofit, and how he represented clients who otherwise couldn't afford private counsel. For the first time, Maddy thought it sounded a little snooty. Again, no one asked Maddy about her work, and they moved on to chat about the children.

Larry asked whether anyone wanted seconds. Maddy planned to take him up on another bowl, but Rose started squirming, and Justin said, "I think that's our cue. Thank you so much for dinner."

"We'll have to return the favor," Maddy added, although the thought of hosting all those boys made her sweat. The women hugged, and the men shook hands.

Maddy's good mood lasted until they reached their porch, at which point Justin said, "Well, that was interesting."

His tone was sharp, and Maddy's defenses flew up. "What do you mean?"

"It was nice of Kelsey and Larry to have us over, but we don't have anything in common with them. Did you see how their eyes glazed over when I was describing my job?"

"Just because they didn't graduate from Ivy League colleges—"

"Did they even *go* to college?"

"You are such a snob," Maddy scoffed.

"Oh, gimme a break. Like you haven't made similar comments a thousand times."

"Actually, we do have something in common," she snapped. "We're neighbors! Duh!" Maddy was so over this conversation. She said she'd go get Rose ready for bed.

That night she stayed awake between Rose's feedings. Justin had been so confident in declaring them different from Kelsey and Larry, whereas Maddy couldn't have felt less sure of who she was anymore.

The next morning she announced she wanted a family day: a picnic at Duck Pond. The spot conjured up pleasant childhood memories. She and Jocelyn had actually gotten along there, racing across the pond, then bundling up in thick towels to snack on Claire's homemade banana bread. It had been different at the beaches, which were packed with summer people and made Maddy yearn to be one of them. She'd covet their stylish swimwear and their extravagant lunches from the upscale seafood joints, and fantasize about the sophisticated lives they'd be returning to after their vacations; meanwhile, Maddy was stuck here, far away from anything. But Duck Pond was usually deserted except for her family, so her longing for a more interesting life didn't flare up there. She could just be.

On the drive over, Justin apologized for how he'd acted the night before, saying he'd been cranky from work. They were both still adjusting to the move, and it was nice that Maddy was making an effort to meet new people. Maddy said a quick thanks, not in the mood to retread that topic; she wanted today to feel relaxed and easy.

The short hike down to the water was just as Maddy remembered it: steep in spots and laden with fragrant pine needles. They passed a grove of scraggly scrub oak before the pond came into view, sparkling and serene.

"Wow," said Justin. Maddy's heart fluttered—she loved that he recognized how special this place was.

They laid out a blanket, and Justin sang to Rose while Maddy unpacked the baguette, tomato, and hunk of Brie. Maddy reminisced aloud, and Justin described a swimming hole near Woodstock that his family had frequented growing up. After eating, Justin strapped Rose to his chest, and they waded in the water, bracing but refreshing. When Maddy had agreed to move back to the Cape, this was what she'd envisioned: their tight-knit little trio together on an outing, sun out and sky blue. She wished she could bottle up the morning to keep.

"So, I want to speak with you about something," Justin said, facing her head-on.

"Okay." Why did Maddy suddenly feel nervous?

"I was talking to your family, and we're all pretty worried about you. You seem to be really struggling."

Maddy's spine went rigid. "You were all sitting around talking about me? Was Jocelyn there?"

"Sure," Justin said. "She's concerned, too. She loves you, Maddy. All of us agree that you could use some help. Your dad got the names of a few therapists."

It was almost unbearable for Maddy to imagine, a conference of her family members gathered to discuss the problem of her. "I'm fine," she said. "I'm just adjusting, as you said in the car. There's been so much change." She was mortified to feel tears prick her eyes.

"Right, of course." Justin placed a palm on her back. "Which is why we thought it might make sense for you to seek out some support. I mean, beyond your loved ones." Maddy recoiled at his phrasing, which sounded lifted from a doctor's office brochure.

"Thanks for your concern," she said tightly. Maddy wasn't against therapy in principle (although she found it ridiculous that her friend Krista paid a shrink $250 an hour to fret over her finances), but it just wasn't something she needed. "I'm fine."

Justin sighed. "Okay, well, you don't have to decide right now. Just think about it. Also, I'm sorry to spring this on you"—*Jesus, there was more?*—"but I have to go to the city next week. You and Rose could come if you want, although I'll be tied up through the evenings. It'll just be a few days."

"We'll be fine here," Maddy replied, wondering how many more times she'd be forced to declare that she was fine. She wasn't, of course. Her family thought she needed fixing, and Justin would soon be abandoning her. A hot nausea spread through her belly, and she was trying not to cry.

"Maddy, come on," Justin said. "Let's talk about this."

"I'm sorry if I'm a little taken aback by you going behind my back to discuss my mental health with my parents and Jocelyn—sorry, with my 'loved ones.'"

"We love you. We just want to help."

"So you keep saying," she said. "And about your trip, I've been taking care of Rose on my own all day, every day, while you work until however late you feel like, so I'll just keep on doing that."

Justin opened his mouth, then closed it again.

"Bring back some bagels from the city, okay?" she added.

"Sure," he replied gently. "Can your family help out with Rose while I'm away? Maybe your mom could take a day off school, or Jocelyn has a few hours to spare."

"Good idea." Maddy didn't want to keep talking about this. "Ready to pack up? It's almost nap time."

"Okay," Justin said. He looked defeated, but Maddy was too humiliated to care.

When it was time to go to her parents' house for Sunday dinner, Maddy claimed she wasn't feeling well. Justin suggested they all stay home then—they could get Thai takeout and watch a movie. But Maddy insisted he and Rose go; she would be fine—*fine!*—on her own. She just needed to rest. After they left, she spotted Kelsey through the window on her stoop and drew the curtains.

Chapter 11

Jocelyn had just dunked in Bee's River when her mother called to ask whether she could watch Rose for the morning. The question dampened the revitalizing effect of the swim. "Why isn't Maddy asking me herself?"

"You know your sister, too proud to admit she needs help. But Justin's away for work, and he asked us to be there for her, given our chat last week."

When Justin had corralled the family to discuss Maddy, Jocelyn was immediately uncomfortable. Claire and Jed were an attentive audience as he laid out Maddy's recent struggles, but Jocelyn couldn't help thinking how much her sister would hate to know they were meeting about her. Justin cited stats about postpartum depression and anxiety, but added that Maddy had been suffering since getting fired last spring. Jocelyn's ears perked up. *Fired? Last spring?* Maddy had told them she'd left her job voluntarily, after having Rose, because of the move. Jocelyn tuned back in: Justin believed sharing their collective concern with Maddy would be a helpful first step. Jocelyn bit her tongue. She didn't want to meddle, even though she was sure that kind of intervention would only make her sister defensive.

She didn't have time to shower before picking up Rose and meeting Betsy at the Blushing Buoy. It was the restaurant's final week, after which it would shut down till April. Betsy mostly avoided the fried fare she served up, except for this last lunch with Jocelyn, an annual tradition. Rose was asleep in her car seat, snoring softly, as Jocelyn carted her into the back booth.

"I wish *I* could nap," Betsy said, nuzzling against the baby's cheek. "Two and a half days till Costa Rica."

"But who's counting?"

"I actually keep a countdown on my phone." Betsy got through tourist season by anticipating the extended vacation she and Jewel took every offseason.

Jocelyn moped as she tied on her plastic bib. "I hate it when you leave me."

Betsy shrugged. "You can snuggle up with Bonnie and Clyde if you get lonely." Jocelyn had agreed to watch the couple's golden retrievers while they were gone; their guinea pigs would become Claire's classroom pets. "Plus, you've got to stay here to find a house for Kyle McDreamy."

"Oh my god, please don't call him that." To hide her blush, Jocelyn ducked her head and worked the word search on the menu. "I so regret telling you about him."

"Come on, I'm your biggest cheerleader. Any updates?"

Jocelyn conjured up her and Kyle's conversation at the old house—but it felt private, almost sacred. "I'm showing him a place in Eastham this afternoon."

Betsy grinned. "Ooh, is it an open house?"

"Don't even think about it, Bets."

"Remember that time I dropped by your open house and sparked a bidding war?"

"Is that how you remember it? I seem to recall you accosting prospective buyers with a rumor that the Kennedys had once owned the property."

"That was genius. You should put me on the payroll."

"Whatever you say." Jocelyn raised her crayon in triumph. "Done."

"You're a word-search prodigy, my friend."

Jewel brought over baskets piled with plump scallops, shoestring onion rings, and the best whole-belly clams this side of the Sagamore, plus two ears of glistening corn. "For my two faves."

"Thanks, love," Betsy said.

They dug into the golden-fried goodness. Betsy pulled a bunch of onion rings over her wrists like bangles. "Let me read your fortune, milady. You will eat until your pants don't zip; then you will close a real estate deal, sealing it with a kiss."

Jocelyn guffawed, open mouth full of corn, just as a girl walked by and recoiled.

"Nina, we're up," a familiar voice called out.

Jocelyn swung around to see the girl join a tall man whose swoop of hair confirmed it was Kyle. "Garden salad, dressing on the side," she told the cashier.

So that was Kyle's daughter. She was striking looking, with wavy red hair framing a freckled face, and nearly as tall as her father. Jocelyn leaned across the table. "That's him," she whispered to Betsy, tilting her head in his direction.

"Kyle McDreamy?"

Jocelyn nodded before sinking down in the booth and taking stock of herself: She wore a plastic bib over a tie-dye cover-up over a damp bathing suit; her hair was matted with salt.

She could hear Kyle trying to reason with his daughter, saying the lobster roll was supposedly to die for (Jocelyn had told him that), growing frustrated as Nina dug in her heels on the salad. Jocelyn wanted to tell him to just order extra and not make a big deal of it. That was what they'd done with Maddy during her dieting spells. Jocelyn herself had always been an eater.

Thankfully Kyle picked a booth across the restaurant. Still, Jocelyn felt the pull of his presence as if they were two magnets.

Rose chose that moment to wake up, lips puckering with hunger, and soon she was wailing. Jocelyn searched the diaper bag for milk, riffling through an explosion of onesies and toys. "Maddy packed enough for a week," Betsy said.

"Seriously." But Jocelyn knew that the smaller the baby, the more stuff they needed.

Finally, out tumbled a bottle—an empty one. "No, Maddy wouldn't forget to pack milk."

Betsy spotted the tub of Similac in a side pocket. "There you go."

"Huh." When Justin had mentioned at their meeting that Maddy was barely sleeping between night feedings, and Claire suggested maybe she switch to formula, he'd cut her off, saying they both agreed breast was best. Now Jocelyn hurried to prepare the bottle, and just as she got Rose to take it, she glanced up and saw Kyle gazing down at her.

"Fancy meeting you here," he declared.

"Hey." Jocelyn waved with her non-bottle hand, then gestured across the booth. "This is Betsy. She owns the joint."

Kyle held out a hand. "An honor to meet you. I'm Kyle Taylor, a client of the wonderful Jocelyn."

Betsy wiped her hand on her shorts before shaking. "Betsy Anderson, best friend of the wonderful Jocelyn. You can call me Bestie Betsy." Jocelyn rolled her eyes.

"Clever. And who's this charmer?" Kyle asked, gazing at Rose.

"This is my very hungry niece, Rose," Jocelyn said.

"Ah, Maddy's daughter." He turned to Betsy. "Man, your lobster roll is out of this world. And my daughter seems to be enjoying the garden salad."

"I call that the teen girl special," Betsy said. Jocelyn shot her a look. "Sorry, bad joke."

"She's beautiful," Jocelyn said.

"I know," Kyle said. "Sorry, I realize I'm not supposed to respond like that. Thank you. She's also very smart."

"I bet," Jocelyn said. She'd been grinning through their exchange, and only now realized there was a corn kernel wedged between her two front teeth—she worried it out with her tongue, discreetly, she hoped. "Well, I've got to get home to clean myself up. I have an important appointment later."

"What a coincidence. Me too," Kyle said, dimples on display. "But first I promised Nina a round of mini golf."

"Fun," Jocelyn said.

"Nina's got some serious competition," Kyle said. "Back in the day, I sank two holes in one in a single game. I bet they still talk about it at the putt-putt place in my hometown."

"What a legend," Betsy said. "Good luck kicking your daughter's ass."

"See you in a couple hours," Jocelyn said. "Why don't you bring Nina along?"

"Sure." As Kyle walked off, Jocelyn felt Nina observing her from across the room. She waved, and the girl held up a tentative hand.

◆ ◆ ◆

Jocelyn almost snapped a picture: Kyle and his daughter on the front steps, framed by glossy black shutters and window boxes bursting with orange chrysanthemums. It looked like they already lived there. Jocelyn greeted them, Nina mumbled hello, and Kyle said, "Don't you clean up nice?" His daughter shot him a look. "What, am I not supposed to say that?" He turned back to Jocelyn. "You looked very nice before, as well. I didn't mean to imply you didn't." To Nina, he said, "Better?"

Jocelyn smiled to herself as she worked the lockbox. She'd changed into a new shirtdress, which she'd told herself she hadn't specifically bought for today.

The house was a classic Cape with a breezy vibe, raw wood floorboards, and plenty of light. Nina plopped onto the couch and began browsing a *National Geographic* from a fan of them on the coffee table, until Kyle urged her to come look around. She sighed, then followed them to the hallway, where she ran her fingers along the bronze sconces and declared them dusty. In the kitchen—charming with shaker-style cabinets and walnut barstools—she opened the fridge and announced that the yogurt was expired.

"Well, I doubt it comes with the house," Kyle said. "Let's go see the upstairs."

"This is creepy," Nina said. "I feel like we're breaking and entering."

"Just entering, actually," Kyle replied cheerfully. Jocelyn admired his composure.

On the staircase landing, he whispered to Jocelyn, "She hasn't said she hates it."

Nina wandered into a bedroom, and from the hallway Jocelyn saw the space light up in electric blue, then purple, then pulsing yellow—LED lights, she assumed. Kyle went to enter, but Jocelyn held him back. "Let's give her a minute."

The primary bedroom extended through pocket doors to an alcove. They stood at the picture window, looking out on an expanse of red oaks, no other houses in sight. "My desk can go right here," Kyle said. "My office back home faces an alley."

"Not a bad upgrade," Jocelyn said. "It's lovely here."

Kyle beamed at her, as if to say, *You're lovely, too.* Her stomach flipped. "I think this is the one," he said. "I'll go find Nina."

"Take your time. I'll meet you out back."

The deck was tidy, with a grill, a few ceramic planters, and a pair of wicker loungers. Jocelyn thought there'd be room for a third.

Nina came outside before her father. "I thought the listing said 'ocean view.'"

"Let's see," Jocelyn said. "Ah, come here." From a corner of the deck, she stood on tiptoes and pointed to a sliver of blue in the distance. "Boat Meadow Beach. You'll be able to see more of it after the leaves fall."

Nina frowned. "Are there really sharks out there?"

"Yeah," said Jocelyn, "but they get a bad rap. Shark attacks are really rare. Statistically, you're much more likely to get in a car accident." Instantly she regretted her words, remembering: Kyle's wife, Nina's mother. "Or to get hit by lightning," she added.

"It would be pretty cool to see a shark, though," Nina said.

Kyle appeared, admiring the grill. "Jocelyn, we'll have to have you over for shish kebabs."

Nina recoiled. "You can just say 'dinner' like a normal human."

Kyle nodded, accepting the feedback. "What do you say, Nina-rina, should we buy this place?"

"Yeah, okay."

"Amazing, let's do it." Kyle hugged his daughter, which she tolerated but didn't reciprocate.

He delivered an equally awkward hug to Jocelyn, all arms, no torso, and Jocelyn could feel Nina eyeing her. She cleared her throat and said, "Okay, we'll talk numbers, and then I'll draw up the paperwork."

"I wish we had a bottle of bubbly," Kyle said.

"Chill, Dad. We could still be outbid."

Jocelyn grinned. "Clever kid you've got there."

Kyle mussed his daughter's hair. "Don't I know it."

They spoke twice that evening, reviewing comp properties and hammering out contingencies. Kyle's offer would be competitive, and Jocelyn had a good feeling about it. Drifting to sleep, she envisioned stopping by to welcome them to the neighborhood. She'd bring a bottle of wine and a string of LED lights for Nina. She'd stay for a toast and some shish kebabs. It would be a happy home.

Jocelyn woke to a message: Kyle's offer had been accepted. She yelped, already dialing his number.

He answered with "You wouldn't be calling so early if we didn't get it, right?" Jocelyn heard Nina in the background telling him to switch to speaker.

"Congrats!" Jocelyn said.

Kyle cheered, and Jocelyn even heard a whoop from Nina. She imagined them jumping up and down, maybe doing some old private handshake that lately Nina acted too cool to perform.

They'd get to the next steps, but now was the time to celebrate. On cue, Kyle cleared his throat and asked, "So, can I take you out to drinks next time we're in town?"

Jocelyn beamed. "I know just the place."

Chapter 12

Maddy was just as nervous about meeting the babysitter as she was about her postpartum checkup. Which of course was happening while Justin was away, and when no one in her family was free to watch Rose. She didn't want to reschedule—it had taken hours on the phone to find a doctor with any availability, and she was weeks past the recommended window for the appointment. So she'd have to leave her baby with a stranger.

Maddy had found the sitter on a Cape Cod moms group on Facebook, where previously she'd only lurked, astounded that the posts were all along the lines of Does anyone have a 3T wetsuit? or Who knows a good baby music class? rather than How on earth is anyone surviving this? or Do the rest of you feel like strangers in your own skin?! (Maddy also still subscribed to her Manhattan moms group news-letter, which she perused when she was in the mood to press against the wound of missing her old life.)

But as soon as she met Tanya, she was put at ease. The sitter was in her mid-forties, her own three kids grown, and she gushed that she loved, loved, loved babies. Maddy's former self would've prepared a list of interview questions, checked references, and con-ducted a background check. But now it was enough to watch Tanya cradle Rose in her arms, radiating affection, and see Rose babble joyfully. Had Maddy ever looked like that while holding Rose? Would she ever come to adore her baby like she knew she was supposed to? Before she could fall further down that quicksand line of questioning, she waved goodbye and slipped out.

Dr. Linnell was around her father's age. Maddy fidgeted in her paper robe, eyeing his thick white eyebrows and large hands, feeling a little ill knowing that they'd soon be inside her. Only out of desperation had she agreed to see a male ob-gyn. She longed for Dr. Feldman, her beloved OB who'd delivered Rose back in New York.

"How are we today?" Dr. Linnell asked, eyes on his handheld device.

"Okay, thanks."

He turned away to strap on plastic gloves. Maddy's view was of his stooped back as he explained that he'd check her vitals and perform a pelvic exam; then they could discuss any concerns.

Dr. Linnell reported each stat matter-of-factly as he typed it into his device: blood pressure, height, weight. Maddy winced at the last number—since Rose was born, she'd avoided the scale.

She gasped as the doctor's fingers entered her. "Some discomfort is normal," he said belatedly. Actually, it was agony. But Maddy hid her torment, enduring the exam in silence, even offering Dr. Linnell a slight smile.

Her mind went to that horrible episode in high school, which she'd never told a soul about. She'd been a freshman, fourteen years old, giddy that her first-ever date was with a charming junior, the star of the lacrosse team. The evening started out even better than her fantasies: snuggling in the back of Ryan Parker's truck as they watched *Ocean's Eleven* at the drive-in, a perfect first kiss under the moonlight, then a winding drive to the parking lot at Newcomb Hollow Beach. Making out was fun and exciting—until suddenly it wasn't, and Maddy found herself squirming away from Ryan's touch, which grew more and more aggressive. It was like he couldn't hear her saying stop, as his hand dug into her underwear and shoved its way inside her. Followed by the rest of him. Thankfully—weirdly—he'd worn a condom. The pain had lasted through the following day, when Maddy's family teased her, trying to extract details of the date, and when a rumor spread to half the school that Maddy made barn-animal noises as she came. It was the same throbbing pain she felt now.

"All set," Dr. Linnell said, pulling his hand out and peeling off his gloves. "Everything's in working order. You're all cleared for intercourse. Would you like a prescription for birth control?"

"Um, okay." Maddy was confused. Was that the purpose of this visit, to get her back to bed with her husband? She hadn't thought about sex in months. Still, she dutifully spelled out the name of the pill she'd taken before.

The doctor was still tapping at his device as he said, "Now, any concerns?"

Heading into the appointment, Maddy had planned to bring up how she'd been feeling, and her worry that she wasn't like other mothers, and maybe to ask about meds. Her husband's confrontation had stayed in the back of her mind, and she wanted a professional opinion. But nothing about Dr. Linnell made her feel comfortable broaching the topic. She shook her head, then added, "No concerns," because he still wasn't looking at her.

Within minutes, she was dressed and out at reception, scheduling an annual appointment that she knew she would cancel. She didn't burst into tears until she was back in her car.

Justin picked up before the second ring, and Maddy gave him the play-by-play, including how the doctor had never once made eye contact. "Oh, Maddy," he said.

"On the plus side, he cleared me for sex." She barked out a laugh.

"Okay," Justin said delicately. "Is that something you're ready for?"

"No! Also, I still have fifteen pounds to lose."

"Maddy, you're taking care of an infant. Weight loss hardly seems like the priority."

"I really miss you."

"I miss you, too. I'll be on the 5:12 Amtrak, home around ten."

"Okay." But there were still so many hours until then.

Justin must've read her mind, because he added, "Can the babysitter stay a little longer? You could go do something nice for yourself." Maddy heard a voice in the background mention a team lunch; then Justin said he had to run. "I love you."

"I love you, too."

It wasn't a bad idea. Yesterday, when Jocelyn watched Rose, Maddy had felt like she had to use every minute. She'd deep-cleaned the kitchen, then tackled the remaining boxes of books. But instead of feeling satisfied by filling the bookshelves, she'd just felt bad about having basically stopped reading since Rose was born. Now she was out in Hyannis, the big city (ha!), and a call to Tanya confirmed that Rose was doing great and it was no problem for her to stay through the afternoon. "Take your time, Mama," the sitter said, her voice so reassuring that Maddy nearly started crying all over again.

She found a coffee shop that, save for the buoys tacked to the walls, could've been in Lower Manhattan. They even had pour-over, strong and dark like Maddy liked it. She settled into an armchair by the window, where she opened the Rate a Doctor app and typed paragraph after paragraph, delighting in describing Dr. Linnell's abhorrent bedside manner. When she clicked "Submit," she felt gratified in the way she remembered from her job after nailing a client pitch. Her review would save other women the indignity she'd endured.

She still had time, so she decided to window-shop. As she strolled the sidewalks, swinging her arms, without even a purse, Maddy felt stunned with freedom, and also like she was missing an appendage. How strange, she thought, that no one else seemed to notice she'd left her baby behind.

Back at Tanya's, Maddy was charmed to see Rose wrapped in a hooded bunny towel, fresh from a bath. Tanya exclaimed at what a sweet baby she was, a cutie even when she got cranky. Maddy marveled at her luck to have happened upon this sitter-saint, the kind of caretaker Rose deserved.

That night, she was half asleep when Justin slipped in beside her in bed. As he recounted his time away, Maddy let the words wash over her. She was here in her husband's arms, safe and warm, and for the moment that was enough.

◆ ◆ ◆

Then Monday rolled around again. It was unseasonably warm, and Maddy decided to take Rose back to Duck Pond. But after the rigamarole of getting out the door, she collapsed into the driver's seat, already exhausted. She peered at her baby, reflected back at her through both the rearview and the car seat mirrors. Rose was burbling merrily, but still Maddy yearned to make the outing alone.

She called Tanya, who said she'd be happy to watch Rose again. So Maddy dropped her off, then continued on to the pond solo. She lay out on the sand, the sunlight caressing her skin. Her jaw unclenched, her mind drained of thoughts, and she felt herself melt into the earth. She must've dozed away half the morning—she never even opened her magazine—and when she came to, she felt cheerful and rested. She hiked out to White Crest Beach and gasped when she glimpsed the towering dunes and the ocean. She'd seen this vista countless times before, but it still astonished her. The world looked so full of promise.

Maddy didn't mean to keep it a secret. That evening she cooked for the first time in recent memory: miso tofu with rice and roasted asparagus. Asking Justin about his day, she found she could focus on his responses. "You seem good," Justin remarked. She was about to respond, *Well, I brought Rose to Tanya's again, and things felt easier after a break*, but he spoke first: "You and Rose are finally finding your groove. What a relief, right?"

Maddy's throat went dry, and she bloomed with shame. *Who spent a random Monday lazing around at a pond?* She nodded silently, feeling the space between her and her husband widen.

But she couldn't stop doing it. She told Tanya a few mornings, once or maybe twice a week. Then she asked about three days a week, then four and five. Next she wondered whether Tanya was free through the afternoons. "Of course," Tanya always replied. "Rose is such a doll, it's my pleasure." These comments stabbed at Maddy, even as they bolstered her desire to flee.

She had no problem filling her time. One day she holed up in the library and read the new Elin Hilderbrand novel from start to finish, crying at the happy ending. Another, she hiked the trails at Nickerson State Park, never encountering another person; the whole park was hers. A third day, she got a mani-pedi and a deep-tissue massage; *I deserve to be pampered,* she repeated to herself as the masseuse worked at the knots in her shoulders. She took herself bowling, a surprise strike sending her jumping up and down like a little kid. She found her old bike in her parents' garage and pedaled the rail trail all the way from Wellfleet to Brewster, her out-of-shape lungs huffing and puffing, her legs delighting at the effort. She lingered at an art gallery, locking eyes with a woman in a baroque portrait and feeling a deep psychic connection. On the Dune Shacks Trail in P-town, she ran down the steep sand and screamed out secrets, like they'd done as teenagers: "I'm a bad mom." "I'm lying to my husband." "I want my old life back." "I'm happy without my daughter."

Meanwhile, things improved with Justin. He was impressed by how much she was getting out with Rose. Now they had real conversations. They posed Rose for pictures and laughed together at her silly expressions. It was so much easier to enjoy her when there was such a short window between pickup at Tanya's and bedtime; for those couple of hours, Maddy could nail the role of good mom. At night she and Justin stood on their deck, holding hands and marveling together at the stars. Maddy kept planning to confess. But then Justin would look at her with such light in his eyes and say something like, "I don't think I could love you any more than I do right now," and Maddy's throat would go dry once again.

She started venturing farther afield. After a morning perusing Edward Hopper paintings at the Provincetown Art Museum, she boarded a whale watch. She'd taken one as a child and remembered the hours of boredom and the insidious creep of seasickness. But this time she loved every minute. She leaned over the railing to watch the land recede to a speck, wind in her hair, sea spray on her cheeks. When the captain pointed out a pod of dolphins, she oohed and aahed along with the other passengers. Next came the whales: a mother and child winding in and out of each other's wake—breathtaking. Inside the cabin she bought Twizzlers and potato chips from the snack bar, and devoured all of it. For the final hour, she lay across a row of plastic seats and slept.

Rose was extra-fussy that evening, and Maddy was exhausted from her big day. She ordered pizza for dinner and zoned out as Justin went on about a tricky client. "Are you okay?" he asked. "Maybe you need a breather from Rosie. Could that babysitter take her one morning?" Maddy nearly laughed out loud. She said she was tired and went to bed.

Keeping up the charade grew stressful, not to mention that Maddy was running out of money. She'd been withdrawing from their joint savings to pay Tanya, counting on the fact that Justin rarely checked that account. The balance was already down to just a few thousand dollars after they'd forked over the down payment on the house, and now nearly all of that was gone, too. But despite the expense, Maddy found she couldn't break her new habit.

The next Monday, she planned to go for brunch at the Wagansett, figuring she might as well treat herself before all the money ran out, but Tanya texted that she'd come down with a cold. The day with her baby stretched out before Maddy. Well, she'd just take Rose with her. But it wasn't the same. *Here I am, taking care of my baby,* she kept telling herself as she picked at her eggs Benedict and Rose banged a spoon against the table; *here I am, doing just fine.* But she felt anything but.

Tanya was sick all week, and the temperature plummeted, ushering in the first whiffs of winter. Maddy knew what was coming: months of bleak gray and most stores shuttered with signs cheerfully declaring, "See you in April!" or "Closed for the Season! Reason? Freezin'!!" She took Rose on a walk, mostly so she could say they'd left the house. But she could see her breath, and she felt sorry for her baby, bundled in five layers; they didn't make it past the end of Blueberry Lane. As Rose napped, Maddy did yoga and tried in vain to slow her racing heart. She thought about knocking on Kelsey's door, but she assumed any conversation of more than two minutes would end in her getting all blubbery, and the thought embarrassed her. When Justin finally appeared, well past dark, she noticed he hugged Rose before her, and she buried her face in his chest to hide her hurt.

By Friday, Maddy was desperate. She stared at her phone for five full minutes before texting her sister, inventing a dentist appointment. Jocelyn wrote right back, saying to bring Rose over whenever; she was stuck at home anyway, waiting on the HVAC guy.

It was nice to be honest with Justin, for once: "I took your advice," she said. "Jocelyn's watching Rose today."

He stroked her hair. "Good, you deserve a break." Shame was becoming Maddy's baseline feeling.

In her sister's living room, Maddy was surprised to find a pot of dried kidney beans on the rug. "Are you cooking out here?"

"It's for Rose," Jocelyn said. She took the baby from Maddy and buried her chubby little feet in the beans; Rose yelped and kicked. "I've got jasmine rice and lentils, too," she said, tickling Rose's toes. "This little lady and I have big plans this morning."

Why hadn't Maddy thought of setting up a sensory bin? "Well," she said, "just don't let her eat any of it."

Jocelyn regarded her. "I think you mean, 'thanks for watching my baby, sis.'"

"Sorry, yes, thank you." Maddy's cheeks burned.

"No problem. And feel free not to rush back after the dentist. My day's wide open, and Rose and I are A-OK, aren't we? Aren't we?" Jocelyn touched the tip of her nose to Rose's again and again, and Rose beamed.

Maddy consulted her watch. "Cool. Okay, I've got to run."

Outside, she crouched in the hedge and spied through the window. The beatific look remained on Jocelyn's face as she played peek-a-boo with Rose. It wasn't an act; Jocelyn was a natural.

Maddy hadn't intended to go all the way to Boston. But she was flying down Route 6, and then just kept going, her thoughts absorbed in all the times Jocelyn had outshone her. Like when Maddy finally got her first boyfriend, sophomore year of college. Jocelyn had been sleeping with guys since early high school, but Maddy had waited, hoping her first time would be special (she didn't count the Ryan Parker incident). Now she'd met an amazing guy, the whip-smart star of her poli-sci seminar who, incredibly, had also become a star in her bed. She'd been floating on a cloud for weeks, dizzy in lust, and when she returned home for the summer, she relished the thought of dropping the news on her sister. But then Jocelyn went and announced her pregnancy, after which Maddy's news seemed silly and small: Maddy had a boyfriend, but Jocelyn had *conceived*.

Maddy was the only one to question her sister's decision to keep the baby, the only one to suggest that motherhood at age twenty would completely fuck up her future. And she was exasperated that her parents didn't back her up. "So you're just gonna let her drop out of school to have a baby?" she'd wailed. "Don't you even care about her education?" Claire pointed out that Jocelyn was her own person, and this was her choice to make. Maddeningly, Jed just nodded along. It was their usual bullshit laissez-faire approach to parenting, letting their kids do whatever. *And Jocelyn was still such a kid*—she often let her laundry pile up so high that she had to wear bikini bottoms for underwear, Maddy happened to know. Jocelyn, in turn, had been furious with Maddy for daring to express an opinion—the obvious, practical opinion!

They never really got past all that upset, and Maddy didn't go home much after that summer. She was busy with school and internships, but also, it was too weird to see Jocelyn with a kid, talking only about baby stuff, making zero life plans beyond being a mom. And then—and even at the time Maddy felt ashamed to be bothered by this—the day before her college commencement came the big tragedy; so, none of her family were there to watch her deliver her big speech. Maddy had been chosen as the student graduation speaker, a major honor; she'd worked on that speech for weeks. Graduation night, she went out hard.

She danced on tables and downed shot after shot, echoing everyone's cheers about making the most of this last night of fun before real life began tomorrow—and meanwhile trying to push away the very real-life stuff happening back home. The more Maddy danced, and the more she drank, the less overwhelmed she felt, until all thoughts of her dead niece receded, leaving her contentedly numb. She stumbled home as the sun came up, then slept through her alarm—missing Juniper's funeral.

◆ ◆ ◆

Maddy pulled off I-93 toward Storrow Drive. She craved an urban setting like she'd craved acai bowls while pregnant. If you squinted, Beacon Hill looked like Brooklyn Heights, with its stylish old row houses and narrow streets lined with gas lamps. Maddy drank it all in: the cars skidding across concrete, the bustling stores, the throngs of people. She circled the block, matching the quick clip of the crowd, thinking, *Here's where I belong.*

Only, not really. She didn't live here—not now or ever. Truthfully, she didn't even know her way around. After everyone else got to where they were going, Maddy was left circling the block.

Well, what about the moms? She spotted a shiny-haired pair pushing strollers, the sleek, made-for-the-city models that she'd researched back in New York. She followed them to a playground and slipped in behind, careful to re-latch the wrought-iron gate.

It was 11:00 a.m. on a Friday. Maybe these women didn't work, or had gone part-time after having kids. Maddy had had a few colleagues who'd done that, and she'd judged them harshly at the time; now she wondered whether they'd found the holy grail of having it all. These playground moms certainly seemed sure in their skin. One held an infant younger than Rose, yet looked in peak Pilates shape; a toddler kept wandering over to her from the play structures, and she'd offer him a water bottle or a peeled tangerine, all while holding up her end of a conversation with another mom. *How?*

If Maddy had stayed in the city, was this the kind of mother she'd be: competent and at ease, too surrounded by community to feel lonely? It was an alluring thought.

"May I help you?" It was the woman with the infant. Maddy pointed to herself with a questioning look on her face. "Yes, you. You've been staring at us. Do you even have a child here?"

"I'm sorry," Maddy stammered, burning with humiliation. She'd assumed herself invisible because that was how she felt. She struggled with the gate's latch, then hurried down the sidewalk, tripping a little, hoping to be out of earshot before the playground moms started talking about her, *that freak*. She bought a Gatorade at an old Italian deli and sat on the curb, gulping it down. She'd imagined herself as part of that crew of shiny, capable mothers, but who was she kidding? She hadn't even washed her hair in a week. She didn't belong here—or anywhere, it seemed.

Anonymous crying in public was another perk of city life. Maddy could just sit there and be miserable while life went on around her.

It was nearly five when she made it back to Jocelyn's. An unfamiliar Prius was parked in the driveway. Maddy wondered whether her sister had invited that client crush of hers over to mess around while Rose slept, like she used to do with guys while babysitting in high school.

But it was only Betsy. Maddy walked in to find the two friends holding up the corners of a bedsheet, with Rose in the center, swinging her to and fro. And what was that sound?

Jocelyn noticed Maddy and lowered the sheet to the rug. "Hey, Mad. What a gorgeous laugh, huh?"

"I've never heard it before," Maddy blurted out.

"Oh wow." Jocelyn smiled wide.

Maddy beamed back, her throat full. For a moment it felt like she and her sister were on the same team, marveling together at one of the great wonders of the world: her daughter's laughter.

Betsy broke the spell: "Nice kid you got here," she said.

"Thanks." Maddy hadn't seen Betsy since the baby shower. She had a tan—she'd been somewhere tropical. "How was she?"

"A little fussy," Jocelyn reported, "but she's a big fan of our makeshift hammock." She lifted Rose and handed her to Maddy. "Here, I bet she missed you."

"Thanks," Maddy said, though she knew it wasn't true. With Rose in her arms, she felt a familiar welling up of emotion at how small and precious her baby was, and how little she deserved a mom like her.

"Hey," said Betsy, "didn't I see you biking the other day?"

Maddy's defenses flew up, her pity party short-circuited. "Me?"

"Yeah, Tuesday morning on the rail trail, near the turnoff to Marconi. I was walking the dogs and called out, but you didn't seem to hear me. Powder-blue bike, purple helmet?"

"I don't think so, no," Maddy said. "I would've been with Rose then."

She could feel her sister's curious gaze; Jocelyn would've known that that description matched the old bike and helmet stored in their parents' garage.

"Huh, I could've sworn it was you," Betsy said.

"I probably *should* start biking." Maddy pinched her belly pudge. "I'm such a fat-ass."

Betsy shrugged. "Or you could try cutting yourself some slack."

Maddy caught Jocelyn stifling a laugh. "Sorry," she said. "Just, that's not exactly your strong suit."

"Well, thanks for today," Maddy said, trying to hide her irritation.

"Of course," Jocelyn replied.

Rose started whimpering as soon as they were out the door. When Maddy blew a raspberry onto her tummy like she'd watched Jocelyn do, causing Rose to explode into giggles, her fussing only escalated. Maddy's head ached, as if she hadn't just spent an entire day away from her life.

Chapter 13

JOCELYN

Jocelyn's bed was piled with clothing rejects. It had been ages since she'd gone out with a guy she was excited about, and it had apparently turned her into someone who took an hour to pick out an outfit. She settled on a slouchy cable-knit sweater and skinny jeans tucked into wedge boots, snapped a mirror selfie, and texted it to Betsy along with the question, Fit check? Betsy replied within a minute: three fire emoji, and an all-caps order for Jocelyn to go flaunt her fine ass and tear off a piece of that Kyle McDreamy. Jocelyn giggled. She was glad her friend was back in town.

Kyle had asked her to meet him at "his place"—the closing was still two weeks away, but Jocelyn had gotten permission for him to go in and measure. Still, she didn't expect that he'd greet her at the door with an actual measuring tape.

"Thank goodness you're here," he said. "I need you to help resolve a very important matter: Namely, will my couch fit in the living room?"

Jocelyn took in the sight of him—dark jeans, well-worn tee, skin a little sweaty—and her body seemed to fill with helium. "If I'd known I'd be doing manual labor, I would've chosen different footwear."

"Sorry, next time I'll send a dress code. Although I think you look lovely."

Their fingers brushed as Jocelyn held the measuring case and Kyle took the yellow blade. He backed up, unspooling it to the wall.

"Ready for the verdict?" she asked.

"Ready."

"Centimeters or inches?"

"Inches."

"Drumroll, please . . ."

"The anticipation is killing me."

"Ninety-two inches," she announced.

Kyle pumped a fist. "It'll fit!"

"Don't you dare let go." Jocelyn steeled herself for the snap of the blade.

"I would never. You come here." Kyle made a beckoning gesture. So, inch by inch, Jocelyn moved toward him, the air between them charged. At thirty inches, she felt her face match his smirk. At twenty, her knees quaked. At ten, she felt flutters. When the ends of the blade spooled back into the case, Kyle took a hold of it, cradling Jocelyn's hand. She felt his breath on her cheek and inhaled his Ivory-soap scent.

Nervous, she stepped back. "What about the rest of the room?"

"Well, let's see." Kyle cleared his throat and lowered himself to the floor. "This'll be my spot on the couch, and this"—he patted right next to him—"will be for my guest." Jocelyn took the cue and sat down. "The coffee table will go here, and the TV above the mantel to watch the Sox games."

"You mean reality shows."

"Right, yes, all the real housewives and aspiring chefs," Kyle said. "And in the corner, I'll put a glass case to display my Little League trophies."

"Classy," Jocelyn said.

"You know me. There, I'm thinking a tiger-print rug."

"Blacklight posters on the wall?"

"But of course. *Architectural Digest* will be beating down my door for a photo shoot."

As they sat riffing in the empty room, Jocelyn felt herself in a pleasant in-between, in this house that wasn't yet a home, with this man who was someone to her but maybe would become more. Kyle asked, "May I kiss you?"

Jocelyn answered with her lips. It was all she'd imagined, how they fit together, and how the taste of him lit up her insides. Her limbs felt like putty. When Kyle pulled away, he cupped her face with his hands and said, "I've been wanting to do that since I first laid eyes on you."

Jocelyn's cheeks burned. It was too much, all of a sudden. She had to stretch her legs. "You should sweep in here," she said, pointing to a string of dust bunnies.

Kyle raised his eyebrows, looking a little confused. But his tone stayed light: "If I'm not mistaken, that's the Realtor's job."

"You're definitely mistaken." They were smiling, but the spell had broken, the temperature lowered. Jocelyn was relieved, but also a little confused herself—she hadn't expected that kissing the person she really wanted to kiss would feel so overwhelming.

"I'm almost ready to go," Kyle said, "but first, real quick, we just need to build an IKEA dining set."

"Cool, you get on that. I'll go hit up the turnip festival, then circle back when you're done."

"Excuse me, the *what* festival?"

"You didn't know Eastham is famous for its turnips?" Jocelyn asked, mock aghast. "It's a big deal around here. There's a turnip cook-off, turnip-themed arts and crafts, and of course, a blessing of the turnips."

"Sounds like the event of the year."

"I still dream about last year's turnip bisque." Kyle gave her a look like he wasn't sure whether she was kidding, and Jocelyn chuckled. The festival was sort of silly, but that bisque really had been delicious.

"Sounds like I can't miss it," he said, following her outside. "Are we really going to the turnip festival?"

Jocelyn winked—she felt at ease again. "Wait and see."

She directed him to drive north, to Truro Vineyards, not a turnip in sight.

They ordered pinot noir from a little hut, then settled onto a bench by a firepit. The sky was streaked peach and lavender, over rows of grapevines in the distance. Kyle draped one of the flannel blankets across their laps as they watched a performer pluck a guitar and sing a Bob Marley song, soft and slow. Jocelyn was thinking how easy this felt, and also strange, and a little thrilling. She could feel Kyle's knee fidgeting beneath the flannel.

"So, this is a capital-*D* date, isn't it?" he said.

"As opposed to measuring for furniture?" she quipped, but the jokey vibe from earlier now clashed with the atmosphere.

"I ought to admit, I haven't been on a real date in a while."

"Honestly, me neither. I'm not really sure how to act."

Kyle raised his glass and clinked it against hers. "To not knowing how to act on a date."

"Cheers," she said.

"There, that's a start."

But he still looked nervous, and Jocelyn thought about how scary it was to try again when you knew so well how it could all go to pieces. It wasn't a coincidence that for so long she hadn't pursued anyone she actually cared about; she'd lacked the courage. But now she felt brave and decided to take a risk—to remind Kyle of what he'd had, even though he'd lost it, and to convince them both that going for it could be worth the gamble. Also, she was just plain curious: "This may be an odd question, but what made you fall for your wife?"

Kyle didn't look taken aback. "Well, Liv was so generous and open. If someone complimented her earrings, she'd give them away on the spot. If someone had too much to drink, she'd be at their side, handing them water, arranging their ride home. Plus, I knew right away she'd be an amazing mother."

"How old were you when you met?"

"Twenty-one. Liv had the campus apartment above mine. She did Tae Bo every morning, and the pounding always woke me up." Jocelyn scrunched up her forehead in confusion. "It was this fitness fad—Billy Blanks in blue spandex?" She shook her head. "Well, it was a different time."

"I guess so," Jocelyn said.

"Anyway, it was another year before Liv agreed to date me. She claimed she wanted no attachments. If only she'd known that a decade later, we'd be married with a baby." Kyle looked wistful.

Jocelyn sipped at her wine, thinking she liked this man very much.

A little bashfully, he asked her to dance. Jocelyn couldn't remember the last time she'd danced—probably years ago, at Betsy's wedding. They joined the small crowd on the makeshift dance floor. Kyle led and she followed. He spun her in and out, then surprised her with a dip and a kiss.

When he pulled her close again, Jocelyn felt vibrations through his pocket. He checked his phone. "Sorry to be rude. It's Nina." He stepped away, phone to ear, and Jocelyn heard, "Yes, honey, it's fine," before he walked out of range.

Back at the firepit, Jocelyn considered how, just like her, Kyle had always known he wanted to be a parent. And just like him with Liv, she'd been in college when she met Luke. It was frightening how fast she'd fallen for him.

They'd met at a booze-soaked party, where Jocelyn had been stuck in a tedious conversation about the problem of misogynist male geniuses. One girl declared that all women should read *Portnoy's Complaint* to understand how men really did consider women just pieces of flesh. Only, her tone was arch, and she was directing the comment at a guy who'd just chugged a forty; she was flirting, Jocelyn realized depressingly. Jocelyn didn't usually interfere with other people's game, but she couldn't help herself; she cut them off with her best Bob Dylan croak, saying you didn't need a weatherman to know which way the wind blew.

The guy behind her laughed, and that was basically all it took. Luke's blue eyes sparkled; his lips parted slightly. He looked as captivated by her as she was by him, and Jocelyn swooned to her core.

They talked about nothing much, communicating mostly in glances. When he touched her arm, she felt a spark. Ten minutes later, they left. It was a frigid February night. Luke held her mittened hand

and pointed at the moon, declaring it a waxing gibbous. Peering up at the sky made Jocelyn feel tipsy and romantic. Later, when she slid off his boxers, Luke referred to himself as a waxing gibbous, and Jocelyn groaned as she climbed on top of him, already a little in love.

Afterward, she cooked grilled cheeses in Luke's kitchenette, and they ate in bed, littering the duvet with crumbs. Jocelyn opened a notebook on the nightstand, filled with tiny black ink; she asked what a tokamak was. Luke explained about powerful magnetic coils and plasma. He sang a verse of that They Might Be Giants song that Jocelyn remembered from her childhood, about the sun being a mass of incandescent gas. When hydrogen turned into helium under all that heat and pressure— that was nuclear fusion, Luke said; he was in grad school studying it. The sun's conditions were perfect for fusion, and if we could get it right here on Earth, we'd solve the world's energy problems.

It sounded like magic. Like how it felt being with Luke.

He finished his food and asked whether she'd cook like that for him every day. She said it depended on the terms. "In exchange for my eternal devotion?" he offered, and she replied, "Oh, sure." It was the kind of talk you could get away with in the liminal stretch between midnight and morning. They sealed the deal in bed.

In the months that followed, when they weren't in class or carrying out the basic necessities of life, they lived in Luke's bed; to Jocelyn, everything else felt like going through the motions. They used condoms, or he pulled out, mostly. Still, Jocelyn wasn't surprised to discover she was pregnant. What surprised her was how unconflicted she felt, and how unfazed she was by the enormous implications of such news. She was happy, plain and simple. She didn't make a plan for how to tell Luke. She just went over to his place that night, as usual. The sight of him still loosened her joints. Her desire pressed up against her chest, almost too big to contain. She leaped into his arms, and he carried her to bed.

She should tell him now, she thought. He'd be shocked but excited. He'd suggest they name her Cleo or Poppy (Jocelyn felt certain it was a girl). They'd banter about her inheriting his cleft chin and her long lashes, then toss around ideas for the nursery.

But Luke had news of his own: He'd been approved to teach his fusion course to undergrads in the fall. He went on about what a great opportunity it was, and the importance of educating people about nuclear energy. Meanwhile, Jocelyn felt like she was receding farther and farther into space. She didn't care about the world's energy problems; she cared about what was happening right here inside this room, inside her.

Luke asked whether she was okay. He was used to her being fun and easygoing. She brought his palm to her belly, and he smiled. She felt a surge of hope that he already knew, until he reached under her shirt and went for her bra.

"Wait," she said. Now was the moment. "I have something to tell you. I'm pregnant." She held her breath as Luke's face went blank.

"How did this happen?" he finally asked. "We've been careful."

Jocelyn wilted.

Luke draped an arm around her. "It's okay. We'll take care of it. I can pay, and—"

The sob that emerged from deep inside her quieted him. This was not how this was meant to go. "You'd be such a good father," she said, barely a whisper.

Luke's eyes went wide. "Wait, you're not thinking of . . ."

"I was. I am."

"Oh."

Jocelyn could see it play out across his face—his belief that it was a woman's body, a woman's choice—his desire to be a stand-up guy. He cared about her, loved her, even. He'd told her so at least a dozen times.

"Listen, you don't have to . . ." Jocelyn stuttered. She wasn't prepared for this. "I'm fine. I just wanted to let you know, since I took the test this morning."

"Oh, so you just found out." Luke seemed to relax. "You must still be in shock."

Jocelyn didn't want this version of this conversation. She didn't want to have to say that she'd never felt more clearheaded in her life, and it was Luke who was in shock.

"I'm tired," she said, lying down, turning away.

They snuggled up the way they had every night since the one when they'd first met, with Luke's limbs wrapped around her own, and Jocelyn let herself feel protected. The next morning she woke to light streaming through the window and Luke watching her.

"So, um, how did you think I'd react?" he asked.

"I thought you'd be happy." Jocelyn could hear how foolish she must've sounded to him. She already knew this was the end.

"It's just, I'm in the first year of a PhD program that I've worked for my whole life. I earn minimum wage. And we've known each other for three months." Luke's voice was gentle, his smile kind, and Jocelyn's sadness bloomed into humiliation. It would've been easier if he were being an asshole. "I love you, Jocelyn. I'll support you in any way I can. But I'm not ready to be a father."

"I understand," she said, trying to. "I'm gonna go."

He wanted her to stay and talk more, but Jocelyn's conviction was strong: This was it. This would be the last time they woke up together, or kissed, or said "I love you." And she was right.

◆ ◆ ◆

"Apologies," Kyle said, returning to the firepit. "Nina's at a sleepover, and she's pissed that I didn't wash her joggers, because all the other girls have their joggers."

"Uh-oh," said Jocelyn, "code-red emergency. So you're driving one hundred miles back to do her laundry?"

"Actually, I told her to suck it up and deal, which is something she likes to say to me."

"I see. Someone should give you one of those number-one-dad mugs."

"Ha." Kyle groaned. "Don't you just wish you had a tween daughter?" It took a moment before his face morphed into a wince. "Sorry."

"It's fine," Jocelyn said. And it was. She took his hand. "But if I did have a tween daughter, you bet I'd make sure her joggers were clean for her sleepover."

"I'm sure you would. Um, this may be an odd question"—it was the same phrasing she'd used earlier—"but do you think you'll have another child someday?"

"Huh, no one's ever asked me that." More notably, Jocelyn realized, she'd never let her own mind go there. Maybe it had seemed wrong, like a betrayal. But she considered it now. "I don't know. Maybe."

"Fair enough," Kyle said. "Personally, I've always wanted two kids. But after Nina, Liv was done."

Jocelyn didn't want to talk about Kyle's late wife anymore, or think about Luke, either. She felt excited about the man in front of her, the sense of possibility in the air. "Hey, do you want to go somewhere?"

"With you? Definitely."

"Snag that blanket."

Jocelyn never remembered the location until the moment she saw it, the dirt enclosure that passed for a parking area off Route 6. She gave Kyle just enough notice to slam on the brakes and swerve over.

"Where are you taking me, wild woman?"

"You'll see."

Jocelyn hadn't been to the Dune Shacks Trail at night since high school, when groups of kids would play terrifying, drunken games of hide-and-seek.

They slipped off their shoes and trudged up the path. After scaling the first peak of sand, Kyle gasped. The dunes looked majestic under the moonlight, stretching out as far as they could see. A great horned owl hooted nearby.

"The rule is," Jocelyn said, "you have to yell out a secret as you run down." It was another game they'd played as teenagers. "I'll go first."

Sprinting down, she shouted out, "I can't stand lobster!"

"Okay, here I come," Kyle said. He ran down hollering, "I really like you."

"I didn't know that was a secret," Jocelyn said when he reached the bottom.

"Sorry if mine wasn't as juicy as your grudge against lobster."

They climbed back up together, both panting at the effort. "My turn." Jocelyn flew down the dune, calling out, "I hate that my sister moved back here."

"I can understand that," Kyle replied from on high. He took off toward her and yelled, "I'm burned out on adulting!"

"I can understand that, too," Jocelyn said, "though I think 'adulting' is a ridiculous word."

"Fair. Down with 'adulting.'" Kyle patted her on the back. "You go. I'm staying put."

Jocelyn trekked back up alone, thinking again of Luke. She could confess that he'd never met his daughter; when Juniper was born, he'd sent a teddy bear. In fact, Jocelyn had seen Luke only once more after that final morning—at their daughter's funeral. She never told anyone about the pain of that breakup, always insisting she was better off on her own. But she felt she could tell Kyle now, how in order to move forward, she'd had to bury that part of her past; she knew Kyle would get it. But knowing that was exactly what made her decide to say something else.

Flying down the dune, she proclaimed, "I really like you, too." She'd built up so much momentum that she flew right into Kyle's arms, and they both toppled over, landing in a heap. Jocelyn could barely see him now in the dark, but she could feel his heartbeat against her chest.

"Please don't make me hike up there again," he said, his words tickling her ear, "but I've got another confession." He looked at her with mischief in his eyes.

"I think I already know."

Jocelyn had thought ahead—she spread out the blanket, and they found their way toward each other, in the bowl of the dune, under a sliver of moon, sand rising up all around them.

Chapter 14

On Maddy's last secret day of freedom, she didn't know it would be her last. It was the Tuesday before Thanksgiving, and for once after dropping Rose at Tanya's, she had no plans for her day. Her anxiety was like a swarm of bees in her belly. Stopping for gas, she noticed a sign on the door to Cumby's: HELP WANTED. Some odd urge made her reach for an application. Ten minutes later, she had an interview for a position that she would've considered beneath her in high school.

The manager looked about nineteen, with bad skin and worse teeth. He didn't ask Maddy for a résumé. Instead, he asked if she could make change, and if she had any physical conditions that would prevent her from lifting heavy boxes. He prompted her to describe herself in three words. "Smart, reliable," Maddy said, then paused before adding, "Tired." The kid looked confused. He asked what hours she could work and how soon, and Maddy said, "Any of them, whenever." He said he'd be in touch. She shook his hand, feeling completely batshit.

Maddy planned to confess to Justin over Thanksgiving: about Tanya, and their dwindled savings, and the turmoil she felt inside—all of it. But then he unboxed a onesie stamped with a cartoon turkey and "My First Thanksgiving" in bubble letters, and the joy on his face nearly broke Maddy's heart. This was all so lovely and simple for him: the three of them together, their baby's first major holiday. Maddy couldn't bring herself to ruin it. So she kept her mouth shut and focused on baking a pie, the smell of cooking butter turning her stomach.

Thanksgiving at the Marx house was always the same. Claire roasted the turkey and prepared the traditional sides, and Jed fried up latkes, a custom that began when Hanukkah had overlapped with Thanksgiving one year. The house smelled like cinnamon and caramelized onions, the centerpieces were pine cone cornucopias that Maddy and Jocelyn had made as kids, and the sisters were responsible for dessert.

But now there was Rose, too. As they arrived, Jed handed his granddaughter a rattle that resembled a turkey leg, and Rose shook it madly, encouraged by the adults' laughter and Rusty's barks. The shake-shake-shake went on and on, fraying Maddy's nerves.

When everyone was seated, Claire raised a glass. "I want to share how thankful I am. Not only is my family all here under one roof, but we all live in the same town. Who would've thought?"

That was another difference this year. Usually Maddy and Justin were visitors, gone by Saturday to return to the city for Friendsgiving at Porter House Grill. This year Maddy's biggest social engagement would likely be stoop beers with Kelsey.

"Okay, my turn," said Jed. "I'm thankful for Claire's cooking, and Rose's giggles, and my son-in-law, and my two daughters, who worked together to bring us dessert today." It was typical Jed, ascribing collaboration to the two of them where none existed. Jocelyn had made a walnut pumpkin torte that looked like it came straight from Martha Stewart's oven; Maddy used a store-bought crust. Luckily, Maddy didn't care about baking, so she was only slightly miffed.

"I'll go," said Justin, squeezing Maddy's knee. "I'm thankful for this new adventure my family has embarked on. And for all of you."

"Hear! Hear!" said Claire.

"Me next," Jocelyn said. "I'm thankful for good health, good food, and good people." Maddy waited for her sister to mention her and Justin's return home, but all she said was, "Mad?"

Maddy's eyes darted around the table. *Say something,* she urged herself. But it was hard to sort out her thoughts over the clacking of that damn rattle. Finally, Justin traded Rose for a spoon. *Blessed silence.*

"I'm thankful you took that rattle away from her," Maddy said with a laugh, and Justin smiled feebly. Everyone was still looking at her with expectant faces. Maddy shifted in her seat. *My baby.* She knew she should've said, *I'm thankful for my beautiful, healthy baby.* So why couldn't she get the words out? What was wrong with her? Then Rose smacked her lips, and Maddy saw that she was licking a dollop of something orange off Claire's finger. "Mom, did you just feed her sweet potato pie?"

"Just a taste for Thanksgiving. Look, she likes it!"

Anger flooded Maddy. "She's not even four months old."

"Babe, it's okay," Justin said.

"It's not okay," she snapped, voice trembling. "Her pediatrician told us to wait; plus, that thing's loaded with sugar and salt."

"Maddy, take a breath," Jed said, placing a hand on her shoulder; she shrugged it off.

"I'm sorry, dear," Claire said. "I didn't realize. I'll go check on the gravy."

Claire retreated to the kitchen, and no one would meet Maddy's eyes. Her stomach swirled with anger.

Jocelyn broke the silence, chanting, "This little piggy went to market," as she reached across Justin to wiggle Rose's toes.

"This is nice," Justin said, touching Jocelyn's sweater sleeve. "Ooh, cashmere."

"Thanks, it's cozy."

Maddy noted how Justin hadn't noticed *her* outfit, a new silk wrap dress from Saks, which miraculously didn't make her look like a cow.

She scrutinized her sister's sweater, which was oversize and forest green, not her usual style. "Is that new?" she asked.

"Nah, it's Kyle's."

Claire reappeared with the gravy boat. "How's it going with you two?"

"Great," Jocelyn said. "He moves into his house next week, and then he'll be out here every weekend. We're having fun." She was glowing like a teenager.

Justin raised his eyebrows. "I *bet* you're having fun." He coughed into his hand and added, "In bed."

"You guys are so inappropriate," Maddy said. "Mom and Dad are here, jeez."

"You're right," Claire said, sounding amused. "No sex talk at the table, kids."

Everyone laughed except Maddy. She felt ganged up on and petulant. She addressed Jocelyn: "I'm surprised you didn't bring Kyle today. Were you invited to his Thanksgiving?"

"I mean, we've been dating for three weeks."

"Still."

As her sister rolled her eyes, Maddy felt a prick of satisfaction; she'd gotten to her.

Jocelyn cleared her throat. "By the way, Mad, I was over here the other day, and it was so nice out, I decided to go biking. I couldn't believe Mom still had our old bikes—those powder-blue ones, remember, and the purple helmets? When's the last time you've been biking?"

"What are you talking about, Cricket?" Claire said. "You ride that old bike all the time."

Both sisters ignored her.

"I don't have time to go biking, obviously," said Maddy.

Jocelyn muttered something under her breath; Maddy thought she caught the word *psycho*. She pushed her plate away. "I need some air."

Jed caught up with her halfway down the road, Rusty shuffling along beside him. For a while they walked in silence. It was late afternoon, the sky gray with dusk. To calm herself down, Maddy counted each house they passed, windows aglow and chimneys wafting smoke.

"So how've you been?" Jed asked.

"Pretty shitty," Maddy answered.

"Well, no shit," Jed said. He honked out a laugh, which made Maddy laugh, too. It felt good. It opened something up in her. She thought of Tanya and how relieved she'd feel to be honest, how the knot that had taken up residence inside her might finally loosen. She'd tell her father, and it would be practice for confessing to Justin. Her heart was beating like mad as she inhaled a jagged breath.

"Listen, Dad, I want to tell you something. I was feeling so desperate for some space from Rose, so I hired someone to help. But for some reason I haven't been able to tell Justin, and I feel bad about it . . ."

Her thoughts were jumbled. She was still sorting out how to explain it when Jed broke in: "Oh, I'm so glad to hear that. Is it one of the people from my list? I wasn't sure if they took your insurance."

"Oh," Maddy said. He thought she was talking about a shrink. "No."

"Okay. Of course, you know the right fit for you. I've heard therapy can make you feel worse before you feel better, since you're stirring up so much stuff at first. It'll get better, as they say."

"Right, that's a good tip." Maddy didn't correct him. It had taken so much energy for her to try to tell the truth, and now she was depleted. It reminded her of when she was a teenager and hoped to confide in her dad about that awful date: She'd nervously broached the subject, saying the night hadn't gone how she'd wanted. Jed had replied that reality often didn't meet expectations and, with a blithe pat on her back, added that it could help to look for silver linings. Maddy had felt herself shrink, realizing what a mistake it had been to try to open up. "Anyway," she said now, "they're probably waiting on us for pie."

"Sure." Jed sounded light, and it pained Maddy to see how relieved he looked to think she was in therapy.

Inside, she made an effort to repair things with her mother, delving into the cleanup. She encouraged Justin to stay to watch football with Jed, and she'd take Rose home. "Happy Thanksgiving," she declared on her way out, realizing she finally felt thankful about something—thankful the holiday was over.

◆ ◆ ◆

Today is a new day, Maddy told herself the next morning, again working up the nerve to talk to Justin. Work was closed and their day wide open—Maddy finally had her husband's undivided attention. At breakfast, she would tell him everything. They were in line at the Hole in One, Maddy debating whether or not to splurge on a cranberry muffin, when someone grasped her elbow.

"Hi!" Before Maddy could process it, Rose was stretching out of Justin's grip and into Tanya's arms, and Tanya was nuzzling Rose's hair. "My little Rosie-Posy," she cooed.

"Hello there," Justin said, his confusion masked by politeness.

"You must be Justin." Tanya extended a hand. "I'm Tanya. It's so nice to finally meet you. I've gotten so attached to my special little companion." She delivered a series of smooches to Rose's cheeks.

Maddy felt paralyzed. She avoided Justin's eyes. How had it never occurred to her that this might happen? Because in her mind, her husband and her babysitter lived in parallel universes, not in the same small town.

"I've got to get these bagels home to my own kiddos," said Tanya, handing Rose back, "but I'll see you Monday morning. Oh, and bring some size two diapers. Rosie's outgrowing the ones."

"Okay, see you." Maddy kept waving even after Tanya was gone. She felt a pit of dread in her stomach for the coming conversation.

But Justin didn't say a word at breakfast. He seemed to be stewing, jaw clenched. Maddy would have to broach the topic herself. After laying Rose down for her nap, she sat beside him on the couch and waited for him to set his phone aside. "I'm sorry, babe," she began. "I couldn't handle it. I needed help, so I got a sitter." She urged herself on. "Full-time."

Justin didn't ask what she'd been doing with her days, or why she'd kept this from him. He didn't insist that he'd tried to help her. Instead, he said, "I'm really sad you've been feeling this way, and also that you didn't feel you could tell me."

"I know. I'm sorry. I've been trying to tell you, but . . ." She trailed off. "Anyway, it's for the best you found out, since I've basically burned through our savings."

"Oh, Maddy." Justin rubbed his brow. "I'm sorry I'm earning so much less than I used to. Maybe it was a mistake for me to leave the firm. And I know I pushed you into this move. I thought it would be a good idea. But maybe it's all been a mistake. I feel like I've failed you." He dropped his head into his hands.

"No, come on." Maddy edged closer. It made her feel worse that he was blaming himself for her screwups. This was not how she'd wanted this conversation to go.

Justin inhaled deeply. "How's this? I'll take a few days off, and then why don't you and Rose come with me on my work trip next month? It might be nice to be back in the city." He smiled wanly.

Maddy nodded, her eyes pricking with tears. A trip wouldn't solve the fact that she no longer recognized herself, but at least her secret was out, and she wouldn't have to sneak around anymore. And Justin wasn't angry—they would figure this out together.

That evening, she got a voicemail from an unknown number. It was the Cumby's manager congratulating her on her new job as an evening clerk; her first shift would be Monday. Maddy deleted the message, laughing to herself—*at* herself—and feeling a little lighter than she had that morning.

◆ ◆ ◆

"Hey, lady," Kelsey hollered from her stoop. She'd traded out her Patriots windbreaker for a Bruins parka and fingerless gloves.

"Be right over," Maddy called back, pulling on her own new parka, because, sadly, her cashmere peacoat wasn't cutting it in the New England cold. "I've got pie."

Maddy was glad to be hanging out with someone who hadn't witnessed her freakout at Thanksgiving or uncovered her big lie. And yet, half a beer in, she was reciting the whole saga. "You must think I'm nuts," she concluded.

Kelsey shrugged. "It explains why I haven't seen you around much lately, or heard Rose screaming. Kidding . . . kind of. But I don't think you're nuts. Or more like, who *isn't* nuts? Anyway, I don't judge."

"That I actually do find crazy," Maddy said, "though I appreciate it."

The front door swung open and a boy ran out, unzipped his fly, and peed an impressive arc into a bush.

"Otis, you animal, use the goddamn toilet." Kelsey turned back to Maddy. "Sorry."

"The thing is, I just don't think I'm cut out for motherhood." She looked nervously at Kelsey to clock her reaction.

Kelsey snorted. "Really, who is?"

"Sometimes I fantasize about my old life like it's an old love affair," Maddy admitted.

"Steamy. Do tell."

Maddy sighed. "Everything was big and important. *I* was big and important—well, not big; I was slim and stylish."

In her head, Maddy replayed the reel of her one perfect morning, beginning with a run along the East River with Krista, the sun rising over the water, followed by cappuccinos at their favorite Swedish coffee shop. Maddy would return to her apartment to find Justin, so sexy in his suit and tie. He'd drop his briefcase and say, what the hell, he could be late for once—he couldn't resist his flushed wife. It would be a quickie, but a tender one. Then Justin would throw a towel in the dryer, to be toasty after Maddy's shower, and she'd stand under the pounding stream, reviewing her day and picking her outfit, assembling her uniform of ambitious urban professional.

"I even loved rush hour, striding down those crowded sidewalks," she told Kelsey. "I know it sounds silly, but I felt like some kind of titan."

"No, it sounds cool," Kelsey said, "although personally I hate cities. So what happened then?"

Maddy waved a dismissive hand. "It all fell apart."

"Ah."

Maddy appreciated that Kelsey didn't probe. "We're going back next week. Justin's got a work thing. But I'm sort of dreading it." Maddy was scared she'd feel out of place—because she'd changed, or the city had changed, or both—and she didn't want the reality to mess with her rose-colored memories. "Anyway, what was your life like before kids?"

Kelsey laughed. "That ancient history? I was an aide at an old folks' home. Most of my patients had Alzheimer's, so I was lucky if they remembered me from one day to the next. But that was all right. I knew I was helping them."

"Wow, good for you," said Maddy, thinking she could never do that job—take care of people with no audience and no validation. Actually, it sounded a lot like parenting.

"It was gratifying work."

Maddy wanted to ask whether Kelsey found parenting gratifying, but then another boy flew through the door, dropped his pants, and farted directly in Kelsey's face. It was loud but thankfully odorless.

"Ashton, you little shit, scram!" He ran back inside, cackling with glee. To Maddy, Kelsey said, "They're barbarians. Except Oliver, my little angel." She called into the house: "C'mere, Ollie." A moment later, a small boy shuffled out, thumb in mouth, and plopped into Kelsey's lap. "Hello, my snuggle bug."

"Hi, Mama."

"He's sweet," Maddy said.

"See, it's not all a slog. Maybe New York will be fun. Of course, you won't catch me there. I'm too happy here, neck-deep in farts."

"And snuggles."

"I truly have it all."

Chapter 15

Jocelyn was used to hibernating at this time of year, when work slowed, stores and restaurants shuttered, and the peninsula went hushed. But this year, with Kyle, she felt like she was living in a rom-com, game to go to all the community choir performances and holiday strolls, so long as her new boyfriend was by her side.

Tonight was the Yarmouth Port tree lighting, where they were gathered with half the town singing "Frosty the Snowman," warming their palms around cups of mulled cider. After a collective countdown, the big fir tree went bright with twinkly lights. Kyle's eyes sparkled in the glow. His kiss tasted like cloves. It was a perfectly sweet scene, marred only by Nina's withering look after Kyle suggested she get her picture taken with Santa. Jocelyn actually appreciated the girl's attitude; otherwise, it might've all felt like too much.

The couple had grown so close so fast, spending every moment of every weekend together. Sometimes Nina would stay with a friend back in Boston, and sometimes she'd join them, and then they had to restrain themselves from touching nonstop. When Sunday night rolled around, Jocelyn would ache at the thought of the coming week apart. How would she sleep without her skin pressed up against Kyle's? How would she experience a fraction of the joy eating a meal without him?

After years on her own, avoiding any serious attachment, Jocelyn was now utterly infatuated. She hardly recognized herself. It was delightful and delicious and slightly distressing.

When Nina wandered off from the caroling to the Edward Gorey House across the street, Jocelyn told Kyle she'd be right back. She found the girl on the front steps. "Want to check out the museum?" It was open late for the event. Nina shrugged, and they went in.

Nina was immediately drawn to the eerie ink drawings on the walls. She looked rapt. The docent offered her a scavenger-hunt worksheet, and to Jocelyn's surprise, Nina took a pencil and set to work. She was the perfect age for Gorey, who'd made children's books that weren't really for children; she, too, was in that in-between stage. Jocelyn tagged along as Nina peered up a narrow staircase, where a rag doll draped perilously off a step. "*A* is for Amy who fell down the stairs."

Jocelyn startled. "Huh?"

"It's the first thing in the scavenger hunt." Nina showed her the sheet, which contained the grimmest possible ABCs: "*B* is for Basil assaulted by bears. *C* is for Clara who wasted away. *D* is for Desmond thrown out of a sleigh."

Nina giggled as she read, "'*F* is for Fanny sucked dry by a leech.' Ew."

Jocelyn scanned the list of so many children felled by so many horrible fates. At *M*, her breath caught in her throat: M *is for Maud who was swept out to sea.*

"What's ennui?" asked Nina, pointing to Neville, who'd died of it.

"Um, like listlessness, because you don't have enough going on."

"You can die of that?" Nina asked.

Jocelyn shrugged, thinking of Maddy.

She decided to wait outside while Nina finished the hunt. She was careful not to come on too strong with the girl, now that she'd become such a fixture in her life. She approached Nina like she approached her clients—making no assumptions, letting her set the terms of the relationship. Thankfully, Nina seemed to like her, and Jocelyn had started to think of her like a little sister.

Unfortunately, things weren't going as well with her actual sister. A new line floated into Jocelyn's head: "*M* is for Maddy who gave birth to a child." It turned out that Maddy had been secretly off-loading Rose to a babysitter each day to go biking and do who knew what else. Of course, Maddy hadn't admitted this to Jocelyn; Claire had told her, who'd heard it from Justin. Now they were in New York for the week. Every day, Jocelyn considered reaching out to her sister. But then she'd remember the times Maddy had called on her for last-minute help with Rose, claiming she never got a break, guilting Jocelyn for being unencumbered. And she'd flat-out denied it when Betsy asked whether she'd been on the rail trail that day back in October. Plus, she'd been indefensibly rude about Jocelyn having a boyfriend. As if only Maddy could have nice things. As if because Maddy wasn't happy, no one else could be happy, either.

Kyle joined Jocelyn on the porch. His arm around her waist steadied her.

Nina appeared a minute later, declaring, "I got all the dead kids."

Kyle started. "Excuse me?"

"It's a scavenger hunt from the museum," Jocelyn said.

Nina explained how hard it was to find Una, who'd slipped down a drain. Jocelyn had never seen the girl so animated, amber eyes all alight. As they were deciding on dinner, Jocelyn ducked back inside to buy her a Christmas present: *Cautionary Tales for Children*, illustrated by Gorey.

A few days before Christmas, Kyle announced it was time to get a tree. They were lying on a mattress on his bedroom floor, a makeshift setup while a custom cedar bed was being built. Jocelyn loved lazing around like this, limbs flopped over each other; it made her feel like a teenager. Kyle mentioned a pop-up shop along Route 6, but Jocelyn knew Betsy's yard was filled with firs, and Betsy was handy with a handsaw.

Watching her best friend and her boyfriend hack away at a tree together, Jocelyn felt her heart fill. The sentiment buoyed her through Christmas Eve, when she, Kyle, and Nina adorned the tree with jewel-colored glass globes and various kids' crafts. Nina seemed embarrassed by her younger self's creations, except for one, which she was picky about finding a spot for. Jocelyn sneaked a look. The Popsicle-stick frame featured a photo of a Nina replica, amber eyes and all: her mother. Later, she noticed Kyle handling the same ornament. How must it be for him to see so much of Liv in Nina?

Having grown up Jewish, Jocelyn had no expectations of the holiday, so it was all a joy. They decorated gingerbread men, sipped eggnog, and watched *It's a Wonderful Life*, which Jocelyn had never seen before. Halfway through, Kyle abruptly slipped out of their blanket cocoon and announced he was heading to bed. Jocelyn finished the movie with Nina, both of them tearing up by the end.

She'd struggled over what to give Kyle, then landed on joint surfing lessons, a bit nervously since they wouldn't happen until June. But when Kyle opened the card on Christmas morning, he leaped up and struck a goofy surfer pose, then pulled Jocelyn in for a kiss so intense it made her toes tingle. Nina rolled her eyes, mortified. Kyle handed Jocelyn a small red box. Inside was a bronze necklace with a heart pendant cracked into pieces and reconstructed. Like both of their hearts, Kyle didn't have to say, as he fixed the clasp around her neck.

Nina got a bike from Santa, and from her father, Lululemon leggings and her first smartphone, which Jocelyn knew Kyle had fretted over. Jocelyn presented her with the Gorey book, and Nina spent an hour poring over the pages. They all slipped into matching slippers from L.L.Bean via Santa's workshop, and the morning passed with cinnamon buns, Sufjan Stevens's holiday album, and a five-hundred-piece puzzle featuring the birds of Barnstable County. Jocelyn was wondering if there could be a more magical Christmas, just as she noticed Nina shove her phone in her pocket, her face blotched and shiny.

"Nina?"

"Be back soon," the girl said, retreating from the room.

"Let her go," Kyle said. But Jocelyn thought she might like some company—someone besides her dad.

She found Nina shivering on the deck. She draped a coat around her shoulders and settled in beside her. They were both quiet until Jocelyn ventured, "So, do you like your presents?" Nina's eyes started to fill, and Jocelyn said, "It's okay to be disappointed. Personally, I didn't want this stupid necklace." She nudged Nina to let her know she was joking, and Nina showed a hint of a smile.

"It's just, everyone else got a smartphone last year. Annabelle would send around these memes at lunch, and they'd all laugh. Annabelle thought it was so funny that I only had a flip phone." Nina pronounced "Annabelle" like it was the name of a fearsome goddess.

"Rude," Jocelyn said. "Annabelle sounds like a dick."

"Well, she's my friend."

"Ah." Jocelyn could picture this Annabelle. Maddy had had friends like that—girls she'd revered despite the fact that (or maybe because) they made her miserable.

Nina sighed. "I thought once I got a smartphone, I'd feel better. And I do, sort of." She showed Jocelyn her screen, already busy with a group chat—someone had shared a photo of a huddle of girls at the bowling alley, Nina notably absent. "But I don't know."

Jocelyn stifled a laugh at the idea that a smartphone would make someone feel better. Also, Nina had owned the thing for all of two hours. "So the reality didn't meet the expectation."

"Kind of, yeah."

"May I?" Jocelyn held out her palm, and Nina passed her the phone. "Check this out." She downloaded the Gem Gulper app, and Nina watched over her shoulder as she maneuvered a princess worm to eat a row of jewels. "It's my favorite dumb game. Looks fun, right?"

"I guess. Must be an old-person thing."

"Rude," Jocelyn said. Nina grinned before her eyes teared up again. "Oh, Nina, I'm only kidding."

Nina shook her head. "I was just thinking, my mom would've liked you. Which is, I don't know, weird. That's her cinnamon bun recipe. My dad doesn't make them as good as she did."

"Then I can only imagine how tasty hers were, since I ate three of your dad's."

Nina rolled her eyes. "I'm glad Dad seems happy, but this whole thing is kinda weird. Sorry."

"It's okay. I know what you mean."

The pensive way Nina was studying the horizon made her seem older.

"Can I tell you something?" Jocelyn ventured. Nina turned toward her. "I had a daughter. She drowned in the ocean when she was fifteen months old."

Nina's eyes widened. "Whoa."

"Her name was Juniper. Junie for short."

"I'm really sorry. You seem like you're a mom."

The remark made it hard for Jocelyn to swallow. "It all kind of wells up sometimes, doesn't it?"

"Yeah."

Jocelyn had an idea. "So, my family's Jewish, but we still had a Christmas tradition: We'd get all bundled up and eat Chinese food on the beach. Any interest?"

"Let's do it."

They were almost inside when Jocelyn said, "Oh, and Nina? Fuck Annabelle."

The girl whispered back, "Fuck Annabelle," a smile on her lips.

In the car, Kyle was slowing to turn into the lot at Nauset Light when Jocelyn snapped, "No." She took a breath. "Let's go to Coast Guard. It'll be less busy."

"Sure." Kyle didn't point out that crowds were unlikely at any beach in late December.

They carted the take-out bags down to the sand, where they feasted until slipping into a noodle-and-teriyaki-chicken stupor. Kyle grew especially withdrawn. He mumbled something about taking a breather. Jocelyn nodded and watched him walk off, wondering whether it was the heavy food or the holiday's history weighing on him. She beckoned

Nina to join her by the water. They lingered at the edge, then ran back like mad when the waves flowed, frosty water biting at their heels. Nina wandered off with a stick, and when Jocelyn saw the names she'd etched in the sand, a lump formed in her throat. Nina said, "I added some verses to the Gorey poem: *L* is for Liv who got hit by a car. *J* is for Junie who swam out too far."

The crash of the waves roared in Jocelyn's ears. Nina wiped the sand smooth with her foot, then set off turning cartwheels down the shore.

When Kyle came back, he looked a bit lighter. He caught a hand around Jocelyn's waist. "Thank you for spending Christmas with us," he said. "I know I can get moody."

"You're fine. I'm happy to be here."

"And I appreciate you talking to Nina."

"She's a great girl."

"*You're* great." His kiss warmed her frozen lips. "So, is Nauset Light where—"

"Yes," she cut him off.

"And you don't go there."

"Not with other people, no."

"Okay." The way Kyle was looking at her, it felt like no one had truly seen her before this moment. "Well, this beach is pretty wonderful—what a good idea."

"I love you," Jocelyn said. It just came out, the words fizzing off her tongue. She felt giddy and scared.

"I love you, too," Kyle replied without hesitation.

His gaze was so intense that Jocelyn had to look away—to the spray of the ocean and the light flashing silver at the horizon. She breathed in the brackish air until her heart calmed, and then she locked eyes with the man she loved, who loved her, too.

Chapter 16

MADDY & JOCELYN

Maddy wanted to stay home. She was worn out from the New York trip, not to mention the endless conversations she and Justin had been having about trust and honesty, and the constant scrutiny over how she was feeling. Plus, she didn't know who would be there besides Jocelyn, whom she hadn't seen or spoken to since storming out of Thanksgiving. Also, who threw a party on December 30? Betsy and Jewel, that was who. Their so-called Old Year's Eve Bash was a long-standing tradition, Betsy had explained, since who needed all the hype of New Year's Eve? The invitation noted that high tide would fall at midnight exactly, a good omen. Justin insisted they go: Maddy's parents had already agreed to babysit, and it would be good for them to get out and meet new people.

Maddy wore her best little black dress with iridescent opal heels and her hair swept up into a loose chignon. Though the dress was snugger than it used to be, she felt confident—right up until the moment they arrived. Betsy's living room was filled with people in jeans, sweaters, and clogs. Maddy didn't want to go home and change; she wanted everyone *else* to go home and change.

After greeting the hostesses, Justin went to hang up their coats, and Maddy made a beeline for the bar. It was covered in fake snow, and a sign by the ice bucket had a penguin with the caption "Quick, take some, before climate change melts it all!" *Jesus.* Maddy poured herself a generous glass of red.

Across the room, she spotted her twin. Jocelyn was leaning against a bookshelf, a coy look on her face, shoulder angled toward a guy who must've been Kyle. He was handsome in a scruffy way, tall and broad, Jocelyn's favorite type. The two of them wore the jeans-and-sweater uniform, but they could've been in black tie or buck naked and they still would've been the most radiant pair there. Jocelyn pressed the length of her body against his, and they kissed, taking occasional breaks to ogle one another. They made smoldering eye contact, and Kyle brushed a tendril of hair off Jocelyn's cheek. Maddy could sense their desire from twenty feet away.

Justin appeared and poured himself a whiskey on the rocks. "Did you see the polar bear cake pops? I'm digging the arctic theme." Maddy tugged him toward her and went in for a deep French kiss.

Justin extracted himself. "Whoa, what was that about?"

"I'm your wife," Maddy said, exasperated. "Can't I kiss you?"

"Sure, yeah." But he looked startled.

Maddy glanced back at her sister, who wore a moony smile as she slipped her hand into Kyle's back pocket. Maddy forced herself to look away.

Justin shook his drink so the ice clinked against the glass, like he always did. It had never annoyed Maddy before, but now it did. They'd been together for so many years—and lately the relationship had felt like so much work. Meanwhile, look how much fun her sister was having. Compared to Jocelyn's new romance, Maddy's own decent marriage felt lackluster. When Justin coughed into his hand, then draped it over her shoulder, she thought she might gag. She excused herself.

After another swing by the bar, Maddy noticed Justin huddled with Jocelyn and Kyle. She swallowed half her wine, steeling herself to go join them. Jocelyn introduced Kyle, who shook Maddy's hand and said he was glad to finally meet her—he'd heard so much about her.

"Likewise," Maddy said, wondering what exactly he'd heard.

"Kyle's a fellow NYU Law alum!" Justin said. "And we're gonna try ice fishing together." The men fist-bumped.

"That's great, babe," Maddy said, not even attempting to sound interested.

Jocelyn nudged her in the ribs. "I saw you spying on us, Mad."

Maddy's cheeks burned. "I couldn't help it. You were making such a scene."

Jocelyn seemed to take that as a compliment—she beamed up at Kyle.

"Anyone else need a refill?" Maddy asked, already on her way to the bar.

She gulped at the cabernet and topped off her glass again. Her chest was now warm and tingly. She greeted an aged version of a guy she recognized from her AP Lit class, then found her way into a cluster of women who turned out to be two couples, friends from the dog park. When Maddy mentioned that she'd just returned to New York for the first time since moving away, a woman named Mariel sighed, saying, "But you can never go home again, right?"

"Exactly!" Maddy replied with such enthusiasm that her wine sloshed onto her dress, which she no longer cared was far too fancy for the party.

All eyes were on Maddy as they waited for her to elaborate. "The truth is," she said, "my homecoming was foiled by my baby's car seat." The line got the laughs she was after, so she continued the story, smoothing the edges off what had arguably been her worst day of motherhood so far.

The drive from Justin's parents' house in Westchester down to the city had started off fine—Rose asleep, Justin humming along to Radiohead, Maddy daydreaming about their old neighborhood. After they passed through the Bronx and Upper Manhattan, the iconic skyline flew up before them, and Maddy went breathless. The view was like a dear old friend, the backdrop to the big life she'd once built.

But then Rose woke up in a rage, and they heard the eruption just as the odor penetrated the car. "So much for subtly expressing your displeasure," Justin quipped, rolling down the windows. But Maddy wasn't in the mood for jokes. They went through a full pack of wipes and finally got Rose changed—and then Maddy discovered a smear across her own shirt. "No big deal," Justin said. "We're surrounded by stores—we'll just buy you a new shirt." But by then Maddy had given up on the day. She encouraged Justin to go to his office and take the train home later; she and Rose would head back now.

Facing the car seat, Maddy nearly vomited. Justin laid down a towel and struggled to buckle Rose in; then he kissed Maddy goodbye and wished her courage. For the whole ride back to Westchester, she craned her head out the window in the whipping wind, her cheeks going numb. She didn't even glance in the rearview mirror as the Manhattan skyline receded from sight.

At the party, Maddy summarized the experience: "I got to enjoy the city for a Manhattan minute"—she'd never once uttered this phrase before, but it somehow seemed fitting now—"before my baby unleashed a literal shitstorm. The day was spoiled—*soiled*. We drew on all our resources, but our best efforts were no match for the digestive system of a fourteen-pound infant. So that was that. I fled back to the burbs."

It had been a humiliating return to Justin's parents' perfectly appointed home. His mother, Carol, greeted Maddy and Rose with a gasp: "Oh my, can I help?" Maddy took one look at her mother-in-law's crisp white button-down, and said, "Thanks, I've got it." She joined Rose in the bath, then Rose conked out in the Pack 'n Play.

Now Jocelyn joined the huddle of women as Maddy recounted the next part of that horrific day: "Then came my battle to clean the car seat. You guys don't have kids, right?"

"Just our dog babies," Mariel said.

"Well, taking that thing apart is like trying to crack the Enigma," Maddy said. "They've got this how-to video where this gorgeous model, definitely not a mom, unclips latch A from latch B, detaches holster

C from holster D, and so on, all the while calmly describing how this sleight of hand you're witnessing is so, so simple. I watched it ten times before declaring defeat, and then I made Justin go buy a new car seat."

The women roared. Who knew Maddy could spin gold out of such misery?

In truth, she'd made it through only two viewings before she'd chucked her phone across the room and collapsed in a pitiful heap. Of course, that was when Carol reappeared. "Knock, knock," she called from the doorway, "just checking in." Maddy's mother-in-law had a way of catching Maddy at her worst. And when it came to mothering, there was no way to stack up: Carol had stayed home to raise her three boys, cooking dinner from scratch each night, or so the story went; she always insisted it was the best job in the world. She was nice enough to Maddy but clearly flummoxed by her struggles as a new mom. Maddy preferred to brush off Carol's offers of help, not wanting to admit to her own shortcomings, but now she felt she had no choice. She asked Carol to stay with Rose so she could go hose off the car seat. But once she was outside, she just couldn't deal with it. She dumped the whole contraption in the garage trash can. *Good riddance,* she thought, feeling instantly calmer.

The new car seat was an upgraded model. Maddy insisted they hide the purchase from Justin's parents, but Carol found the discarded box and made a wry remark about throwing money at every little problem, when who knew how they could afford it. Justin clenched his fists—he never stood up to his mother. Maddy demanded they leave that afternoon, a day earlier than planned, and Justin started packing.

"The takeaway is," Maddy told the group now, "don't have a baby, 'cuz I bet you'll regret it."

It was a good line, even if she didn't really mean it, and she certainly didn't mean to make eye contact with Jocelyn at that moment. She was maybe going to say something to temper it, but Jocelyn slipped out of the huddle, probably to go make out with Kyle again. Mariel urged Maddy to tell another story, so she forgot about her sister and began riffing on how she had to plan Rose's naps around the neighbor's coyote-hunting schedule.

Maddy was having fun. She could've done this all night.

◆ ◆ ◆

Jocelyn tried to find Kyle. Or Betsy, or even Jewel. She couldn't believe her friends had invited Maddy to the party. But before she located someone she could lean on, she bumped into her sister. "Taking a break from your adoring audience?" she spat.

"Loosen up, Joss. It's a party." But nothing about Maddy's expression looked loose.

They were standing in a hallway that was too narrow for a conversation, but Jocelyn pressed on: "Can I ask you something, Mad? Why did you have a kid? I mean, seriously."

Maddy shrugged. "Oh, I dunno, everyone else was doing it, and I had FOMO." As Jocelyn suppressed a scream, Maddy barked out a laugh. "Look at you, so worked up. I know that's what you expect me to say, right? You always assume the worst of me. But whatever. I don't have to justify my decisions to you."

"Fine," said Jocelyn. "I guess I know, anyway. It's so you could entertain strangers with stupid anecdotes about the nightmare of motherhood. If you think your desperation is hidden under some kind of charm, you're sadly mistaken. And no wonder you chose a group of nonparents to regale, so none of them could call you out on your bullshit."

Jocelyn's heart was hammering in her chest. She went on with her little speech: "Babies poop—so what? They're also the most incredible thing ever, and if you can't appreciate that, something is seriously wrong with you."

Maddy balked. "Excuse me for not annotating every sentence with 'hashtag grateful.' You're unbelievable."

"*I'm* unbelievable?" Jocelyn could hear her voice rising. "Mad, I'm not the one who secretly hired a babysitter to go live some clandestine life of, what, biking down the rail trail? And then flatly denied it even after Betsy saw you! It's so typical of you to cook up this elaborate scheme rather than own up to any weakness. Not to mention, who knows what happened with your job? You certainly didn't tell the truth about that."

Maddy scoffed. "Why do you even care? None of this is any of your business."

"Are you kidding? You're the one who came barging back into my life! You really haven't changed one bit." Jocelyn shook her head. "By the way, Mad, don't talk to me like I've never had to deal with a car seat. Just because you weren't around to see it doesn't mean it didn't happen."

Maddy looked indignant. "I was in college, living two hundred miles away!"

Jocelyn dug in: "How many times did you meet your niece, would you say? Twice, three times?"

"Because every time I came home, it was the Jocelyn-and-Junie show! No one gave a shit about anything going on with me, as per usual."

"Seriously, Mad?" Jocelyn's voice cracked. "So what about after she died? What about when you were too busy reveling in all your achievements to even show up to her funeral?"

"Jocelyn." Maddy's eyes closed. "Please. You know how much I . . . I can't rehash all that right now."

"Oh, why not? Because you can't even admit to yourself how utterly shitty and selfish you've always been? Even back in high school—"

Maddy's eyes snapped open and narrowed with fury. "Oh, you want to talk about high school? How about when I was violated on my first date, and afterward you were so desperate for me to dish, you roped Mom and Dad into chanting 'Maddy and Ryan sitting in a tree.'"

"Wait, what?"

"Nothing. Never mind."

"I seriously don't know what you're talking about, Mad. What—"

"Just forget I said anything," Maddy said, cutting her off again. Apparently that was the end of her disclosure. "It's just, you're not the only one who's been through it, Jocelyn. You're not the only one who's suffered loss. Like, I don't remember you rushing to my side after my miscarriages."

Jocelyn coughed with scorn. "That is so not the same."

"I'm not saying it's the same, but it also wasn't nothing. And you barely acknowledged it either time."

"Well, you've got your kid now, Mad, not that you seem to care."

"Oh my god, can you get off your high horse for even a second?"

Jocelyn shook her head, so done with this conversation. "You know, you've been acting like everything is so miserable and impossible, when the solution is beyond obvious."

"Oh yeah? Please enlighten me, oh wise sister of mine."

"Stop lying, stop pretending you're cut out to be a full-time mom, and get a fucking job." Jocelyn took a breath—she wasn't done. "While you're at it, how about quit it with the pity party you've been throwing yourself for, like, two decades."

Maddy stood there, blank-faced and mouth agape, and Jocelyn thought maybe she'd gone too far. But then Maddy snapped out of it, screwed up her face, and said, "Thanks for the advice. Here's some for you: It's been a decade since Juniper, so maybe it's time to move on."

Somehow Jocelyn's legs carried her outside. She was trembling and gulping for air. How could her sister say such things to her? How could she be so cruel? Although after all this time, she didn't know why she expected anything different. Maddy had always acted like her own life mattered so much more than Jocelyn's.

Jocelyn thought back to her early months with Juniper, when Maddy would call the house and Claire would pass her the phone. Jocelyn would share Junie's latest milestone—her first laugh, her first time rolling over—and Maddy always sounded distracted, like she was checking her email. Until it was time for her to gush about her latest A-plus or some prestigious new internship, at which point she'd grow chatty and animated. It was baffling to Jocelyn: So what if Maddy had aced another exam or landed some temporary job? Jocelyn was raising a human!

Still, one of the marvels of motherhood was that Jocelyn became twinned with someone new. Mothering Junie, she felt less yoked to Maddy, less drawn in by the push and pull that had defined their twindom. Even as babies, she and Maddy must've competed for their mother's attention. It wasn't like that with Jocelyn and Junie. They were perfectly paired, their symbiosis seamless.

Until Junie was taken from her. And then Maddy blew off the funeral. And her apologies were so laden with excuses that they never really sounded like apologies.

Jocelyn wasn't ready to go inside. She stood in Betsy's yard, peering up at the ancient oaks, their bare branches rattling in the wind. She watched those branches a long time, waiting to feel steady on her feet.

◆ ◆ ◆

Maddy got another drink and stood in a corner, sipping it. She wasn't sure whether people had overheard her and her sister, or how convincing she was now acting as someone simply taking a moment for herself. Inside, she was roiling, shards of anger piercing her chest. She thought of the day she'd gone whale watching, how she'd been miles out to sea and no one had known. How glorious that had been.

Justin sidled up to her. "Hey, where have you been?"

"Fighting with Jocelyn." The tremble in her voice belied her attempt to sound blasé.

"Oh, babe." Justin touched her cheek. "I wish you two would give each other a break."

"Ha." Maddy coughed out a bitter laugh. Replaying her sister's stream of invective nearly knocked the wind out of her. She was especially horrified at the accusation that she hadn't changed a bit—she knew she'd been monstrous recently, but surely this wasn't her true self. As much as Maddy hated to admit it, Jocelyn knew her better than anyone, so her words cut deep. And she still felt such shame about missing Junie's funeral. Was that why she'd brought up Ryan Parker—to change the subject? The old hurt had just gushed out, along with her yearning for someone to know about it and understand. Clearly her sister was not the right someone.

"They're handing out wet suits," said Justin. "Everyone's heading to the beach to count down to midnight."

"But it's not even New Year's Eve," Maddy said.

Justin shrugged. "I guess that's part of the fun of it. Come on, who would ever think we'd do a polar bear plunge?"

"Fine, although I doubt I can squeeze my fat ass into a wet suit."

"I love your fat ass, and of course you can."

◆ ◆ ◆

Jocelyn was contemplating how she'd break it to Betsy that she was leaving early. But then there was Kyle approaching her with two wet suits.

"I'm not really up for the plunge," she said.

"Are you okay?" Kyle asked. "I lost track of you. Jewel was giving me a tour."

"It's my sister. We had a fight. She's . . ." Jocelyn couldn't come up with a word that encapsulated it. She settled on, "I wish I didn't have to be in the same room with her for a long, long time."

"I'm sorry." Kyle enveloped her in a hug. Then he held up the wet suits and tried out a British accent: "May I suggest the sea cure? Take the waters to heal thyself?"

Jocelyn sighed. "Your accent is terrible. But all right."

◆ ◆ ◆

The water was bracing. Maddy assumed that a wet suit would act as a barrier against the cold, but really it just made her mind it less. She thought only briefly of swimming off toward the horizon, like the character in that Kate Chopin novel she'd slogged through in college. "Isn't this fun?" Justin asked, floating next to her, and she had to admit it sort of was. Most people jumped in and out, but Maddy lingered beside her husband, feeling her sour mood dissipate as she gave over to the sensation of weightlessness.

◆ ◆ ◆

Jocelyn dove right in—the best way to face the cold was to embrace the shock of it. Letting the water wash away her fury toward her sister, she turned her attention to Kyle: how nice it was to drift with him under the stars. Although she was surprised to discover he was a poor swimmer, wagging his arms inefficiently—they'd have to work on that before their surf lessons. It excited Jocelyn to realize how much they still had to learn about one another. "This is wild, and I love it," Kyle said. "I love you." He'd started tossing off the phrase so easily, and each time it left Jocelyn breathless.

◆ ◆ ◆

The feeling of neoprene on neoprene was strangely pleasant as Maddy wrapped her legs around her husband. "You know I'm here for you," Justin said, kissing her forehead, "always."

She really did know. Since Thanksgiving, along with initiating those hard conversations, Justin had been ending his workdays promptly at five. He'd set up a schedule for her parents to help with Rose, and Tanya still took her once a week. He'd joined Maddy to watch half a dozen rom-coms set in Manhattan, letting her marinate in missing the city, even if she'd never actually ridden the Central Park carousel or ice-skated at Rock Center. When she quoted John Updike to him, the thing about how real New Yorkers believed living anywhere else was a joke, he pointed out that Updike had lived only briefly in New York—he'd spent most of his adulthood in Ipswich, a coastal town in Massachusetts; that made Maddy laugh out loud. And when she finally admitted that she was open to exploring professional help, Justin got a referral for a clinician at Mass General specializing in postpartum care; her appointment was next week.

Maddy was okay, or at least she felt she would be. She spun around and caught a glimpse of Jocelyn, and her sister's words surfaced like a drumbeat in her brain: "The solution is beyond obvious: Get a fucking job." Well, Maddy thought grudgingly, maybe she would peruse some job boards, just to see.

◆ ◆ ◆

Jocelyn noticed Maddy entangled with Justin nearby, so she took Kyle's hand and led him to dry land.

"Listen, I have this out-there idea," he said, wrapping them both in a giant towel. "You mentioned your work slows down at this time of year. And Nina's babysitter is going abroad for the semester. What if you came back to Boston with us?"

Jocelyn was still processing—*was he asking her to move in with him?*—when he added, "Sorry, that came out weird. I'm not trying to hire you to babysit. It's just, you said you could use some space from your sister, and it might be a welcome change of pace. I'd love the company, and I know Nina would, too. We could just try it out."

His earnest bumbling charmed Jocelyn. Unlike Maddy, whose words always hid some ulterior motive to offend or undermine, Kyle was the opposite—whatever he said, Jocelyn knew he meant well. His offer was appealing, if a little daunting. Jocelyn had called Cape Cod home her whole life; she'd only ever left for a couple of years of college. As she was pondering what it would be like to live in a city, Maddy's so-called tip invaded her thoughts: "Maybe it's time to move on."

"Okay," Jocelyn said. "Let's do it."

Kyle looked surprised. "Really?"

"Why not? I'm up for a change. And I love you, Kyle Taylor." That his kiss could warm her insides after she'd dunked in the icy Atlantic on a December night made Jocelyn feel like anything was possible.

◆　◆　◆

The countdown began all around them. "Ten, nine, eight . . ."

"This is so stupid," Maddy said.

"Oh, shut up and count down with me," Justin said, pulling her toward him.

So she did, hollering as loud as her lungs would allow, giving over to the group's elation. "Three, two, one, midnight!" She topped it off with "Happy almost 2019!"

◆　◆　◆

The partiers' whoops and cheers echoed over the ocean. No one among them was immune to the magic of the moment. It wasn't quite the new year, and as the minutes ticked by, it was no longer quite high tide. But to Jocelyn, these not-quites felt better than if they'd been the real thing. She felt almost perfectly happy, and could you ask for anything more than that?

PART 2

Chapter 17

Winter in the city may as well have been a different season from the one Jocelyn knew. On the Cape, winter was for retreat. The landscape emptied out, and those who remained hunkered down. But in Boston, the world grew only more crowded. Mountains of snow obscured half the sidewalk, forcing pedestrians into narrower and narrower paths, their vaporous breath in each other's faces. On the Cape, the afternoon sunset signaled time to trade in boots for slippers and cozy up by the fireplace. In the city, everyone just continued on with their lives in the dark, no matter how low the temperature plunged.

Maddy must've loved this nonstop urban pace, Jocelyn thought, the badge of honor you could claim for trudging through extreme weather to get on with your agenda. Jocelyn didn't feel that sense of urgency about anything, especially when faced with sleet and black ice. Nevertheless, she'd promised Nina that she would attend her swim meet. So she pulled on two sweaters and a parka and trekked to the pool.

At the blast of chlorinated steam, Jocelyn raced to shed layers like they were on fire. She climbed the bleachers, past the mom posse, none of whom gave her a second glance (at pickup last week, one of them had referred to her as Nina's nanny, and Jocelyn hadn't corrected her). From the top bleacher, she looked out at the sea of girls in hydrangea-blue swimsuits and canary-yellow caps. She spotted Nina, a head taller than her teammates, hips more pronounced in Lycra than they looked in her slouchy everyday clothes. She caught her eye and waved. Nina waved back, bouncing a bit on her feet.

A litany of races preceded Nina's. Jocelyn checked her phone, but the service was bad. She observed an influencer wannabe shooting a "swim mom" video, dramatically revealing the contents of her bag: a quick-dry towel, an energy bar, a bottle of leave-in conditioner. She tried closing her eyes, but the room's acoustics made dozing difficult. So she simply sat there and let the time pass, growing sluggish in the soupy air.

This seemed to be the essence of parenting a tween: showing up and standing by. Kyle insisted that Jocelyn didn't have to serve as Nina's personal chauffeur and cheerleader, but she'd embraced the role. Compared to parenting a baby, it was a muted form of care, with occasional crescendos. Like watching Nina crouch on the block until the starting pistol's blast propelled her into the water and she began undulating like a dolphin, arms soaring in sync above the surface, possessing so much power and grace. For the entire lap, Jocelyn was rapt.

Nina placed fourth out of six. She'd explained to Jocelyn that the swimmers in the center lanes were the fastest, and she'd had the outside lane. But Jocelyn didn't care about the other swimmers. She leaped up and shouted Nina's name until the girl glanced up, eyes alight but shoulders slumped, both pleased and embarrassed.

Kyle showed up five minutes later. "Did I miss her?"

"There's still the relay."

"Right, good." He pecked Jocelyn on the cheek. Then his phone pinged, and he was drawn into its depths, frantically typing through the next two events.

Just like winter in Boston, Kyle was different here, too—more serious, often stressed. He worked a lot and could get snippy after a long day. Of course, Jocelyn had known he had a whole life off

Cape, but she hadn't quite realized that he considered it his real life, versus the Cape, which was a break from it.

And wasn't that what this stint in Boston was for Jocelyn—a break from her real life? At first, while Nina was in school, she'd played tourist, strolling through Faneuil Hall and Newbury Street, exploring the ICA and the MFA. Next she'd had a phase of scouring specialty markets and cooking multicourse meals, morphing into a housewife extraordinaire. Then she'd researched breaking into the local real estate market, but she knew so little of the area (was Southie not the same as the South End, and how did anyone navigate downtown—had this city been planned by toddlers?), and quickly set the idea aside. Each evening when Kyle came home and kissed her hello, Jocelyn experienced what she'd dubbed a David Byrne moment—thinking, *This is not my beautiful life.*

She wasn't sure whether she missed the Cape. She longed for the ocean, but when she thought of home, she felt uneasy, the image clouded by the incident with her sister at Betsy's party. Her mother kept encouraging her to come back for a visit. Kyle liked the idea, too—they could do a weekend trip, or she could go on her own. But Jocelyn wasn't ready.

The roar of the relay began, and the spectators stood. Nina was second, and when she dove in, Kyle squeezed Jocelyn's hand. Her flutter kick motored her down the lane, elbows poking up in quick succession, cheeks turning for occasional sips of air. Her flip turn was a marvel. After completing her leg, she hopped out and looked to the top bleacher, grinning up at her dad. He cheered, full of pride, and Jocelyn grinned up at him, too.

When she looked back to the lane, Nina was no longer among her teammates. She scanned the pool deck—still, no Nina. She nudged Kyle, and he couldn't locate her, either. Nina didn't reappear for the announcement of scores or the handshake line between the two teams. "She probably got a jump on her shower," Kyle said.

"Maybe."

They stood in the corridor outside the locker room, where the cluster of moms closed in on Kyle. Their apparent leader detailed an ice-skating fundraiser for team spirit wear and a coach-appreciation dinner, her tone flirtatious. She reminded Jocelyn of Maddy, who would probably run the PTA one day. Jocelyn wasn't included in the conversation, which was fine with her; she had no desire to break into the mom clique. Plus, she understood the appeal of the hot single dad, one of the few men who showed up to school events (albeit late). Kyle eventually extracted himself, and when he shrugged an arm around Jocelyn, she felt a satisfying sense of possession.

One by one, wet-haired girls with gym bags emerged from the locker room and found their people, until Kyle and Jocelyn were the only ones left in the hall. "Nina always takes forever," he said, getting sucked back into his work email.

Jocelyn decided to go in. The locker room smelled of chlorine and mildew. She wandered the empty aisles until she heard shuffling by the bathrooms. "Nina?"

"Who's there? Jocelyn?" Her voice came from the leftmost stall.

"Yeah. Are you okay in there?"

"Yep." Nina sounded uncertain, so Jocelyn waited. "It's just, I can't figure out this whole tampon thing." She said it in a tone like, *Stupid me*, and it took Jocelyn a moment to catch on: *Nina had her period—for the first time?*

"They're tricky, right? Hang on." Above the sinks was a sanitary-napkin dispenser. Jocelyn inserted a quarter, and predictably, a pad an inch thick popped out. She passed it under the stall. "Try this. Stick it in your underwear. We'll pick up better ones later, okay?"

"Okay." After much crinkling of plastic, Nina said through the stall, "After the relay, Annabelle pointed to my leg. It was all bloody. I'm such an idiot, I thought I had a cut. Annabelle said, 'It's your period, dummy.' I would've figured it out in, like, another minute."

"So that's why you disappeared," Jocelyn said.

"The only other girl who's gotten her period has these giant boobs. Annabelle threw a bunch of tampons in my stall, and everyone laughed."

Jocelyn wouldn't do that unhelpful adult thing of telling a kid that something mortifying was totally normal and nothing to be ashamed of. She wouldn't point out that those girls were laughing out of their own insecurity, nor would she get on a soapbox about the insidiousness of internalized misogyny.

"That must've been really embarrassing," she said instead.

"I don't think I can face them again."

"Well, they're all gone for now. Are you ready to come out?"

The stall door creaked open. Nina washed her hands, and they exited the locker room together. "Hey, kiddo," Kyle said. Nina mumbled a reply.

When they passed CVS, Jocelyn told Kyle they'd be just a minute. They found the right aisle, and Nina surveyed the shelves of products with wide eyes. Jocelyn grabbed a package of pads. "We'll tackle tampons another day."

Outside, Kyle shot them a quizzical look. "Dad, I got my period," Nina said. "Please don't say a single word."

Kyle made a lips-sealed gesture, glancing meaningfully at Jocelyn.

"What do you say?" she asked Nina. "Are you up for the team dinner?" The pizza place was across the street.

"I guess." Nina stared at her feet. "Thanks."

"No problem."

Kyle saluted his daughter, breaking his vow of silence only to remind her to be home by nine. He went quiet again after they parted ways with her. At home, he prepared a simple dinner of pasta with red sauce, but then said he didn't have much of an appetite. "You enjoy," he told Jocelyn. "I need to finish a contract." So Jocelyn ate on her own, replaying her interactions with Nina, feeling proud of how she'd handled the situation.

Nina appeared at nine on the dot and went directly to her room. Jocelyn waited five minutes before knocking, then entered when Nina gave her the okay. "How was pizza?" she asked, sitting at Nina's desk.

"Fine." Nina was scrolling on her phone.

"That's good. Did you try one of the new pads?"

"Lily said pads are awful for the environment. Everyone uses those cup things or period underwear."

"Oh, okay," Jocelyn said. "We can get you that stuff. So it sounds like some other girls have gotten their periods, too."

Nina's nod was barely detectable. Her whole demeanor had changed. Clearly unwelcome, Jocelyn stood to leave. "Well, let me know if you need anything."

Nina didn't look up from her phone. "Close the door on your way out."

"Sure thing."

Now that Nina had gone frosty, Jocelyn felt silly for having thought she'd handled things so well before. Even her wisdom on period products was evidently antiquated. She shuffled back to Kyle's office. He was sitting at his desk, staring into the middle distance, his laptop closed.

He noticed Jocelyn. "Hey. How's she doing?"

"I don't know. Different."

"You never know what you'll get with Nina. Do you think I should check on her?"

"I have no idea." But then she did have one. "Hey, when Liv had her period, did she get any cravings?"

Kyle's smile carried a touch of melancholy. "Brine, big-time. She could eat half a jar of pickles."

"Good. Go tell Nina that."

Kyle left, and Jocelyn remembered when she'd first gotten her period, at age twelve. It was before Maddy got hers, which drove Maddy nuts. Jocelyn's cramps had been so bad, her mother let her stay home from school, tucking her into bed with a heating pad. Maddy pouted at Jocelyn's special treatment, then pretended not to care when Claire took just Jocelyn out for celebratory ice cream. Over mint-chip cones, Claire walked her through the menstrual cycle. "Now you're part of a special club," she added, "because one day you can have a baby." Jocelyn felt the magnitude of the moment. When Maddy got her period a few months later, for her it was all about the accessories. She bought a special case for her Tampax and was quick to criticize girls who used inferior brands or, god forbid, pads. Of course, Jocelyn had been the one to teach her sister how to use a tampon.

Kyle was gone for a while, and when Jocelyn passed Nina's door on her way to the bathroom, she could hear Nina whimpering, along with Kyle's soothing voice. How hard it must've felt for her to reach this milestone without her mother. How hard for Kyle, too, to witness his daughter missing her mother and not be able to erase the hurt.

After becoming a mother herself, Jocelyn didn't get her period back for years. That wasn't unusual while nursing. Then, after Junie was gone, she couldn't eat. "Amenorrhea due to malnutrition," her doctor reported. Jocelyn ignored the directive to drink protein shakes. It seemed right to her that her body had shut down in that way, becoming inhospitable to growing a baby. Then, after months of feeling nauseous at the sight of food, she began eating a nightly pint of ice cream, and her period returned. Her doctor declared it a victory, her body returning to "normal." To Jocelyn, it felt like a loss.

When Kyle finally came to bed, he curled his body around Jocelyn's and whispered in her ear: how good she'd been with Nina, how grateful he was for her, how he couldn't do this without her. Jocelyn's eyes pricked with bittersweet tears. She couldn't help thinking it should've been Liv here with Nina, while she herself should've been with Junie, helping her through her first period. What a strange situation Jocelyn had found herself in: mothering this girl who wasn't her daughter, living in this place that wasn't her home. She felt a welling up of homesickness. That night she dreamed of waves crashing against dunes, the scene so vivid it was like a memory.

Chapter 18

"Resolved: College athletes should receive salaries," Maddy announced. "This group, start working on affirmative arguments; this group, negative." She circulated the stage, checking in with each huddle of students as they typed up notes.

A senior named Kim called her over. "Did you know at some colleges, the football coach earns more than the president? It's sickening."

"Yeah, but who's bringing in all the money?" asked a junior named Gus.

"It's an interesting issue, huh?" Maddy was channeling her own high school debate coach, Mr. Everly, who'd never revealed where he stood on an issue.

After twenty minutes, she said, "Okay, everyone, time to partner up. We're focusing on affirmative and negative constructives today."

"Ooh, my favorite." This was Layla, dripping with sarcasm. "Why does anyone care about sports? You'll never catch me wearing shorts." She'd apparently spent her prep time writing a ditty. "Actually, Ms. Marx, can I abstain? Sports are so stupid."

"Get in line, Layla." Maddy still wasn't used to being called Ms. Marx, more than a month into her gig as interim debate coach, a maternity leave fill-in.

Layla grudgingly obeyed, picking Kim's name from the basket. Kim's arm shot up for their pair to go first, making Layla groan. Kim was affirmative, so she approached the podium. She'd perfected the mile-a-minute patter; her six minutes were filled with facts about the prominent role of sports at colleges and in our culture, and stats about the historical exploitation of students. Layla took no notes, and when it was her turn to rebut, she cracked her knuckles, then launched into a tirade about how paying college athletes would only entrench them in our messed-up capitalist system, when sports should be the last sacred realm of play—no one should be paid, games should be free, everything just for fun.

Kim won, by a mile—teammates offered "glows" and, as usual, had trouble coming up with "grows"—but her victory was Pyrrhic, since Layla's "glows" were so much more enthusiastic. Kim fumed in the corner, channeling her frustration into notes. Maddy wanted to give her a hug. She reminded her of herself as a teenager.

"Who's on for endnotes?" Maddy asked, after all the pairs had gone.

Gus stepped forward. "I brought a quote from this old-timey French dude named Joseph Joubert: 'It is better to debate a question without settling it than to settle a question without debating it.'"

The kids clapped, and Maddy beamed at the community they'd forged, with her at the helm. "Strong session," she said. "Tomorrow we'll focus on key rebuttal tactics."

As the auditorium emptied out, Maddy hung back, inhaling the sawdust smell, unchanged since her own days as a high school debater. Her teenage self would be sorely disappointed to know she'd ended up right back where she'd started. And the irony didn't escape her that she was living out the exact scenario Jocelyn had hurled at her as an insult and a threat, on this very stage, back before the move. Not to mention that every dollar of her measly paycheck went to childcare. But despite all that, Maddy liked the job—she really, really liked it.

In the art room, Maddy found her mother rinsing paintbrushes. "Greetings, colleague," Claire said. "Here to help?"

"Sure." It had become Maddy's routine to visit with her mom after practice. As she dried paintbrushes, she told Claire about Kim. "She's whip-smart and works so hard, but there's a lack of inspiration."

"You know what I remember about you as a debater?" Claire said. "You were best when you let yourself relax."

"True." Maddy could conjure up those times—when she felt buoyed but not overtaken by her prep, how she could tune in to her instincts and project confidence. "Maybe I can convey that to Kim."

Claire smiled. "Look at you, thinking like a teacher."

"Come on, I'm just an after-school temp."

"Don't sell yourself short. Those kids are lucky to have you."

Maddy put away the brushes, thinking how strange it was to spend time in this classroom. Back in high school, it was home base to an alternative crowd, Jocelyn among them. Maddy never set foot inside unless she had to. Then she'd note the ease of the group, and how effortlessly they joked around with Claire, their den mother. Maddy once overheard a girl with stringy blue hair say, "I couldn't make it through the week without Mrs. Marx." She'd wondered what it would be like to feel that way about her mom.

"I just never thought I'd end up back here," she told Claire now.

"Well, life's not a straight path."

"It sure seemed like it was before."

Claire shrugged. "That was then, this is now. And as you said, it's temporary. Who knows what the future will bring? In the meantime, isn't it nice to be working again?"

"It is." Her mom was right. Ever since Maddy had taken this job, things were looking up. She'd seen a new doctor, who prescribed her antidepressants. She'd finally unsubscribed from her New York moms group newsletter, and deleted Facebook. And she no longer woke up dreading her days. Instead, she'd slip into the nursery and watch Rose start to stir, wiggling and babbling in her crib; she'd recently caught her rolling from belly to back, and clapped at the achievement.

"I remember how relieved I was to go back to work," Claire said. "No offense. But you were like Rose as an infant—furious at the world, hardly ever sleeping."

Maddy was surprised. "Why haven't you told me this before?"

Claire tilted her chin in consideration. "I guess I didn't want to be the type who's like, *You think you have it bad? Here's what I went through!*"

"But you always seemed just like Jocelyn, so in love with motherhood all the time."

Claire chuckled. "No one's in love with motherhood all the time. But you just keep showing up and trying your best. Even when your kid's in her thirties." She winked.

Maddy was moved almost to tears. Lately she'd been feeling like she'd survived something harrowing and was finally safe on the other side.

Claire scrutinized her. "I know you wanted to be easy-breezy about having a baby, like something that was hard for everyone else would be a cinch for you, as per usual. And it was a shock when it wasn't. But I always knew you'd get through that tough time."

Maddy hugged her mother. It was nearly five, time to pick up Rose. She pictured her baby's outstretched arms and scooping her up and hugging her close.

◆ ◆ ◆

On her walk to the parking lot, Maddy was enjoying the sun on her skin and the mild breeze; she caught herself humming Bill Withers's "Lovely Day." Halfway past the soccer field, she spotted Chad, her Realtor, now in a tracksuit instead of a tailored suit. Heat welled up inside her, taking her by surprise. It had something to do with his boyish stance and his gravelly voice as he yelled out to the players. Maddy wanted to pounce on him, tear off that tracksuit and her own clothes, too. When Chad noticed her staring, his attention felt like a spotlight: dazzling. *Holy shit.*

"Hey, it's Maddy Marx," he called out. "What a nice surprise. I coach the boys' soccer team. Do you work here, too?"

The twist of his lips made Maddy tremble. Her heart raced, and she found she couldn't quite close her mouth. "Yes," she said finally. "Debate."

"I knew you were a smarty-pants." He flashed her an ironic smile. "How's the crib working out for you guys?"

"Good. Thanks." Then she fled, Chad waving after her.

She made it to her car. In the driver's seat, she took several deep breaths. She felt stripped bare, dizzy with desire—a feeling of the past, she'd assumed, buried and done. She'd noticed Chad's good looks back when they were house hunting, but it wasn't accompanied by any inner stirrings; she'd been a thousand months pregnant then, preoccupied by her aching ankles. Even now Maddy suspected it wasn't really about Chad, but her own sense of aliveness.

The feeling stayed with her as she drove off. When Tanya handed over her daughter, Maddy rubbed her cheek against Rose's silky skin and breathed in her milky scent, hypersensitive to every touch and smell.

At home, Rose played with chunks of avocado and banana in her high chair, and Maddy poured two glasses of cabernet. When Justin walked in, she kissed him deeply.

"Well, hello," he said. "How are my loves?" Together they giggled at the sight of their daughter, whose face was a Jackson Pollock painting of mashed-up food.

Justin handled bath and bedtime, then returned to the kitchen and ribbed Maddy about her dishwasher-loading technique. He was no longer treating her like a fragile vase, thank god. These days he complained about work and snapped at her sometimes, when for months, Maddy realized lately, he'd swallowed it all; now she could handle it, and it made her feel like his partner again. He reached his arms around her from behind, and Maddy caught a whiff of Old Spice. Her skin tingled at his touch, and she felt an excitement between her legs. She spun around, abandoning the dishes. Justin hoisted her up onto the counter, and they began making out like teenagers, lust blooming in Maddy's body. She pulled off her shirt.

Justin's eyebrows lifted. "Are we really doing this?"

Because they hadn't done it, not yet, not since Rose. Justin had broached the topic occasionally, but as soon as Maddy expressed any hesitation, he changed the subject, not revealing disappointment or impatience. Her gem of a husband, her guy.

Now Maddy hopped off the counter and led him to the bedroom. Their first sex in six months was going to be the good old-fashioned kind, on their bed, and with plenty of lube, as her new doctor had advised.

"Whoa." Maddy flinched. It felt like shards of glass.

"I'll go slow," Justin said.

It kept hurting, but less and less. Maddy breathed through it, and when she winced, Justin kissed her and rolled off, saying, "That's enough for now." Then they lay side by side, getting themselves off. It took Maddy forever, and Justin stroked her arm and told her how beautiful she was. Her orgasm was weak, barely there, but it was a start.

"That was nice," Justin said, draping an arm across her stomach. "So, um, where'd that come from?"

Maddy flashed on Chad in his tracksuit, the electricity coursing through her body. Justin probably wouldn't have minded if she told him—he wasn't the jealous type—but she kept it to herself anyway. She shrugged, suddenly shy. "I guess something just got stirred up in me."

"Well, I heartily approve," Justin said, delivering a pat to her hip.

Soon he was asleep. But Maddy stayed awake—the Lexapro had exacerbated her insomnia. She lay there thinking what a relief it was to discover that her desire had just lain dormant for a while, and not disappeared altogether. It was good to remember that things could change.

Still, ten minutes of staring at the ceiling soon stretched to thirty, and Maddy's gratitude gave way to anxiety, unwelcome thoughts nipping at the edges of her brain. She decided to distract herself with Instagram (an app she couldn't yet bring herself to delete). Three posts in, she came across her sister's face pressed up against Kyle's, beaming over a spread of sashimi.

Swipe, swipe, swipe—a whole carousel of the pair posed before elaborate meals, against aesthetically pleasing backdrops. The caption read, Stepping up our dinner game. Jocelyn had posted two hours ago, and already her hearts were in the triple digits.

Envy surged through Maddy. When was the last time she'd gone out to a meal like that? She examined the photos again, Jocelyn's and Kyle's bedroom eyes, their bodies magnetized together. She wondered about their sex life: whether they were doing it daily or more, which positions they'd tried, what peaks of satisfaction Jocelyn had reached. Maddy replayed her own bedroom rendezvous that evening, and a pool of embarrassment settled in her stomach, tinged with fury at her sister. No, she realized, the fury was at herself, for scrolling so late at night, for letting herself get so worked up about something so trivial.

Enough. She placed her phone face down on the nightstand. The clock confirmed that Rose would be up in a couple of hours. Maddy sighed and pulled on her sleep mask.

Chapter 19

JOCELYN

Rounding the rotary to the Outer Cape was the sign to roll down the windows, no matter how blustery the April wind. Jocelyn took a whiff of the brackish air, realizing how deprived she'd felt of it. Kyle winked at her from the driver's seat. It was good to be back after a tough drive, and a tougher few months.

Nina had grown extra moody lately, trying on cruelty like a new pair of jeans, and directing it more often than not at Jocelyn. Kyle urged her not to take it personally—even to be flattered by it—since Nina was only a terror to those she loved. Spring break was approaching, which overlapped with Nina turning twelve. She and her mother had always spent her birthday with Liv's parents in Rhode Island, but now, for the second year, Nina would be visiting her grandparents on her own. Jocelyn had planned a playlist for the drive, all the songs she'd heard blasting from the girl's bedroom that winter, in yet another attempt to connect with her. But when she cued up Ariana Grande's "No Tears Left to Cry," Nina declared the song played out. Same attitude with the next track, and at the opening notes of the third one, Nina scoffed and put on her headphones. So Jocelyn and Kyle were left listening to teen pop on their own. Kyle made a joke of it, crooning "I'm in love with your body" along with Ed Sheeran. But Jocelyn felt stung, though she tried not to show it; she sensed Nina clocking her reaction from the back seat.

Her honeymoon period with the girl was over. During the first big snowstorm that winter, Jocelyn had shown up at Nina's school with sleds, and they'd spent the afternoon flying down the hill in the common, then breaking for cocoa when their lips turned blue. But the next time Jocelyn suggested sledding, Nina mumbled that she had too much homework. Once, at school pickup, Jocelyn spotted her enmeshed in a group of girls and slowed her gait. Nina was posed in a studied slouch, gazing at Annabelle the Asshole, as Jocelyn had come to think of the queen bee. Annabelle grabbed one of the girls' phones, maneuvered her thumbs, and then tossed it back. Observing a look of alarm pass over Nina's face, Jocelyn sped up to extract her. She asked about the incident on the walk home, unsure whether Nina would share or shut down. Nina got this conspiratorial look as she said, "So, Lily likes this guy, and Annabelle was sick of her just talking about it, so she took Lily's phone and texted him, 'I wanna lick your dick.'"

Jocelyn stopped herself from laughing, and also from demanding that Nina exorcise this she-devil from her life. "That sounds pretty mean," she said. "How do you think he'll respond?"

Nina giggled. "That's the thing. Annabelle can be a real bitch, but she always makes things interesting." Jocelyn waited for more, and it came half a block later. "At Josie's party last week, she kept pushing me to kiss this guy, Wyatt, saying it was obvious he likes me. When I wouldn't do it, she told everyone I must be gay. I should've said, 'So what if I am?'"

Jocelyn held her breath. She was conscious of the air between them, of Nina's footsteps and her own, and of the seconds ticking by as she scrambled to formulate a response. Because she wasn't sure if what might've been happening was actually happening. She decided not to risk it: "I always think of the best comebacks hours later." As the words left her tongue, she sensed their inadequacy. She added, "I think people like Annabelle must be unhappy, so they wield their power to make other people unhappy, too."

Nina nodded like she wasn't really listening. At home, she retreated to her room.

Kyle had a work dinner, so it was just the two of them that evening. Jocelyn kept turning Nina's words over in her head. She thought about Betsy, who hadn't come out till college. Wasn't this new generation of kids supposed to be so progressive, fluid with their gender and sexuality? Jocelyn felt out of her depth. But she also thought it was better to try than not to. She knocked on Nina's door. After hearing a clipped "Yes?" she went in and perched on the edge of the bed. "You know my friend Betsy, right? When we were in school, some kids were really unkind to her. She dressed different, and she never dated guys like the rest of us."

"Oh my god," Nina snapped. "It was just a stupid story. Which obviously I regret telling you now."

Jocelyn grew warm—had she totally miscalculated? She tried again: "I'm sorry, Nina. I'm just trying to tell you I care about you, and I'm here for you."

"Cool, thanks," Nina replied curtly.

Jocelyn yearned to get through to her: "I know it must be hard to be this age and not have your mother around."

Nina narrowed her eyes. "So that's what this is about? You barging into our lives so you can pretend to be my mother?"

"No, that's not—"

"Because you're not. And guess what? I'm not your daughter. I'm Nina, remember? Not Juniper. And I'd like to be left alone."

At the sound of Junie's name, Jocelyn broke out in a cold sweat. She stood up and managed to stave off the tears until she was behind her own closed door. She climbed into bed, where she remained through the night.

Nina mumbled an apology over her bowl of cereal the next morning, but Jocelyn remained unsettled. All day she ruminated on Nina's accusations, questioning her own motives for being there. Then came Junie's birthday. She would've turned eleven—Nina's age. Would she have been just as temperamental, just as ruthless?

Or would Jocelyn have done a better job of connecting with her? She didn't mention the date to Kyle. She spent the day on her own, walking around, screening calls from Betsy and her parents. It was frigid out, but soon it would be spring. Work would pick up again, and it would be time to go home.

Jocelyn was mulling all of this on the ride to Providence, stealing glances of Nina in the rearview mirror. As they pulled up to her grandparents' house, Nina's whole demeanor transformed into that of an eager kid. She called out "Mee-Maw! Pop-Pop!" and bolted from the car, reveling in their hugs. Seeing how fiercely the three of them clung to each other tugged at something in Jocelyn.

She was nervous as Kyle introduced her to Eleanor and Stuart, Liv's parents. Stuart was a gracious host, friendly in a grandfatherly way. He offered them iced tea and asked Jocelyn how it was to live year-round on the Cape. Then he suggested Eleanor give her a tour of the house, adding with a chuckle, "So long as you don't try to sell it out from under us." As she was led out of the kitchen, Jocelyn glanced back and saw Stuart and Kyle leaned together closely, talking. It looked like a reunion of close friends.

The house was a stately colonial, but Eleanor said little about it as they moved through the well-appointed rooms. She remarked how it must be nice for Nina to have Jocelyn in her life; it was a kindness, given that the girl hadn't made eye contact with Jocelyn since they'd arrived. Jocelyn noted a familiar vacancy behind Eleanor's eyes. She'd recognized grief in Kyle from the moment they met, and it was there in Stuart, too, but Eleanor was different: It was like meeting a mirror image of herself, two mothers in mourning. Part of Jocelyn wanted to hold her tight, and another part wanted to shake her and demand she snap out of it. Instead, she followed her into the next room, where they came upon Nina, cross-legged on the rug, surrounded by rabbit figurines and dollhouse furniture. Jocelyn imagined her as a younger girl playing with these toys, maybe with her mother. Nina looked caught out. Jocelyn apologized and stepped out, regretting the intrusion.

She and Kyle left soon after the tour, and they both were quiet for the rest of the drive.

Jocelyn's cottage was right where she'd left it, only now, pale-green leaves dotted the oaks and daffodils burst from the soil. The tinkle of wind chimes welcomed her home. Jocelyn thought of her second-home clients returning to the Cape each spring to open up their houses, the warm months stretching out before them like a sumptuous buffet.

Inside, the air was stale, and there were gatherings of crispy bugs in corners, inevitable after months away. Jocelyn moved around, throwing open windows and observing her things: her comfy old couch, her mother's paintings on the walls, her pale-purple bedspread. She'd bought this place after years of selling houses to other people; it was simple and snug, but it was hers. She face-planted on the bed and spread out like a starfish.

Kyle came and joined her. He trailed kisses along her shoulders and the nape of her neck, and her body responded to his touch. Soon their clothes were in a heap on the rug. "I'll go grab something," he said, but Jocelyn stopped him. "Are you sure?"

She nodded, feeling a wild streak of joy, of being brave and open to the future. A flood of happiness overcame her along with the waves of pleasure—to be here, home, with her love.

"So, no condom, huh?" Kyle asked afterward. They lay supine, peering up at the parabola-shaped crack in the ceiling.

"I guess not. Is that okay?"

"Sure," he replied, grinning, and Jocelyn couldn't help but giggle at the nonchalance of the exchange. They'd talked about it occasionally—Kyle going on about how he hoped to have another child, and Jocelyn getting more and more comfortable with the idea. These conversations secretly thrilled her. Though they hadn't been dating all that long, Jocelyn felt like she'd known Kyle for years; he'd opened up possibilities that she hadn't previously let herself hope for. She also suspected the only way she'd go for it would be spontaneously. So who knew? Though in truth the chances were slim, since her period had just ended that morning. She rolled off the bed and gathered up her clothes.

They'd intended to open Kyle's house next. But on the drive over, the sliver of aquamarine through the branches beckoned to Jocelyn, and suddenly she couldn't wait another minute to see the ocean.

"A little brisk," Kyle remarked on the path down to the beach. Jocelyn went to feel the water, anticipating the first day that would be warm enough to plunge in. Spring's arrival usually brought on a mix of anticipation and foreboding in her, but all she felt now was optimism and joy.

Drunk on the scenery, she blurted out the thought filling her head: "Would you ever move out here full-time?" She knew Kyle planned to spend the summer on the Cape, and weekends until then, but they hadn't yet talked about the fall.

"Sure, maybe," Kyle said.

"The schools are really good, you know."

"Oh yeah?" But he sounded far away. To him, they were just dreaming aloud, talking hypothetically. Anyway, as strong as the Nauset District was, it probably didn't measure up to Nina's prep school in Boston. Jocelyn dropped it. When a gust of frigid wind cut across the shore, they jogged back to the car and blasted the heat.

Jocelyn leaned into the week. After a corn muffin at Cod Coffee, she conducted a market analysis on a property, then visited a new build site in Chatham. She practiced yoga with Betsy, walked Rusty with her dad, and visited her mom's classroom to assist with still-life drawings. When Claire asked whether she could stay a little longer, since Maddy's debate practice was about to end, Jocelyn begged off—she was due to stage a house in an hour. Well, how about Sunday dinner, then? her mom asked. Jocelyn said she had an open house on Sunday (never mind that it ended at three), so maybe the following week. "You know, you've got to see your sister sometime," Claire said gently. Jocelyn didn't reply, thinking, *Says who?*

At day's end, she reunited with Kyle, who regaled her with his latest attempts at DIY home projects. They traded off in the kitchen—one cooked, the other cleaned; then they swapped the next evening. On

Kyle's final night, they took a bath together in Jocelyn's too-small tub. "I don't want you to leave," she said.

"I know." Kyle wrapped his arms around her. "I'll be back next weekend."

"Right." But he'd be returning with Nina. Jocelyn had relished their time alone, without the girl who'd been punishing her for trying to be her mother.

Kyle nuzzled her neck. "I can't tell you how much I'll miss you in the meantime."

The coming week looked gray to Jocelyn. The thought of a bath by herself almost made her cry. "It's getting cold," she said. She stepped out of the tub and wrapped herself in a thick towel, but she couldn't stop shivering.

Chapter 20

Maddy's new favorite part of the week was her Saturday-morning swim at Duck Pond. She'd strap on a wet suit, cap, and goggles, and plunge into the clear, cold water. Crossing the kettle pond, she felt every muscle working. But it was peaceful, and it quieted her mind in the same way that running once had. Maddy had tried to return to her old exercise regimen, but even a light jog led to an ache in her right hip and twinges in her back. She'd pushed through a few short runs before reluctantly accepting that nine months of growing a human had rearranged her body in a way that required a gentler kind of tending to. Hence: swimming.

Maddy usually had the pond to herself, save for an occasional fisherman, but today she was dragging Kelsey along—Kelsey, who called her a freak for swimming outside in April. "Two minutes in and you won't even feel cold," Maddy assured her. Kelsey shook her head as she packed her towel. Something Maddy had learned about her neighbor was her total open-mindedness—she'd give anything a shot. Like, she'd belly-laughed when Maddy described her love of true-crime podcasts, then asked which ones she should download. Now, each weekday morning, after Kelsey dropped her youngest at preschool, they met up to walk the Salt Pond Trail, earbuds in and Rose in Maddy's carrier, pressing play simultaneously on the next episode of *Darkest Before Dawn*. At each shocking reveal, Maddy would gasp and Kelsey would wag her arms and bounce on her toes, and it was in those moments that Maddy felt happiest to have found this friend.

Kelsey drove, blasting Taylor Swift, and they sang-shouted along to "Look What You Made Me Do." Both of them were Swifties, but only Kelsey was embarrassed by it. As the truck bumped its way down the twisty dirt road, she asked, "Are you taking me into the woods to off me?" That very plotline had appeared on a recent episode of their beloved pod.

"I guess you'll find out," Maddy said. She was surprised to hear that Kelsey had never been to Duck Pond, a staple of her own childhood. Just as Kelsey was shocked that Maddy had never gone clamming before she'd taken her. Maddy liked that there were worlds within worlds even in such a remote place—it reminded her of the city's micro-neighborhoods, how moving just ten blocks changed all your local spots.

Kelsey shrieked as she dipped a toe in the water, but then dove in before Maddy had even secured her goggles. Kelsey had a decent stroke, flutter kicks creating tiny ripples on the pond's surface. Maddy waded in, the shock of the cold catching in her throat. "Let's do this," she whispered to herself before setting off.

She hated the start of the swim. There were no distractions underwater, nothing to mask her burbling thoughts. Like how the end of the school year was fast approaching, which meant the end of her stint as debate coach—and what would she do next? And the fact that she needed to start earning real money again. And how her sister had been back on the Cape for a week already but had made no effort to get in touch. Not that Maddy had reached out to her, either.

It took maybe five minutes before the chatter in her head receded and Maddy was fully in her body. She circled the pond two and then three times. Only when her limbs felt like spaghetti did she head back to shore. There Kelsey was wrapped in a towel, skipping rocks. "I was trying to nail you, but lucky for you, I've got crap aim. No death by pebble today."

"Maybe we need to lay off the true crime."

"Never."

Maddy especially loved the afterglow of swimming—her body spent, her head humming pleasantly. On the drive home, they didn't chat or listen to music. Maddy scanned the passing marshes through the window and came to a decision.

◆ ◆ ◆

The next afternoon she buckled Rose into her car seat, then copied the Zillow address to Google Maps. "Let's do this," she told herself, just like before her swim. The house was in Orleans, overlooking Nauset Harbor: modern architecture, six beds and four baths, thirty-six hundred square feet, list price $2.8 million. Maybe if Maddy could land a top-notch consulting job and convince Justin to join a corporate firm again . . . well, they probably still couldn't swing it, but a girl could dream.

The property was even more stunning than it looked in the listing. Bursts of hydrangeas flanked the winding driveway, and when Maddy pulled into the parking area, already crowded with Teslas and Audis, she took in the towering structure on the hill, a wall of windows overlooking the bay. "Ooh, ahh," she murmured to Rose in her carrier as they crossed the terraced stone patio, passing an oblong pool that twinkled turquoise. "Should we live here?" she chanted. "Let's live here." Rose cooed back. Entering the foyer, Maddy felt like her daughter was protective armor, literally strapped to her chest.

There she was: across the room, chatting with a couple in their fifties. Maddy scrutinized her sister. She wore a floral sundress and espadrille wedges, her hair in loose waves down her back. Anyone would call her pretty. Was Maddy that pretty? She was certainly in better shape, after all the swimming. But Jocelyn was glowing; it reminded Maddy that she needed to level up her skin-care game—invest in some retinol now that she'd stopped breastfeeding. The couple laughed at something Jocelyn said. Was her sister good at her job? Probably, Maddy conceded, although she couldn't imagine Jocelyn negotiating in the cutthroat way she assumed was required of Realtors.

When Rose grew squirmy, Maddy automatically began swaying and humming "Do-Re-Me." Did Jocelyn still have her intuitive sense for babies—was that why she noticed them right then? Maddy raised a tentative hand, and Jocelyn nodded back. Then a man pulled her aside, and she disappeared down a hallway.

Maddy hadn't considered this possibility—that her sister would see her and then just carry on. Searching for something to do, she grabbed a tear sheet and read about the house: the bedroom balconies, the steam shower and sauna, every amenity you could imagine.

Maddy moseyed into the kitchen, where Jocelyn was holding forth to a small group. She pointed out the quartz countertops and custom cabinetry, the tile backsplash imported from Spain, and the same light fixtures Gwyneth Paltrow had in the breakfast nook of her Hamptons house. Maddy felt like she was in a Nancy Meyers movie. Could anyone possibly be unhappy in a kitchen like this?

Finally, Jocelyn approached. "You found me," she said.

"Well, Mom said you weren't coming to dinner tonight because of an open house."

"So you sleuthed."

Maddy shrugged.

"Or are you already antsy in your own house and ready for the next big thing? You need a walk-in closet the size of your living room?"

"That sounds splendid, actually."

"I'm sure it does, to you, Mad. I didn't realize your salary as a substitute debate coach could finance a seaside villa."

"Nice, Joss." Maddy rocked on her heels. This wasn't what she'd wanted out of coming here. She tried again: "Actually, I should thank you for suggesting that I get a job. It's really helped me. I feel like I'm finally settling in."

"Well, good for you. Congrats."

Maddy tried to ignore the tightness in her sister's voice. "I had no idea you represented houses like this."

"Why wouldn't I?" Jocelyn asked, defensive.

"I don't know. Just, it's cool."

"Okay." Jocelyn seemed to be searching Maddy's face for signs of sarcasm. "Well, I've got to get back to work."

"Sure. Will you come to Sunday dinner next week?"

Jocelyn hesitated before saying she'd try to; then she squeezed Rose's foot. "I've missed this girl."

Maddy smiled—it was something. "You know, it occurred to me that Rose is a nature name, like Juniper. Maybe subconsciously we picked it as a tribute to her."

"Huh. That's nice."

"Anyway, I'll talk to my accountant about scrounging up a down payment for this place. Maybe we've got an extra hundred grand hiding in some account."

"Sorry to burst your bubble, but I just got an all-cash offer from this Silicon Valley tech bro."

"Good for you, Joss." Maddy was proud of her sister.

"Thanks," Jocelyn said, sounding more sincere than skeptical.

Since she was here, Maddy decided to check out the rest of the house. Wowed at every turn, she was suddenly full of ideas for her own modest house, which she'd grown quite fond of. They could finish the basement to put in a playroom; if they wired the shed with electricity, it could be her home office. There were plenty of branding firms in Boston—if Maddy went in once a week and earned even half her old salary, they could probably afford some renovation. It was exciting to consider.

Back home, Maddy spotted a small package by the front door. She opened the card bearing her name and read: "To stay safe on your swims! —K." Inside was a fluorescent yellow buoy, the kind used for open-water swimming. Duck Pond wasn't big, but who knew if she might get a cramp or encounter a snapping turtle out there alone? The gesture from her friend made Maddy feel the opposite of alone—she was becoming part of a community. And she'd made peace, or at least a step toward it, with her sister. She went inside singing "Ring Around the Rosie" to her baby, voice resonant with hope.

Chapter 21

JOCELYN

At Sunday dinner, Jocelyn was on edge. Her sister greeted her with a hug, saying, "I'm so glad we're good now." Jocelyn couldn't conjure up a response. Since when were they good? She'd missed the part where Maddy apologized for saying what she'd said—that after so many years, it was time for Jocelyn to get over Juniper already. The words had lodged themselves in Jocelyn's gut, amid a stew of hurt and anger, where they remained months later. It was typical Maddy, to believe she got to dictate the shelf life of grief. And now to decide unilaterally that they'd moved on, without considering Jocelyn's perspective or taking any responsibility for her viciousness.

It also happened to be Mother's Day. It was a stupid manufactured holiday that Jocelyn was choosing to ignore. She didn't ask Maddy how she'd celebrated, and to her relief Maddy was mindful enough not to share. Jed presented bouquets of irises to his wife and daughters, and that was that.

The conversation turned to another May occasion that Jocelyn would've liked to skip past: her and Maddy's impending birthday. It was Claire's idea to throw a party. Maddy proposed a clambake on the beach, saying she and her neighbor could dig up the clams. Jocelyn was thinking, *Since when is Maddy a clammer?* just as Claire clapped her hands and declared, "Perfect."

Jed beamed. "Celebrating your birthday together, it'll be just like the old days."

Justin chimed in: "I love me a beach bonfire."

"Who doesn't?" Maddy added, and Jocelyn nearly choked on her water.

Claire turned to her. "What do you think, Joss?"

"Fine," she replied. She didn't want to be the party pooper, nor did she want to have to remind her family why it actually wasn't fine. Because shouldn't they realize they were coming up on the tenth anniversary, or was everyone experiencing collective memory loss? Well, Maddy must've remembered, given the invective she'd spewed at Betsy's—basically, *It's been a decade, move the fuck on!* Before Jocelyn could propose that they at least limit the party to adults, Justin piped up to say he'd get sparklers for the kids, and Nina could help pick them out.

"Excellent," said Claire. "That's settled, then."

Jocelyn pushed her plate away, appetite vanished. She couldn't remember ever having felt more distant from her family. And the mention of Kyle's daughter put her even more on edge.

Since spring break, Nina had been joining Kyle for weekends on the Cape, although the fact that she'd rather be anywhere else had become pretty much her whole personality. She moped around, whining about missing soccer and sleepovers back home, and Jocelyn bore the brunt of her irritability—it was because of *her* that Nina was dragged here every Friday. In fact, Nina seemed to relish demonstrating how blameless she considered her dad. She and Kyle would take long bike rides or go browse the flea market, but if Jocelyn proposed an outing, like to check out the herring run, she refused to leave the house. Jocelyn was actually sympathetic—being a middle-school girl was a nightmare under the best of circumstances—and she didn't even blame Nina for trying to drive a wedge between her and Kyle. The problem was, she was very good at it. Kyle understood that Jocelyn was in a tough spot. But Nina was going through a hard time, he said, and she needed him right now. So father and daughter would head out, leaving Jocelyn behind.

This left Jocelyn feeling unmoored. She spent her weekdays anticipating Kyle's arrival, lighting candles just to see flickers of movement in the house, but then their weekends together were tricky. Not only was it tough to connect with Kyle during the day because of Nina, but in the evenings, the girl would plop herself on the couch and dominate the remote, staying up till ten or later. Meanwhile, Jocelyn started fading at nine, her body like sludge. She had a passing thought that maybe, possibly . . . but no, there'd been just that one time, and the timing was wrong. So she chalked up her exhaustion to the Nina situation. Something would have to give, and soon.

◆ ◆ ◆

In the meantime, there'd be a birthday party. The morning of the big day, Jed insisted that both daughters come over to receive their gifts. When Jocelyn arrived, he and Maddy were already by the garage. "Ready?" he asked, relishing the drama, before rolling up the garage door to reveal two cherry-red kayaks. "Ta-da!"

"Thanks, Dad." Jocelyn accepted his hug. It was an extravagant present, and classic Jed to give the two of them something meant to be done together. When they turned ten, he'd presented them with tennis rackets and joint lessons (Jocelyn gave up after a month; Maddy played through high school). For their eighteenth, he'd given them matching hiking boots and bus tickets to Mount Greylock; Maddy had been busy all summer at her precollege enrichment program, so Jocelyn ended up taking the trip with Betsy. Her dad's gifts always made Jocelyn feel a mix of gratitude and guilt.

"I love this," Maddy said. "I'll go with Kelsey to the bay."

Of course, Maddy didn't want to go kayaking with Jocelyn any more than Jocelyn wanted to go kayaking with Maddy. Jocelyn avoided her dad's face. That was the problem with gifts that carried agendas: You couldn't force people into camaraderie.

"I'll strap them to your cars, and you can bring them tonight," Jed said. "I'd love to take one out for a spin."

"Sure, Dad."

Jocelyn searched for clouds on her drive back to Kyle's, but the sky was a clear-blue sheet—no hope of a rainout. Still, she decided to pretend it was crummy weather, to justify napping away the morning.

She awoke in a foul mood. She heard Kyle and Nina out in the living room engaged in what sounded like a negotiation: Nina mentioned a soccer clinic, and Kyle said maybe, but they'd definitely be out here for August. As far as Jocelyn knew, Kyle was planning to spend the whole summer on the Cape. She'd been holding it out for herself like a carrot—this was a rough patch, sure, but soon they'd be together for two whole months. Now her heart sank, realizing that Nina's needs would always come first. Which was how it should've been, but what did that mean for Jocelyn? Would she forever be left scrounging for scraps?

"You look tired," Nina said upon seeing Jocelyn, before griping to Kyle, "Do I really have to go to this thing?" Evidently she was dreading the evening as much as Jocelyn was.

"It'll be fun," he insisted. "And it's not just 'this thing'—it's Jocelyn's birthday party."

"Will there be anything to eat besides clams? They're so disgusting, like, primeval." Nina made a gagging noise.

"Nina Taylor, you're being rude," Kyle said.

Nina rolled her eyes as her thumbs flew across her phone screen.

"Gimme that thing." Kyle snatched the phone away. "Apologize to Jocelyn, now."

"Sorry," Nina mumbled before stalking off to her room and slamming the door.

"I'm sorry she's being like this," Kyle said. "I'll go talk to her."

But Jocelyn wanted him to stay and talk to her. She wanted to ask whether he'd be spending half the summer in Boston. But she didn't have the energy to get into it, so she nodded and watched him walk away.

A glance at Nina's phone revealed an unlocked screen. Curious, Jocelyn picked it up. An Instagram post showed a girl posed in a gymnastics leotard, a gold medal hanging from her neck. Under the photo was a string of congratulatory comments, but the one with the most attention was from @annabelleoftheball, a.k.a. Annabelle the Asshole: first place for longest leg hair? zoom in and check it out lol. Nina's reply was posted six minutes ago: omg grossss. its so long it curls! Jocelyn stared as someone marked it with a laugh emoji.

She dropped the phone. When had Nina become such a monster? Was Kyle to blame, for being so easy on her? Their muffled voices through the door turned to laughter—so this was his big talking-to with his daughter? It struck Jocelyn that lately all the people in her life were disappointing her. What was going on with everyone?

◆ ◆ ◆

That evening, so much felt similar to the evening nearly a decade ago. The tide was rising, the ocean surface choppy. At dusk, the sun softened to pastels, and then they got the bonfire going. At least they were gathered at Coast Guard, not Nauset Light. Still, Jocelyn couldn't quite get a grasp on where and when she was—it was like she was seeing the scene through a fun-house mirror, and time felt unreliable. The past ten years expanded and collapsed, seeming like an eternity and then nothing at all.

Jocelyn's mother kissed her on the cheek. Her father offered her clams swimming in butter and lemon, the sight of which turned her stomach. When Stevie Wonder's "Happy Birthday" thumped from the speakers, Kyle shimmied over. He asked if she was all right, and Jocelyn said yes, because she didn't know how to explain. He took her at her word and began dancing circles around her. Well-wishers abounded, raising their drinks when they caught her eye. Nina handed her a sparkler, a kind of peace offering, and Jocelyn held it and watched it burn down until someone blew it out, warning, "Careful there."

She scanned her surroundings. Shadows flickered around the dancing fire. A dog barked and took off running down the beach. A bob of seals peeked up from the water, a sign perhaps of a lurking shark. Sparklers sizzled and popped. And there was her sister.

Maddy looked luminous in a teal dress, neck low and slit high. She welcomed guests warmly, throwing her arms around a stout woman trailed by a line of boys. She slurped up clams, moaning melodramatically. She danced with abandon, flitting around Justin and swinging Rose in the air in sloping figure eights, then setting her down and gaping as she crawled away quick as a crab. In the glow of the firelight, Maddy looked happier than Jocelyn had ever seen her.

Jocelyn, meanwhile, wondered whether she'd eaten a bad clam. Nausea pooled in her belly. Her unease festered as she weaved through the party, ducking conversations and looking for Kyle. She spotted him down the beach with Nina, two tiny figures in the distance. She wished Betsy were here, but her friend had texted last minute that she'd come down with some kind of stomach bug.

Jed announced a speech. "To my daughters on their thirty-second birthday." Jocelyn showed her face in the firelight long enough for him to raise his glass in her direction. "You've both grown into your own and found happy new beginnings this past year. Isn't it wonderful, after so much time, to be all together again? Everyone I love is here with me tonight. Cheers!"

No, Jocelyn screamed inside, *we're not all together again, we're not all here tonight. My most important person is gone—and has been for a decade. Don't you know that? Don't you remember?* As cheers resounded around her, Jocelyn stumbled away from the group.

That was when she saw it: Rose. Everyone was toasting and shouting "Hear, hear!" and, meanwhile, her niece was crawling down the shore, at least fifteen yards off. Jocelyn searched the crowd for Maddy—there she was, tossing back champagne with her friend by the fire. She looked for Justin—he was over there, too, engrossed in conversation.

Jocelyn's chest went tight. She couldn't breathe. She ran down the beach and scooped up the girl, just feet from the waves, the knees of her onesie damp. Jocelyn hugged her close, and Rose gurgled contentedly, having no idea how close she'd come to catastrophe. Jocelyn held her tighter, chanting, "You're safe, you're okay, you're safe." She scanned the party again, and there was Justin's back, Maddy nowhere in sight. She fled the beach, clutching her niece, heart racing and head buzzing with the past.

◆ ◆ ◆

The last day of Juniper's life had been just as fair and bright, the sky painted azure. Jocelyn's high school friends were trickling home for the summer, college now done for good. There was a graduation party on the beach, and Jocelyn was told Junie would be welcome.

She'd been excited and a little nervous. It wouldn't be like last summer, when things had felt awkward around her old friends, all of them just home on hiatus from their real lives back on campus, and Jocelyn with a newborn. A year later she'd grown confident as a mom, and she'd be starting classes at Cape Cod Community College in the fall. She was on her own track and felt good about it.

Only, when was the last time she'd been to a party? Especially with her crew from high school? As teenagers, they'd spent countless nights on the beach, drinking and goofing around, but that may as well have been a century ago.

Jocelyn shrugged on a seersucker dress and put Junie in a frilly yellow jumper. She packed a six-pack of Sam Adams, plus an applesauce pouch and a bottle. She wished Betsy were coming, but Cornell finished late, its commencement still a week away.

In a way it was just like old times. They drank beer and roasted hot dogs and chatted by the bonfire in the golden-hour light. But it was even better now, because Jocelyn had her daughter, her little companion. She toasted a marshmallow for Junie, and it was hilarious watching her gum at it until most of it ended up on her cheeks and chin. Jocelyn's friends took turns holding her, singing her songs and dancing her around, everyone so enamored with this precious girl. To the soundtrack of her daughter's peals of laughter, Jocelyn flirted with the guys she'd dated back in high school, sensing her body awaken in that old familiar way.

Junie was determined to move. She'd recently learned to walk, and then run. Jocelyn watched her fly down the beach chasing a flock of seagulls, tummy out and jumper flashing like sunbursts. *That's my Cape Cod girl,* she thought. Junie would grow up with salt in her veins, just as Jocelyn had—there was nowhere better to raise a child, she was sure of it.

She wasn't drunk, just a little tipsy. And she didn't walk off to hook up, despite the rumors that spread later. She just had to pee.

"You go, it's fine, we'll stay with Juniper," they said. *Who said?* Well, everyone—a chorus of reassurances. *But who, specifically?* the police wanted to know after the fact, trying to identify a culprit. *It wasn't like that,* Jocelyn replied, struggling to un-jumble her thoughts, rambling on—about how it took a village to raise a child, and this was her village, and surely she should be allowed to perform a basic bodily function—and on and on. Each new interview brought a fresh round of questions, but the looks on the cops' faces remained the same: wary, pitying. When they brought in Child Protective Services and the interviews turned to interrogations, Jocelyn realized that she was being blamed. *But you don't understand, I'm a good mother,* she kept pleading, petrified she wasn't convincing anyone, least of all herself. It took weeks before they dropped the investigation, clearing her of wrongdoing. Officially, it was no one's fault.

But although they hadn't pinned it on her, Jocelyn knew she had been the one to let go of her daughter and walk away. She had made that choice. Because the light of the fire was far reaching, and she didn't want to be seen. Because it was lovely to walk down the beach on her own, enjoying the mild evening air. She cherished being with Juniper, but when was the last time she'd been alone and unencumbered? She felt almost like a teenager at a high school party again, wild and free. So she kept walking—she walked until her bladder was about to burst. Then she popped a squat, did her business, and turned back.

She was only gone ten minutes, tops.

The bonfire was blazing, the music blaring, and someone passed Jocelyn a beer. She felt a twinge in her belly, a sudden sense that this wasn't her place and these weren't her people. When had she last seen them, anyway? Who among this group had she even thought about in the past year? It took her a minute to realize what was wrong—and she would never forgive herself for that lapse, that moment of unease when she stood at the edge of the crowd and didn't yet realize that her life as she knew it was over.

Because where was Juniper? When she first asked the question, it was casual, to a small huddle of girls. They shrugged and pointed—maybe those guys knew, or those ones over there. Jocelyn circled the bonfire, her question growing more insistent, more desperate. She barely heard the answers, the "I thought they were watching . . ." and "Wasn't she just . . ." and "Wait, ask him, I swear . . ."

After that night, she would never speak to any of these people again. Her so-called friends, who'd treated watching Juniper like any other party activity, fun for a while until it was on to the next thing, who had no idea the kind of responsibility it took to care for a child. But the fury she felt at everyone else masked the knowledge that she'd been the one to fail her daughter.

She called out Junie's name. Who was nowhere. Whom no one had seen. The party quickly morphed into something else.

The shouts of "Juniper" would haunt Jocelyn for years. The blinding beams of cell phone flashlights, the frantic searching. A boy she'd made out with years ago sprinted off to call 911, since there was no cell service on the beach.

The search and rescue team arrived, and soon after, Jocelyn's parents. Some people left; some stayed. A guy Jocelyn vaguely remembered from her freshman homeroom wrapped his forest-green fleece around her and stuck to her side all night. They yelled out "Juniper" until their throats were raw, until the tide went all the way out again. Sometimes Jocelyn still thought of that forest-green fleece.

It was a bleak, rainy morning, the fog heavy on the horizon. Eventually Jocelyn was taken home and told to get some rest. Somehow the days passed. She remembered the police station's stale coffee smell, the worn flannel of her childhood sheets, her mother's fingers through her hair. Watching the light change through the window, pinned down by the crushing weight on her chest of how she would possibly live with herself. The news from the chief of police that they'd found her body—not *her*, her *body*—half a mile offshore. The undertow was strong out there. *You're talking to me about the undertow?* Jocelyn wanted to scream. It would've been fast, drowning at that age. *Fifteen months,* he didn't say, or didn't know. Was she sure she didn't want to press charges?

Wasn't it obvious? The only thing she wanted was her daughter back. She was Juniper's mother, period, end of story. And who was a mother without her child?

Chapter 22

MADDY

It was shaping up to be a fine birthday celebration. It wasn't the Soho House, where a slew of Maddy's friends had gathered on her thirtieth, then crashed in adjoining rooms at the Jane Hotel; or even Vinegar Hill House, where she and Justin had enjoyed a quiet dinner on her thirty-first, when Maddy was well into her second trimester. But tonight there was the beach and the bonfire, clams and champagne, Justin's well-curated playlist, and people Maddy liked and loved—all in all, not so bad.

One improvement she could imagine would be not having to pee in a porta-potty, but the bathhouses weren't open this early in the season. Up in the parking lot, cell service suddenly restored, Maddy's phone buzzed and buzzed. She scrolled through the birthday texts—from relatives and former colleagues and an especially sweet one from Krista, with a bunch of GIFs about how much she missed her; Maddy replied with an invite to come visit this summer. She was headed back to the party when she opened the last text, from Jocelyn: Don't worry, I've got her.

Huh? Maddy texted back a string of question marks but received no reply. When she called, it went straight to voicemail.

She found Justin by the fire. "Where's Rose?" Last Maddy saw, he'd had their daughter up on his shoulders, bopping around to Regina Spektor's "Folding Chair."

"She's down the beach with your sister. I was watching her play in the sand, and then Jocelyn went and got her."

They both looked to where Justin was pointing, but the only creature in sight was a fat seagull ambling across the shore. Maddy scanned the party. No Jocelyn. No Rose. Her hands started trembling. She showed Justin the text.

"That's odd—why would she send you that? Did you ask?"

"Of course, but she must've turned off her phone. Did Jocelyn leave with our daughter?"

"No way," Justin said. "They probably just went for a walk. Why would she do that? Come on, she wouldn't do that."

"She would, and she did." Suddenly Maddy was sure of it. Her fury was like fuel, launching her into action. She grabbed her parents and read them the text. "Jocelyn took Rose," she said.

They exchanged a worried look.

"It must be a misunderstanding," Jed said.

"Ask Kyle if he knows anything," Claire suggested.

Kyle, too, insisted there had to be a reasonable explanation—the Jocelyn he knew wouldn't take off with someone's baby.

"Well, maybe you don't know her as well as you think," Maddy barked. She was annoyed at having to bring everyone else up to speed, when they should be focusing on finding Rose.

Nina piped up: "I saw them. Jocelyn had Rose and was running up to the parking lot."

Kyle clasped his daughter's shoulders, demanding details. It was about ten minutes ago, she said; she'd assumed Jocelyn was going off to change Rose's diaper, or something like that.

Maddy mobilized. She divvied them up into search crews: Justin would hang back in case Jocelyn reappeared. Jed and Claire were to go by her house, then to Betsy's and the Blushing Buoy, and then onto the bay beaches. Kelsey wanted to help, too, so Maddy instructed her to check the town's bars and restaurants. Maddy would team up with Kyle, and they'd rack their brains for out-of-the-way spots, anywhere they could think of that Jocelyn might go.

Kyle looked stunned, like he wasn't fully taking in the facts. Maddy wanted to tell him to snap out of it; wasn't it better that he realized now that Jocelyn was like this? He was far from the first man to fall under her spell—she'd charmed half the guys in high school into believing she was their fantasy girl, when in fact it was always, invariably, 100 percent about her.

"Even if it's not what we think," Maddy told Kyle, "we should find her, right? It's her birthday, after all." Lowering the stakes would help keep him focused.

Kyle nodded. "Of course, yes. We can drop Nina off on the way."

"But I want to come," Nina pleaded. "Please?"

"Fine, let's go," Kyle said. The three of them piled into his BMW.

Kyle first proposed Cod Coffee, that quirky little café Jocelyn liked. But it was closed, the lot deserted. Next, Nina suggested Bob's Sub and Cone; no sign of them there, either. Maddy tried Jocelyn's phone again—still straight to voicemail—then she shot off a litany of texts, a dozen variations on Where the hell is my daughter? and What the fuck is wrong with you? She checked in with the others: no news. Justin kept texting reassurances: He loved her, he was sure Rose was okay, this would all get resolved soon.

They continued on to Duck Pond, where Maddy prayed they weren't. It was a sacred spot to her, one she decidedly did not want to associate with her unhinged sister abducting her daughter. They parked and walked down to the pond. The surface was painted with pines, reflections in the shimmering moonlight. Maddy thought of her and Jocelyn as kids in this water, playing Marco Polo and diving for coins. She felt a pang for her sister—was she okay?

"Wow," exclaimed Nina.

"It's beautiful," Kyle said. "But no one's here. Should we try the Dune Shacks Trail?"

It was the best idea yet. Maddy could imagine her sister escaping into that strange, majestic landscape. They drove north, just past the border to Provincetown, and pulled into the little lot off Snail Road. Theirs was the only car, but maybe Jocelyn had parked elsewhere. They hiked up the path until the dunes came into view, looking otherworldly under the stars.

"This place is creepy," said Nina.

"We used to have parties here in high school," Maddy said. Privately, she'd always disliked those nights: kids tumbling drunkenly down the dunes in the misty dark, Jocelyn ducking behind one of the artist shacks with whomever she was hooking up with that week, Maddy all nerves until she returned.

"Jocelyn brought me here on our first date," Kyle said, a smile spanning his face. "It was a special night."

"Gross, Dad," Nina said.

"Come on," Maddy urged, "let's keep looking." They trekked across the sand, hollering "Jocelyn" and "Rose" until they went hoarse. Scaling each dune, Maddy got her hopes up, only to have them dashed all over again at the revelation of yet another empty vista. When she felt she couldn't take a single step more, she plopped down onto the trail.

"This is hopeless. I just want my daughter back."

Kyle sat beside her as Nina took off running down a dune. "Do you think something happened to them?" he asked.

Maddy scoffed. "Yeah, something happened to Rose, or more like some*one*: my sister."

Kyle paused before responding. "Why do you think Jocelyn would take her?"

The words flew out of Maddy's mouth: "Because she's broken. Because she lost her own baby, so now she can't let me have mine."

Kyle furrowed his brow. "Well, they're not here." He extended a hand to help her up.

They'd run out of ideas, and it was past midnight, so Maddy texted Justin to meet her back home. In the passenger seat, she kept feeling phantom vibrations in her lap, holding out a sliver of hope that her sister would call. They passed through Truro and Wellfleet in silence, and then Nina asked to borrow her phone. A moment later she pointed out a new icon on the home screen. "It's this game where you're a worm princess and you have to eat up all the jewels. It sounds stupid, but I dunno, it's sorta fun. I play when I'm upset."

"Thanks, Nina."

As he swung onto Blueberry Lane, Kyle gasped. Then Maddy spotted it, too: Jocelyn's car in the driveway. She flew out of the SUV and into the house, sprinting back to the nursery.

A sob gathered in her throat. There was her baby, asleep in her crib, snug in her penguin sleep sack. "Rose," she whispered like a prayer. She picked up her daughter and inhaled, hungry for her scent. "It's okay, Mama's here." Rose nuzzled into her mother's neck, sighing in her sleep.

Only then did Maddy see her sister, curled up on the rug, also asleep. A mighty rage roiled up in her. She pelted Jocelyn with a stuffed hedgehog, hitting her in the jaw and jolting her awake. She sat up and rubbed her eyes. "Mad, hi. Listen, I'm sorry."

"You're sorry?" Maddy wailed. Every muscle in her body was tense with fury. Rose began fidgeting in her arms, still half asleep, and Maddy rocked her as she whisper-yelled, "I don't even know what to say to you right now."

Then Justin was in the room, crying out in anguish and relief. He hugged them close, their little trio reunited. He addressed Jocelyn, voice ragged: "Has she been fed?"

"I gave her a bottle about an hour ago, when we came in."

"All right," he said. "You should probably go now."

Jocelyn nodded and got up. Maddy squeezed her husband's hand, handed over their daughter, and then followed her sister to the front door.

Now it was just the two of them.

"Seriously, what the fuck, Jocelyn?"

"I told you I had her."

Maddy scoffed. "Oh, so as long as you tell me you're doing it, it's fine for you to steal my child? That's what hostage takers do—they kidnap someone and send a note. I can't believe I ever let you near her."

"I said I'm sorry." Jocelyn's voice was small. "But she was crawling away. A few more seconds and she would've been in the water."

"Justin was watching her. He saw you pick her up."

"He was so far away, and distracted—that's not how you watch a baby by the ocean."

Maddy shook her head. "Okay, so you went and got her. Problem solved. Why not end it there, bring her back to us?"

"I brought her home eventually."

"Oh, good job, Joss. Hats off to you for not taking off with my daughter for good. Do you hear yourself?" Maddy felt like she was in some upside-down world where logic was absent. This was how it was dealing with her sister, who acted impulsively, never considering the consequences, and mostly got away with it.

Jocelyn stared at her feet. "You don't deserve her."

"Excuse me?"

"You of all people should know what can happen to a baby crawling by the ocean, and meanwhile you were off frolicking with your friends. You think because you're the incredible Maddy Marx that nothing bad could ever happen to you. You're so arrogant, it makes me sick."

Maddy shook her head. "What are you even talking about?"

"You treat Rose at best like some cute accessory, and otherwise she's an obstacle to you living your best life. Ever since she was born, you've been complaining about how tough it is for you, or else working so goddamn hard to prove that you're the same old you, unchanged by motherhood. It's like Rose isn't even a real person to you."

Maddy was stunned. "This is all *your* shit, Jocelyn! Stop dumping it on me and accusing me of being a bad mother. You're the one who couldn't keep your baby alive! Not me!" Her shouts echoed through the room.

Jocelyn was silent. Finally, she said, "You really are the worst."

"*Me?* You kidnapped my child!"

Maddy didn't need a mirror to know that her face was a replica of her twin's: tears streaming down, salt on their tongues. She flashed back to their fight at Betsy's Old Year's Eve party—would the two of them always return to this, forever tethered together in this age-old knot?

Jocelyn cleared her throat. "Do you know that I'd kill to have what you have? Being a mother was the greatest joy I've ever known."

Maddy inhaled deeply—she was so sick of this narrative, and of everyone tiptoeing around the truth, for years and years. "Do you know what I think? You loved your daughter, and a tragic accident happened, and it was unspeakably horrible. But you've used that as an excuse to stay stuck for a goddamn decade. To not finish college or move away from home or grow the fuck up."

Jocelyn narrowed her eyes. "Oh, fuck you, Mad, and your dumb ideas about what it means to be a grown-up. You're the least grown-up person I know. You devoted your life to the vapidest career, climbing the corporate ladder and collecting all your gold stars. Then you had a kid and threw a monthslong tantrum, because for the first time you didn't get to have everything you wanted exactly when and where and how you wanted it. How could you be thirty-two years old and still such a brat?"

Maddy clenched her fists to stop herself from slapping her sister. "You can keep insulting me, but the fact remains that you're the one who took my baby, and we both know it's because you don't have one of your own. Like a fucking toddler stealing another kid's blocks."

Jocelyn glared. "Actually, Mad, I was keeping her safe, because no one else was."

"Right. You keep telling yourself that. In the meantime, I'm going to go be with my daughter. *My* daughter. And you'll be lucky if I let you lay eyes on her again."

The slam of the door was indistinguishable from the hammering of Maddy's heart. So big was her anger, she feared it might consume her. She drew the drapes, thinking, *Good fucking riddance.*

In the nursery, she found Justin leaning over the crib, singing softly to their sleeping daughter: *You'll never know, dear, how much I love you. Please don't take my sunshine away.* For a flash, Maddy considered her sister's perspective—that Justin hadn't been vigilant enough with Rose. But Jocelyn was the irresponsible one, not him.

Maddy slipped to the floor, and then the sobs came. It was as if they'd been gathering inside her this whole horrific night and were finally flooding out. Justin sat beside her and held her.

The next thing she knew, she was waking up on the rug as a thin band of light streamed through the shades. Justin was asleep at her side, and Rose was standing up in her crib, gripping the railing and calling out, "Ma! Ma!"

"Hi, baby." Maddy picked up her daughter, shaking off the previous night like it was all a terrible dream.

Chapter 23

JOCELYN

When Jocelyn spotted Kyle in Maddy's driveway, her heart fell—he was the last person she wanted to see. He stood there arranging and rearranging his stance, finally settling on a lean against his SUV, hands in pockets.

"How are you?" he asked as she approached. He was squinting at her like he was trying to figure out how he knew her. Jocelyn shrugged, trying not to cry. "Can I give you a lift home?"

"No, I'll be all right," she said. "I'm sorry for tonight."

Kyle nodded. He seemed to hesitate before offering a tentative embrace, and Jocelyn didn't feel her usual sense of safety in his arms. She worried he would insist she explain what had happened, but when all he said was "We'll talk tomorrow, okay?" she was disappointed. She retreated to her car.

Jocelyn drove past the turnoff to her road and continued on to her parents' house, where she went inside and tucked herself in to her childhood bed with her old stuffed seal. Rusty trudged in and curled up at her feet. The clock flashed 2:00 a.m. For hours Jocelyn had driven up and down the road overlooking the dunes, singing Rose lullabies and listening to her breathing as she slept in the car seat that Jocelyn kept in the trunk; there'd been no destination, only the desire to keep her close, to keep her safe.

It must've been late morning when Jocelyn woke to a gentle tapping sound. Claire stood in the doorframe with a cup of hot tea and a message that Kyle was outside. It seemed easiest to let him in.

Kyle sat gingerly on the edge of the bed, observing Jocelyn like she was made of glass. Ashamed, Jocelyn squeezed her eyes shut. "Did you get some sleep?" he asked. She murmured an mm-hmm. "Good. So, do you want to talk about it?"

How could she explain? How scared she'd been, and how she'd acted on instinct, just trying to protect her niece. She knew she'd messed up, and she got how reckless it must've seemed from the outside. But she couldn't figure out how to say any of it, and she was so tired. "I don't think so. Not right now."

"Okay. Um, would you like to come home with us this week?"

Taking a trip seemed inconceivable, Boston another planet. Plus, Jocelyn assumed Kyle didn't really want her to say yes. "No. I'll just stay here and rest." He nodded. "I'm sorry," she added.

"I'll call you later, okay?" He kissed the top of her head.

Jocelyn watched him leave. She knew she didn't deserve him. She'd thought she could move on and be in a real adult relationship, but she'd been wrong. She should just let him go, for his own sake and for Nina's, too. Jocelyn was still so lost and frail—and even her body knew it. She kept experiencing waves of nausea, sending her darting to the toilet. But no matter how much she expelled, she couldn't seem to get rid of what was making her sick—as if it were a part of her.

When she finally turned on her phone, it was filled with texts from last night, all panic and fear, confirming that she'd done a terrible, crazy thing. The messages from Maddy were like shrieks in her ear, escalating from blame and insult to pure venom. Jocelyn swiped them away. She texted a colleague, asking him to cover her upcoming house tours; then she powered the phone off again.

She was next startled awake by her father's humming. "You're up," Jed said, from the bedside chair. He asked whether she was hungry, and she said not really. "Fair enough."

For a while they were both quiet. Jed peered out the window at what Jocelyn assumed was a Baltimore Oriole—she heard its signature whistle. Eventually Jed cleared his throat. "You know," he said, "sometimes I find it tough to be around Rose. She has certain gestures that are identical to Juniper's. Like, when she hears upbeat music, that hokey way she bounces from one leg to another, and her hiccup-y little laugh. Do you know what I mean?"

A lump formed in Jocelyn's throat. The description conjured it up like a video clip: Junie bopping around and giggling to Lady Gaga. *How had she forgotten that?* It was heartening to be reminded that memories of her daughter lived on not just in her but in others; it also made her ache. Jed patted her arm, and she thought, *We're alone in our suffering, and then for a moment, we're not.* "Thanks, Dad."

"You and Maddy," he said, shaking his head. "I always hoped you'd come to see what a blessing it is to have each other. When I was growing up, all I wanted was a sibling."

"Oh, Dad."

"But that hasn't been fair to you girls—I see that now."

Jocelyn blinked away tears.

"Anyway, you acted out last night, and it wasn't good. But you'll figure out how to repair it."

"I just wanted Rose to be safe," Jocelyn croaked, tears spilling over.

"I know, Cricket." Jed squeezed her shoulder. "If you explain that to Maddy, I think she'll understand. Will you go talk to her?"

Jocelyn tried to respond, but the thought of approaching her sister made her throat constrict. Jed broke the silence: "Do you want to come to the Audubon Center? Someone spotted a bay-breasted warbler this morning."

"No thanks, Dad."

After that he popped in a couple of times per day, inviting her to come walk Rusty or to help in the garden, and offering to bring her over to Maddy's. But Jocelyn needed more rest. Her mother would deliver chamomile tea and chicken soup, patting her on the head and then retreating, never asking when she planned on getting up or how long she planned to stay.

Kyle texted that sadly they wouldn't make it to the Cape that weekend—Nina's soccer team had made the playoffs. Again, he asked her to consider coming to Boston. Jocelyn congratulated Nina, but declined the offer.

◆ ◆ ◆

Betsy was the one to finally get her up and out of the house. "We're going paddleboarding," she declared, leaving no room for debate.

The bay was glassy, and Jocelyn concentrated on pulling her paddle again and again through the water. She asked Betsy about the Blushing Buoy, which had just reopened for the season.

"Oh, who cares about that?" Betsy said. "Tell me what's going on with you. You haven't been answering my texts. What on earth happened at your party?"

Jocelyn sighed. She didn't want to talk about that. "The thing is," she said, "I thought I'd reach a point where everything would feel okay. That I'd get over Maddy moving back and having a daughter. And that falling in love would fill me up"—she faltered—"like having a baby did. But instead, it's like, fine sometimes, and even good a lot of the time, but then other times it isn't, not at all. Some nights, when I'm lying in bed and Kyle's asleep beside me, I feel petrified at how far away he is and how I can't reach him. So I wake him up, and he holds me until I calm down. But after a while, inevitably, he falls asleep again."

"Wow," Betsy said. "Jewel would kill me if I woke her up like that."

"My point is, it's not enough. It doesn't fill the hole."

"Right. Well, maybe nothing ever will completely. Maybe you'll have to live with that, alongside all that's good."

"I guess." Jocelyn stopped paddling and sat on her board. "Lately I don't even feel like myself. It's like my body's rebelling against me, letting me know how wrong I was to think I could be in a relationship."

Betsy sidled her board up to Jocelyn's. "Um, this might sound nuts, but is there any chance you're pregnant?"

Jocelyn's heartbeat quickened. The thing was, she hadn't been sick at all while pregnant with Juniper, and she'd been clinging to that distinction whenever the suspicion arose in her thoughts. But of course it was possible. "Well, sure," she said to Betsy.

"But you haven't taken a test?"

"No."

"Instead, you stole Maddy's baby?"

Jocelyn shot her a look. "What? No. She was right by the water, and Maddy and Justin were distracted." But she could hear how it sounded like a flimsy excuse.

Betsy was nodding emphatically. "This is all starting to make sense, Jocelyn Marx. No wonder some twisted maternal Spidey sense kicked in and you went psycho with your niece. And no wonder you're terrified. This is a huge deal. Okay, here's what you're gonna do. You'll go home and take a test. Then you'll go to the doctor to confirm it. Next, you'll talk to Kyle and really explain things. And he'll understand, trust me."

"Yes, ma'am," Jocelyn replied. It was helpful to be ordered around by her friend, to think that if she simply followed each item on her list, everything would turn out all right.

◆ ◆ ◆

Jocelyn's doctor had an opening the next morning, and another one later that week; she opted for the second one, to give herself time to prepare. In the meantime, she called Kyle. It was better than doing it face-to-face. Fearing she'd lose her nerve, she launched right into it: "I told you my daughter drowned."

"Yes," he replied.

"But that's all I said, right?"

"I figured you'd tell me more when you were ready."

His words spurred her on: "It was at a bonfire on the beach. I had to go to the bathroom, and people at the party said they'd stay with her. Everyone thought someone else was watching her. Junie loved the ocean, the feel of the crashing waves. I took my time walking back. I remember feeling so free, finally alone, and meanwhile . . ." Jocelyn's voice cracked. "It was an accident."

"Oh, Jocelyn, how awful."

"I don't think I'll ever be over it."

"No, of course not."

"I'll think I'm okay, more or less, but then it all wells up inside of me like this big wave, and I . . . I don't know, I take off with my sister's baby."

She heard Kyle clear his throat. "That wasn't your finest hour."

But he didn't declare her crazy or unforgivable—which only strengthened Jocelyn's resolve that he was too good for her. "Anyway, I don't think it's fair to you to have me in your life."

"Oh." He sounded surprised. "Is that what you want?"

"Of course not." She tried to explain: "It's like, if things are going too well for me, if I've been too happy, then the feeling that I don't deserve it, that I haven't been punished enough, starts to creep back in."

"That's a terrible way to feel."

"I just don't know if you can trust me." Jocelyn shook her head. "I can't even trust myself sometimes."

"I hear you," Kyle said. "But I've known loss, too, remember?"

"It's not the same." Jocelyn was barely getting the words out, she was so choked up. "You still have your daughter."

"You're right; of course it's not the same. But I know the sorrow that can rear up all of a sudden and just take over, so you act out and really screw things up. I once left Nina stranded at school, not because I forgot to pick her up but because I couldn't bear to look at her, she reminded me so much of her mother. I did that more than once, actually."

Tears were streaming down Jocelyn's face.

"I also know that those moments pass," Kyle went on. "Think of all the times you've been a wreck and then gotten through it. So, can you know that it'll probably happen again and that maybe you'll do stupid, irrational things, but still be kind to yourself anyway? Can you try to repair the damage, ask forgiveness from the people you hurt, and then forgive yourself?"

"Maybe," she managed. "I can try."

"Good. Because I know that my love for you, Jocelyn, is rooted in how deeply you feel. I know it's a vital part of you and a way that your daughter lives on in you, too. And you deserve happiness."

Jocelyn was now weeping.

"I'll be back this weekend. I'll have Nina stay with a friend." Jocelyn nodded, even though she knew he couldn't see her over the phone. "I love you, Jocelyn. We'll be together soon."

◆ ◆ ◆

She finally went home. She faced her work inbox and her laundry, and it felt good to get things done. The doorbell rang, accompanied by the barking chorus of Betsy's golden retrievers.

"I was in the neighborhood," said Betsy from the welcome mat. "I brought you this." She held out a box: a pregnancy test. "I figured you probably haven't gotten one yet, right? I'll stay while you take it."

It was a demand, not an offer, and Betsy barged her way inside with the dogs, then prodded Jocelyn into the bathroom and shut the door behind her. Jocelyn stood there on legs like toothpicks. "Are you still there?" she called out.

"I'm here," Betsy replied, from right on the other side of the door.

Jocelyn scanned the instructions, took the test, and then waited, sitting on the edge of the toilet and watching the stick from the corner of her eye.

Two blue lines appeared, confirming what she'd already known in her gut. She blinked at herself in the vanity mirror. She detected a slight smile, though she wasn't sure whether to trust it.

The word felt stuck in her throat as she emerged from the bathroom. "Pregnant," she spat.

Betsy clapped her hands together, and the dogs began barking again. "There, now you know. This will be good, you'll see. And I'll help."

"You better."

"Obviously." Betsy gathered up the leashes. "For now I've gotta jet before these girls pee all over your rug."

Then she was gone, leaving Jocelyn alone, but not quite.

◆ ◆ ◆

Jocelyn pulled up Kyle's name on her phone three times, and three times she couldn't complete the call. It would be better to tell him in person.

In the meantime, she'd stay busy. She drove to the high school, where her mother was cleaning out her classroom for the last time—thirty-five years' worth of supplies, and just one week of school left. Claire showed her the bins for donation and dumpster, then went back to clearing shelves.

"Look at all this handmade paper," Jocelyn said, running her fingers along the velvety surface. "You don't want to keep it?"

"Take it or toss it," Claire said. "I'm moving on, welcoming the beautiful unknown." She snorted and rolled her eyes. "Look at me, trying to sell myself on retirement."

Her mom's words had a familiar ring to them. "Hey, do you remember that poem 'Good Bones'?"

"Of course," Claire said. "I sent it to you and Maddy a couple years ago. Even though half the lines are about shielding your kids from all of life's awfulness."

"Well, it was a little late for that," Jocelyn said.

"I have it printed out. Check over that bookshelf."

The laminated sheet was tacked to a corkboard, "Good Bones," by Maggie Smith in bold across the top. Jocelyn read to herself, lines about how dreadful the world was, full of stoned birds and kids sunk in lakes, but also so full of potential. She whispered the last bit aloud, about how this place could be beautiful—how you, the reader of the poem, could make this place beautiful. Those words had stayed with her. "It's a hopeful poem, don't you think?"

"I do," Claire said. "Because I'm an optimist, just like you."

"Me?"

"At heart, I think you are." Claire opened a cabinet and started tossing out bottles of dried-up paints. "Like, I think you know you can make things right with your sister." Jocelyn caught her sly glance. "Have you two spoken?"

Jocelyn didn't answer, her mind on something else. "Mom, I have to tell you something."

Claire stopped her sorting and faced her daughter.

Jocelyn gulped in a breath, then said it: "I'm pregnant."

"Oh!" Claire exclaimed.

"I'm freaking out."

"Of course you are, Cricket." She took Jocelyn's hands and looked her in the eye. "Whatever you decide to do is the right thing."

Jocelyn raised her eyebrows. "You didn't tell me that the last time."

"Well, back then you were so clear about what you wanted."

"Huh." Jocelyn felt her throat catch. "Aren't we supposed to get clearer about things as we get older?"

Claire scrunched up her face. "Who gave you that idea? The very opposite, I'd say."

Jocelyn was quiet, taking that in.

"Can I share something?" Claire said. "So, with a baby, things are pretty straightforward, right? Are they fed, are they clean, have they slept? You know what you need to do, not to say it's easy. A baby's basically still an extension of you. But then they get older—an experience that was robbed from you with Junie. They grow separate from you, with their own personality and preferences, and more complicated needs. I know a lot of moms struggle early on before finding their footing, like Maddy. But for me, the later years were tougher."

"How so?"

"Like, I often worried I was unfairly comparing you girls, or not giving one of you enough attention, or being there for you but not Maddy, or vice versa—the list goes on. It's a tricky business, motherhood."

"How come you're telling me all this now?"

Claire tilted her head in thought. "I guess to reassure you that it's okay to feel ambivalent. If you're not up for having another child, that's totally understandable. But if you decide you are, it'll be different this time around, and I think that'll be both a relief and a challenge."

Jocelyn was considering her mom's words when Claire added, "Anyway, what does Kyle say?"

"I haven't told him yet."

Claire's eyes went wide. "No?"

"I was remembering when I told Luke about Junie." How excited she'd been to share her news, and how completely Luke had shut her down—and then how quickly he'd been out of her life.

"Oh, honey," Claire said. "You kids were so young. Plus, Kyle couldn't be more different from Luke. Still, you tell him when you're ready. And you're lucky, because I was about to ask you to move those boxes, and now you're off the hook. Would you round up the colored pencils instead?"

"Sure, Mom."

Jocelyn pictured Kyle's face, and the joy that would spread across it as she described their future.

◆ ◆ ◆

The sun was high in the sky when Jocelyn arrived at Nauset Light. She flung off her sandals and took in the view: sparkling sea, steep cliffs, iconic red-and-white lighthouse in the distance. There was a reason travel brands named this one of the world's most beautiful beaches. Bright bursts of umbrellas dotted the shore, along with chairs and blankets and all the accoutrements for a day at the beach. A cluster of kids was building an impressive drip castle in the wet sand, and a couple of skiffs bobbed out in the water.

Jocelyn spotted Kyle down the shore. He noticed her and waved, and as he came closer, she was reminded of the first time they met: those kind eyes and how she'd felt she already knew him.

"Hi," he said, and kissed her. "I missed you."

Jocelyn basked in his gaze, feeling lit up from within. "I missed you so much. Can we not be apart again?"

"Sure, let's always stay together."

They walked along the water, flowing waves rinsing their feet and then retreating.

"So, this beach," Jocelyn started. "I only come on my own, at night, when there are no people." No mothers and children, she meant.

Kyle nodded. "But today you invited me here, in the afternoon."

"Yes." Jocelyn squeezed her fists, then launched in: "You know what's crazy? I've told myself a million times that what happened to Junie was a senseless tragedy. And it's been a long time since I devoted my days to beating myself up over it. But I also never truly let myself move on. It's like I have to keep pressing on the wound to make sure it's still there."

"That doesn't sound crazy to me," Kyle said.

"I don't really remember the aftermath. I mostly slept away the days, or tried to. Junie had been my anchor, and without her . . ." Jocelyn couldn't describe the feeling, which was more like the absence of feeling, how without her daughter it seemed as if she might float away and evaporate. "But the nights were different. I'd be wide awake. I'd come out here, hoping, bargaining, thinking impossible thoughts. Like, if I just kept returning to the place where I'd last held her in my arms, soon enough she'd come running back to me."

Kyle took her hand.

"One night I dove right into the water. I was searching and searching, my eyes peeled. I don't know how long I was out there, but at some point the sea spit me back out. I was numb and sluggish, which wasn't so unusual back then. But it turned out to be hypothermia. A mild case, luckily."

Kyle frowned. "Oh, Jocelyn."

"My dad suggested we scatter her ashes here. After that, my mom started coming to the beach at night, to watch over me, I guess. She'd stay in her car, but I knew she was up there. Sometimes I'd go sit with her. Somehow a year passed."

Kyle squeezed her hand.

"When I got my real estate license, everyone was so relieved, like thank god I was finally moving forward with my life. But I felt like I was just standing by, watching other people move forward, into their new houses, and their new lives. And I never stopped coming out here."

"Grief doesn't have a timeline," Kyle said. "You love your daughter."

Jocelyn was grateful he hadn't used the past tense. She was grateful for him. "Kyle," she said, "I'm pregnant."

A flash of excitement passed over his face before she saw him temper it. "And are you happy about that?"

"I think so. A little scared, too."

Kyle brightened. "Oh, good. I feel exactly the same." He placed a palm over her belly and laughed. "Well, so much for surfing lessons this summer."

"You and Nina can take them."

They came upon a pile of driftwood configured like a bench. They sat down and looked out at the water. "How will we do it?" Jocelyn asked.

There was so much to work out—practically, logistically—but that's not what she meant, and Kyle knew it. "We'll figure it out," he said. "We've both done it before, and we both have so much love to give. Truly, what else matters?"

He was right. Jocelyn was full of loss and full of love—both things were true.

When the light began leaching from the sky, they walked back to the parking lot. "So, have you spoken to your sister?" Kyle asked.

"No, not yet." The thought of talking to Maddy still scared Jocelyn—would her sister slam the door in her face all over again? But she felt hopeful, too, imagining their reconciliation.

"Well, in your own time," Kyle said.

They parted ways, driving caravan-style to his house, then reunited on the front steps. Kyle's fingers graced the small of Jocelyn's back, and they walked through the door together.

Chapter 24

MADDY

The last week of school had a strange charge to it: everyone energized with their coming freedom, but wistful, too, for all they'd be leaving behind. Maddy was feeling as sentimental as the seniors—she wouldn't be returning in the fall, either.

The debate team was gathered one last time to live stream nationals. Maddy watched the kids as they watched the screen: Gus ribbing Kim for taking notes, Layla cracking jokes. They'd built something special together, and now it was over. The live stream ended, and the group disbanded.

Except Kim, who hung back to help Maddy with the finicky projector screen. She rolled her eyes as a woman entered the auditorium. "Mother, I said I'd meet you outside."

"But I wanted to meet the famous Ms. Marx. Hi, I'm Christine, Kim's mother."

"A pleasure to meet you," Maddy said. "Kim's a star, as I'm sure you know."

"She's such a fan of yours," Christine said. "You've helped her enormously." Kim was turning red, and Maddy quelled the urge to muss her hair. "So Kim tells me you used to do branding in New York. I own a little outfit called Kanoodle."

"I love that place," said Maddy. Kanoodle was a local gift shop slash café whose coffee had a cult following.

"Well, we're expanding, and I'm looking for a marketing person. I'm sure it's small potatoes compared to what you're used to, and just part-time for now, but I can pay well: city rates." Her laugh made the gold bangles on her wrists jangle.

"That sounds intriguing," said Maddy.

"Fabulous, here's my info." Christine handed her a card, which Maddy clutched like a golden ticket. "Shoot me an email." She patted Kim's back. "Let's skedaddle, kiddo."

Now Maddy was alone on the stage, telling herself she wouldn't cry, but doing it anyway. One last time, she shut off the lights and left.

Back home the aroma of garlic and ginger carried her to the kitchen. There was Justin stirring at the stove, with Rose underfoot. Maddy scooped up her daughter and kissed her husband hello. Since the birthday incident, they'd closed ranks: staying home in the evenings, focusing on their little family. They ate dinner with Rose's high chair nestled between them—everyone within reach.

Over a shrimp stir-fry, Maddy related the interaction with Kim's mom.

"Sounds like a great opportunity," Justin said.

"Yeah. But I was also looking forward to my summer with Rose."

Justin smiled. "A few months ago I never could've imagined you saying that."

"I know." Maddy touched her nose to Rose's. "Everything feels different now."

"I guess we should thank your sister for making us appreciate our kid so much."

Maddy screwed up her face, and Justin held up his hands in defense. "Sorry, too much. But I will say, that terrible night gave me a glimpse into what it would be like to really lose your kid. I give Jocelyn a lot of credit for picking herself up and rebuilding her life."

"Yeah." Maddy shifted in her seat. She knew she could never grasp how much Jocelyn had suffered, but she also didn't want to talk about her sister right now. "Well, everyone finds ways to manage after loss."

"True," Justin said. "I think back to when we were trying to get pregnant—all that false hope and disappointment, for all those years."

His words pressed at something tender in Maddy. She'd worked so hard to move past that time, when she'd walked around like an open wound, shot through with sadness. "Do you remember when my mom sent me that awful poem, about how life is short and miserable? After I'd just miscarried again." Maddy had scanned the lines about a stoned bird and a child sunk in a lake, her indignation rising, thinking, how could Claire have been so insensitive?

Justin shook his head. "And my mom suggested I return to my old firm—get back on a real career path, given that the whole baby thing didn't seem to be happening."

"What a bitch," Maddy said. "Sorry."

"And your boss gave you an Edible Arrangement."

Maddy groaned. "Who on earth wants a bouquet of overripe fruit?" She'd pictured pelting Susan with those pineapple flowers and stabbing her with the toothpicks.

She swallowed hard—all that anger had masked such sorrow. And Justin hadn't wanted to talk about it back then, but here he was, talking about it now. She clasped his hand, and they each took one of Rose's chubby fists. "Well, look at us now, right?" she said.

"We're lucky," Justin said.

"So lucky."

◆ ◆ ◆

Justin was cleaning up the kitchen and Maddy had just put Rose down when her phone pinged. She did a double take at the text on-screen: Hey, can I stop by?

She'd been waiting weeks for Jocelyn to reach out and apologize. But now that it was probably happening, Maddy realized she wasn't ready to face her sister. "Sorry, it's late," she typed, pressing "Send" before she could second-guess herself. She watched the bouncing ellipses appear and disappear in Jocelyn's reply bubble, then disappear altogether. She set her phone aside and went to read her book.

She was plugging in her phone before bed when she saw the new message. She held her breath as she read: I'm so sorry, Mad, truly. This isn't an excuse, but it turns out I was newly pregnant that night and it had me all messed up. I think the baby stuff will always be tough for me. I can't really explain what I was thinking, but I know I fucked up. I understand if you don't want me around Rose, though I'll miss her terribly. Hopefully we can talk soon.

Maddy's mind spun. She felt hollow. The only word she could really take in was *pregnant. Jocelyn was pregnant.* When Justin climbed into bed, she tried to sound neutral as she related the news.

"Holy cow," Justin said brightly. "I'm happy for her."

"Me too." Maddy *was* happy for her, but it was cut through with a creeping envy as familiar as her twin's face. "It's just, I'm worried she'll do it better than me."

"Oh, babe," Justin said, and left it at that. Maddy appreciated how he listened to her without judgment; how he'd never insisted it didn't have to be a competition between her and her sister—because how could it not be?

Back when they'd started dating, Justin had asked what it was like to have a twin. Maddy hadn't sugarcoated it: She'd described the envy that was her constant companion, almost like an extra limb. She'd expected Justin to be shocked or disgusted, but instead he looked sympathetic, saying, "You know, Socrates called envy the ulcer of the soul." Maddy had never felt more understood.

She still thought of that exchange. But now it occurred to her, there were probably treatments for ulcers.

Chapter 25

JOCELYN

"Are you sure you want to do this now?" Betsy asked, leading Jocelyn to the storage space in her basement. "With your mother's party later?"

"That's the point," Jocelyn said. "I've got two hours, tops, and I already put on mascara, so I can't get too emotional."

"Whatever you say." Betsy flicked on the light and pointed. "There."

It was a small stack of boxes, ordinary as could be. Jocelyn had been down here dozens of times over the years, to grab a light bulb or a paper-towel roll, and she'd never suspected that right there, boxed up in the corner, were her baby's things.

Betsy first admitted to the existence of the boxes just last week. For months after Junie died, Jocelyn hadn't disturbed the mosaic of toys and stuffies scattered across the nursery; she hadn't displaced a single onesie or shoe. Until the morning when suddenly she couldn't stand to look at any of it. She'd brought in garbage bags, and Betsy to help. As they purged the room of every totem of her pain and loss, Jocelyn hadn't realized her friend was secretly saving stuff, predicting that Jocelyn might want it later.

Now it was later—a decade later. Jocelyn's mouth went dry when Betsy related the fact of the boxes. She wasn't sure she wanted to see them, but Betsy encouraged her to at least look.

She sliced open the first box, and her breath caught in her throat. There was the white muslin dress with the Peter Pan collar. Claire made the dresses for every baby Marx girl—for her own daughters, and then her daughters' daughters. Jocelyn ran her fingers along the embroidered forsythia and remembered Junie wearing it at her baby naming. Cradling her in her arms, Jocelyn had given a little speech about how *Juniper* means "young and evergreen." The memory was almost too much to bear.

"It turns out I'm not ready for this," she told Betsy. "Also, I really hope I'm having a boy."

"Here, try this one." Betsy beckoned her to a box filled with toys. Peeking out was the stuffed dolphin Junie had dragged everywhere, its dorsal fin worn thin.

Jocelyn hugged the stuffie to her chest just as Junie had always done while drifting off to sleep. "I'll take this."

"Good, that's a start."

◆ ◆ ◆

An hour before Claire's retirement party, Jocelyn still hadn't heard back from Maddy. Her silence was stressful. Jocelyn refolded her sweaters, then checked her phone; she organized her junk drawer, then checked her phone again. Was her sister planning on ignoring her indefinitely? Was Jocelyn to be punished forever?

She was going to be late. She threw on her batik maxi dress and examined herself in the mirror; she turned sideways, pulling the material taut across her middle, even though it was too early to be showing. She felt a flash of déjà vu: She'd worn the same outfit to Maddy's baby shower last spring. So much had gone wrong between the sisters since then—since always, really.

But tonight was their mother's night. Jocelyn was proud of her mom for having touched so many kids with her teaching. Although, to her, Claire's most important role was as her mother, which thankfully she wouldn't be retiring from anytime soon.

The party was already underway in her parents' backyard. Kyle and Nina went to scope out the food—a team of cater-waiters was setting out trays, and Jed was at the grill, sporting his "Proud Hubby" apron. Jocelyn found Claire by the coolers, nursing a beer and squinting at the "Happy Retirement" banner hanging askew from the deck.

"Nice party, Mom," she said, digging a ginger ale out from the ice.

"It's very lovely, and I look forward to when it's over," Claire replied.

The party had been Jed's idea, naturally—he'd said closure was crucial. And despite Claire's reluctance, Jocelyn agreed with her dad that Claire would be glad to have spent an evening celebrating her career with her community.

Claire peered up at the sky. "Rain's on the way. I can feel it in my hip." Just a few clouds mottled the sheet of blue, but the air was near solid with humidity. "Just like at your high school graduation party, remember?"

"Right." It came back to Jocelyn in a rush: Jed pontificating about her and Maddy turning over a new leaf, gesturing to the flipped-over maple leaves, and right on cue, the downpour had begun. "Maddy's friends all ran for cover. Mine had a dance party."

"Of course. You girls." Claire waved to a pair of women, then turned back to Jocelyn. "Cricket, have the two of you talked yet?"

"I tried," Jocelyn said. "She wouldn't see me, so I texted her an apology. No reply."

"I see." Claire finished off her beer. "Why not give it another try? Look, she's right there." She pointed with the neck of her bottle, then nudged Jocelyn practically right into her sister.

Jocelyn uttered a hesitant "Hey."

"Hi," said Maddy, her mouth set in a line.

"End of an era, huh? Mom retiring." She was feeling out her sister's mood.

Maddy rolled her eyes. "Can we not with the small talk? I got your text. I haven't had a chance to write back."

Jocelyn nodded tentatively. "I wanted to tell you those things in person."

"Well, here we are now." Maddy's jaw was clenched. "Anyway, I see you're drinking ginger ale. How are you feeling?"

"Not great, actually." At the moment Jocelyn's insides were even wobblier than they'd been in recent weeks.

"Yeah, well, you're not twenty anymore."

Jocelyn swallowed the sting—Maddy's words were flippant, but true. "To be honest, I'm all mixed up about being down this path again. That's what was going on at the beach that night—I was confused, and scared. I know how scared I made you, too. I hope you can forgive me. I'm really sorry."

"Thanks," Maddy said. It was an acknowledgment, if not absolution. "And you'll be fine, Joss. You were born to be a mother."

"You know, our kids will grow up together." It was the first time Jocelyn had thought of that—their children would be cousins. "They could be close."

"Or they might hate each other." Maddy shrugged, and they both laughed a little. "So, what about Kyle? Where will you guys live?"

"We're still discussing it. Of course, I hope they move out here. We haven't told Nina yet. We're waiting till the second trimester."

"That makes sense," said Maddy. "I can pull together some of Rose's things for you."

"Thanks. Apparently Betsy saved a lot of Junie's stuff, too. I started going through it earlier."

Maddy's eyes widened. "How was that?"

"Oh, a breeze." Jocelyn's eyes filled and she blinked away the tears. "It's just, I'm scared I won't be able to do this again. There's all this shit from before that's been bubbling up."

"Grief is weird, Joss." Maddy held out a tissue, and Jocelyn wiped her face.

"Do you remember after Junie died, how you tried to send me on that spa weekend?" Maddy nodded. "I know you meant well, but it felt like you hoped I'd get a massage and a facial, then just get over it." Tears were streaming down her face.

Maddy watched her intently. "I'm sorry, Joss. I was younger than you back then—I mean, more than the eight minutes. I didn't have a clue about what you were going through, or what I should do. I was terrified to face you. I'm so sorry I didn't go to Junie's funeral. It's my biggest regret."

"Thanks," said Jocelyn. "You know what, though? I was so full of anger, and the easiest target was you. Much easier than being angry at the world, where random, senseless tragedies occur. Or at myself, for making one decision that ruined everything. Or at Junie, who dared abandon me." She let out a sob. "I was actually so fucking furious at her. Can you imagine, being furious at a baby?"

Maddy nodded. "Uh, definitely. I was furious at Rose for months. And at you, too, for having done it so well, when meanwhile I was such a wreck of a mom. Honestly, I'm worried you're gonna show me up all over again. I know it's awful, but I kind of can't stand that you're pregnant."

"I get that," Jocelyn said, smiling a little. "And frankly, I like knowing you have these petty thoughts, so I can feel superior. Obviously my own thoughts are perfectly pure."

"You're a goddamn angel," Maddy said.

Jocelyn took a deep breath. "I shouldn't have been so hard on you when you were struggling after Rose was born. I should've been there for you."

"I appreciate that," Maddy said. "It's okay."

Jocelyn flashed on something Maddy had said in the heat of their fight at Betsy's party. "Hey, and about what went down with that guy back in high school—I never knew." Maddy hadn't elaborated on what happened, but Jocelyn got the gist. "How awful."

"Yeah."

Jocelyn held up her fists. "Should we track him down and unleash some Marx-sister vigilante justice?"

"Great idea. I'll check my calendar."

Maddy wore a crooked semi-smile, and Jocelyn felt her own lips twist up into the same expression. Replicas of her own hazel eyes stared back at her. Had the two sisters ever faced each other so squarely, or spoken so directly? Jocelyn felt she could go on looking at her twin like this forever—at the profile she knew better than her own, at the constellation of freckles she could map from memory.

And then the rain began, a sprinkle at first, growing steadier. Someone turned up the music—Vampire Weekend's "Walcott"—and Jocelyn grabbed Maddy by the arm. "Dance with me."

"We'll get drenched."

"So?" Jocelyn was already bopping to the beat.

Maddy started moving, and soon the two of them were flailing and twirling, dredging up dance moves from their youth. Jocelyn thought again of their graduation party—how as each song ended, the two of them would trade off darting to the boom box to switch out the CD, so the soundtrack ping-ponged between indie rock (Jocelyn) and top-forty pop (Maddy).

Rose crawled over, and Maddy picked her up and bounced her on her hip, despite her muddy knees. Jocelyn didn't dare reach for her niece, but after a moment, Maddy handed her over.

Jocelyn hugged Rose tight and spun her around, singing along to the lyrics about wanting to get out of Cape Cod tonight, even though she herself was totally content right where she was.

Chapter 26

MADDY

Dancing in the deluge with her sister like a couple of maniacs, Maddy suddenly sensed something was wrong. It was a blip at the edge of her vision—but what? She searched around and saw guests dispersing, Jed taking down decorations, Kyle closing deck umbrellas, and Justin helping with the waterlogged food. She looked up to find her mom framed by her bedroom window; it was classic Claire to slip away from her own party to observe it from afar. Finally, Maddy spotted what she was looking for: Nina, slumped in an Adirondack chair at the far end of the yard, crying in gasps.

Maddy flashed back to her conversation with Jocelyn. She could now sense the shape of the girl hovering nearby as Jocelyn mused about her pregnancy and future plans. Maddy grabbed her sister— still swaying with Rose—and indicated Nina. "I think she overheard us talking."

"Oh no," said Jocelyn.

They found Kyle on the deck. When Jocelyn filled him in, a stricken look passed over his face. "I'll go talk to her."

The sisters hung back and watched. As soon as Nina noticed her father approaching, she stood up and started yelling. Kyle seemed to be trying to calm her down, but a moment later, Nina overturned the Adirondack chair and darted from the yard.

Kyle slumped back toward the deck. "She said if I went after her, she'd run out onto Route 6."

Jocelyn rubbed his back. "I'm so sorry. She's probably just blowing off steam. She'll be all right."

But Maddy felt compelled to act. She grabbed her keys, and Jocelyn's sleeve, and they strode to her Range Rover. It took about two minutes to catch up to Nina, who was trudging along the side of the road, head down and hoodie soaked through. Maddy rolled down the passenger-side window. "Hey!" she called out.

Nina glanced over and rolled her eyes. "Oh my god."

"Are you okay, sweetheart?" Jocelyn asked. "Why don't you get in the car?"

"I'm fine. Leave me alone."

Jocelyn persisted: "It's pouring out. Come on, Nina, hop in."

"Go away, I'm begging you."

Maddy drummed her fingers against the steering wheel, thinking. "We'll leave you alone, but we're not leaving. You don't have to get in until you're ready."

Nina pulled her hood tighter and kept walking. The car crawled along to match her pace, and Maddy rolled up the window to stop more water from leaking in.

"This was a good idea," Jocelyn whispered. "Nina's been so mad lately."

"Well, what do you expect?" Maddy whispered back, not that Nina could've heard them now. "Is there anyone moodier than a tween girl?"

"Still, I can't believe I was so careless," said Jocelyn. "I mean, to find out your father's having another kid, and you might have to move, and the whole thing's been kept a secret from you. Plus, to hear it from me, who Nina is not exactly a fan of these days—what a betrayal."

"It was a mistake, Joss. It's okay to make a mistake. She'll forgive you." Maddy's eyes told her sister, *Just like I have.*

The rain held steady, and they let Nina plod along for several more minutes. It was nearly dusk. Finally, Maddy rolled down the window again. "Nina Taylor," she commanded with as much authority as she could muster, "get in this car right now."

It actually worked. With a dramatic sigh, Nina flopped onto the back seat, probably soaking the leather. Maddy passed her a box of tissues. "Are you ready to go home now?"

Nina's voice was a squeak: "Um, can we go to Duck Pond instead?"

Maddy considered it. "I don't see why not." Jocelyn looked confused, so Maddy explained, "We searched for you and Rose there."

"Ah."

They drove in silence to the turnoff, then bumped along the narrow dirt road, tires sending up cascades of water at each puddle. In the parking area, they stayed in the car until the rain let up to a drizzle.

Maddy gestured for Jocelyn to hang back, as she got out to follow Nina to the pond. The two of them stood watching raindrops pelt the surface, and a flock of gulls taking flight.

Nina must've sensed that Maddy was trying to figure out how to address what had gone down earlier, because she crossed her arms and said, "I don't want to talk about it."

"You don't have to," Maddy replied. "But I think you heard some things you weren't meant to hear. And I get it, you're mad."

"I'm frickin' furious," Nina spat. "I can't believe they didn't tell me. I'm not a little kid. It's not fair! I don't want to move again. And I definitely don't want my dad and Jocelyn to have a baby."

"Yeah, siblings are pretty terrible," Maddy said. She saw Nina stifle a smile. "But it probably won't be as bad as you think."

"Oh my god, spare me. I'm so sick of grown-ups saying, 'It'll get better.'"

"I hear you. I for one think that's bullshit." Nina looked up a little. "Sometimes things get better, but sometimes they get worse—much worse. Life isn't a straight path, and a lot of the time, you don't have any control over it, which is totally infuriating." Maddy knew she was talking in platitudes, but there was truth to her words—which she herself had only recently come to accept. She didn't really expect any of it to sink in for Nina. "Anyway, I'm sorry things feel so shitty right now."

"Hey, guys," Jocelyn said, coming down the path. "Anyone up for skipping rocks?"

"The water's pretty choppy," Maddy said.

Still, Jocelyn set about foraging for ammo. The rock she handed Maddy was perfectly flat and round.

Both sisters' attempts plopped right in the water.

"You try," Jocelyn told Nina, holding out an ideal skipping rock. Nina hurled it overhand—she had a strong arm—then glared back at Jocelyn, as if to suggest where she really wanted to throw it.

Jocelyn didn't react. Instead, she held out another rock and demonstrated the wrist-flicking motion. "Try it like this."

Maddy held her breath for Nina's next move. After a moment the girl took the rock and flung it out, imitating Jocelyn's form. Incredibly, it skipped twice across the water's skin.

"Look at that, you're a natural," Jocelyn said.

Nina's grin was barely perceptible.

Maddy clapped. "Okay, folks, I think it's time to haul out."

They hiked back to the car, the sisters flanking the girl.

"You know," Maddy said, glancing to the back seat before she veered onto Route 6, "a lot of people assume this place is dead in the offseason. But if you end up moving here, you'll find out that that's the best time. The locals have the run of the place, and you should see the beach covered in snow—it's like a different planet." This was another thing Maddy had recently learned, or, actually, relearned: the magic of the Cape all year round. She was looking forward to summer, of course, but it was cozy here in the fall and peaceful in the winter.

Jocelyn shot her a look, like, *Enough with the Cape Cod relocation campaign.*

As they pulled into their parents' driveway, Kyle ran toward them. Maddy urged Nina out: "Go on, you'll be fine."

She watched the reunion through the windshield—Kyle clutching his daughter.

"Thanks for this, Mad," Jocelyn told her, "really." Maddy was about to say no problem, but Jocelyn was already out, approaching Kyle. Keeping one arm around Nina, he pulled Jocelyn in with the other; then Jocelyn placed a hand on Nina's back. Maddy thought, *Now there's a family.*

Justin emerged from the house with Rose in his arms, and Maddy's heart surged at the sight of her own family. Everyone was here, okay, back in their rightful places.

Chapter 27

JOCELYN

Nina had soccer camp for the month of July, and this time when Kyle asked Jocelyn to join them in Boston, she agreed. She was strolling through the Public Garden, the roses in such full bloom it was almost obscene, when her obstetrician's name flashed on her phone. Jocelyn steeled herself to answer.

"Congratulations," the doctor said, "your fetus is female."

"Oh. Thanks." Jocelyn hung up and dropped onto a bench, where she didn't move a muscle. Around her people were jogging and playing Frisbee and setting out picnics; kids were racing around the green and squealing from the swan boats. How did they all have such energy? And did doctors ever make mistakes about such things? Jocelyn doubted it. So, she'd be having another girl.

It took her a while to get up and moving again, and soon she spotted the *Make Way for Ducklings* sculpture. She patted Mrs. Mallard on her bronzed head and thought of the picture book her mom had read to her as a child—about the brave mother duck leading her ducklings home through downtown traffic. As she stepped off the curb to Charles Street, Jocelyn told herself that she, too, could be a mother who bravely navigated the world to take care of her daughter. She'd done it before, and she could do it again.

◆ ◆ ◆

That evening Jocelyn cooked her mom's Moroccan chicken and rice. "That smells good," Nina said in her new subdued way.

Since Claire's retirement party, they'd come to a gentle détente. Kyle had grounded Nina for a week for running off, and she'd accepted her punishment without complaint. She got herself up and off to the camp bus each morning, and when she returned in the afternoon, she kept to herself in her bedroom until dinner.

"I have news," Jocelyn announced to the table. Kyle regarded her expectantly, while Nina kept her eyes on her plate. "Nina, you're going to have a sister."

Kyle's gasp made up for Nina's nonreaction. "A baby girl, wow!" Jocelyn tried on a smile, willing his enthusiasm to wash over her; it worked, mostly.

Nina piped up: "We don't actually know if they'll be a girl or a boy or nonbinary."

"That's true," Jocelyn said. They didn't know much of anything about this being growing inside her, which was oddly reassuring.

"Well, whoever they end up being," Kyle said, "they'll grow up in a home full of love, and with the best big sister."

"Also true," Jocelyn said.

Nina asked to be excused. Moments later, Billie Eilish's breathy voice emanated from her room.

Kyle poured two flutes of grapefruit seltzer. "I know you were hoping for a boy," he said, "but I think this'll be wonderful. Cheers!"

"Cheers," Jocelyn echoed.

"How are you doing with the news?"

"Well, earlier I found myself communing with Mrs. Mallard, trying to draw inspiration from an inanimate duck."

"I mean, Mrs. Mallard is a badass," Kyle said. "Although I've always felt bad for Mr. Mallard, getting the shaft on that statue."

Jocelyn had forgotten all about the ducklings' dad. He was out of frame for most of the storybook, off finding a home for his family. It occurred to her that she wouldn't be on her own this time around, raising a child—things would be different in all kinds of ways.

Kyle leaned in for a kiss. "Thanks for including Nina in your announcement. I'm sure she appreciated it, even if she didn't show it."

"Of course," Jocelyn said. "We're family."

The day after Nina stormed off from the party, Jocelyn had sat her down and explained why they hadn't yet told her about the pregnancy: Miscarriages were so common early on, and they hadn't wanted to share something so big when it might've all come to nothing. Nina seemed to understand; still, she'd asked, if you had a miscarriage, wouldn't you want your family to know you were sad? Jocelyn was touched by the question.

"I'm okay, all in all," she told Kyle now. "You don't have to worry."

"Good. I think Nina's okay, too, right? All things considered."

"Sure. It probably helps that she can work out her rage on the soccer field all day."

"Definitely." Kyle laughed. "So when are you heading back?"

"Crack of dawn. I've got a showing at nine."

"I'll miss you. We'll be out there on Friday."

"I'll be waiting." Jocelyn recalled their original plan, for Kyle and Nina to spend the entire summer on the Cape. She was glad they'd changed it, that Nina wasn't on her own all day, at the beach or wherever, at loose ends.

Jocelyn herself felt at loose ends at the moment, her mind filled with the question of their future. She didn't get up the nerve to say anything until she and Kyle climbed into bed. She was staring at the smooth slab of ceiling—free of the cracks that crawled across her own bedroom ceiling—when she ventured, "You won't be able to move to the Cape full-time, will you?"

Kyle sat up, eyes bright. He'd been broaching the question of where they would live for weeks now, and Jocelyn had been putting him off. "You're ready to discuss this?"

She nodded, nervous, thinking how fond she was of those cracks in her ceiling.

"Well, it would be tough," he said.

"I get it." And she really did. "Nina's got her whole life here, and there's so much other change coming."

Kyle spread a palm over the slope of her stomach. "Have you given any more thought to moving up here?"

It was one thing for Jocelyn to face the fact that Kyle couldn't relocate to the Cape, but quite another for her to commit to moving off Cape. "I'm thinking about it."

Kyle kissed her cheek, then flicked off the bedside lamp. "Sounds like a plan."

It wasn't a plan, actually. But it was probably the solution, even if Jocelyn wasn't yet ready to admit it out loud.

◆ ◆ ◆

The baby started kicking her as they crossed the Sagamore Bridge, as if she shared Jocelyn's relief to be back on home turf—another Cape Cod girl. Only, not really, because she wouldn't grow up there.

And what about Jocelyn? How would she say goodbye to this strip of land, the ocean, her heart? And what about her work? She'd always considered real estate the thing she did to pay the bills. But the thought of *not* doing it made her realize how much it meant to her to find people their homes, to usher them from one chapter of their lives to the next. Maybe she'd try it in Boston—or, who knew, maybe she'd try something new.

She'd postponed discussing the future for so long, and Kyle hadn't pressed her. It wasn't just about leaving the place she'd always called home. Jocelyn knew that once their plans were set, she'd have to start nesting in all the usual ways: setting up a nursery, organizing the gear. Meanwhile, she was still busy readying her mind—excavating memories, like the tunes of lullabies, and the twists and turns required to tie a baby wrap, and trying to remember how on earth to move through the world when your heart was living outside of you.

A wistfulness for the present welled up in Jocelyn. She reminded herself that she still had half a summer left on the Cape. After that, she'd figure out how to let go.

◆ ◆ ◆

Maddy was late. Jocelyn couldn't remember a single other instance in their lives when her sister had been late. All month, they'd been meeting for sunrise walks at Fort Hill, and now August was nearly over. The days were shortening, and there was a crispness in the air. Jocelyn idled in her car, considering her day ahead: a showing, a stack of paperwork, and then Kyle and Nina would arrive around dinnertime. The sun was already peeking up over the salt marsh when Maddy's Range Rover roared into the lot.

"Don't even say it, I know." Maddy hopped out, assembled the stroller with a push of a button, and retrieved Rose, ready to go in less than a minute, though her face was all flushed. Jocelyn liked this version of her sister, not perfectly put together.

She held up her hands. "I didn't say a word."

"Well, I can tell what you're thinking," Maddy said.

"No, you can't." (She could.)

They set out on the trail, which wasn't really stroller-friendly, but Maddy seemed to relish the challenge. The reason she was late, it turned out, was that she'd been up past midnight finishing a presentation for the National Park Service, her newest client. She'd been tasked with revamping the national seashore's social media strategy. "We launched this tick awareness campaign with the park rangers—"

Jocelyn cut her off: "Wait, Tick Talk on TikTok? Nina's obsessed with those videos, all the rangers doing those dorky dances. You're the one behind that?"

Maddy nodded. "It's really been blowing up. The health department is tracking the rates of Lyme disease to see if it's making a difference."

"That's amazing, Mad."

"Also, I've got news: I'm starting my own branding business. Now that I've landed a few big clients."

"Like the bird-watchers' store?" Jocelyn quipped.

Maddy rolled her eyes. "Dad won't drop that. He keeps pressing them to hire me, claiming I'm an intermediate birder."

"In his dreams." One thing the sisters had always shared was a lack of interest in their father's favorite hobby. "But hey, look." Jocelyn pointed to a green heron taking flight from the salt hay, and they both tracked its arc across the sky. Like a football with wings—that was how Jocelyn would describe it later to Jed.

"You know what's funny?" Maddy said. "Back in New York, when I told my pregnancy group I was leaving the city, I felt all this pressure to justify it, so I invented a job I was moving for. And it's basically what I'm doing now, a year later."

"You must've manifested it," Jocelyn said, mostly kidding.

Maddy rolled her eyes again. "Something like that."

"I'm proud of you, Mad."

They stopped at a bench to watch the tail end of the sunrise: a fuzzy yellow ball against a blazing orange sky. It would be a clear day. Usually they had this view to themselves, but today a trio approached to ask directions to the Captain Penniman House. Both sisters pointed up the hill.

When the tourists were out of earshot, Maddy said, "I feel bad for them. They have to go back to wherever they live, and we get to stay here. We could watch the sun rise over the ocean every day if we wanted."

A lump formed in Jocelyn's throat.

"Hey, what's the matter?"

"Oh, everything makes me emotional these days," Jocelyn said. But that wasn't it. It was the secret she'd been harboring all summer, not yet ready to tell her sister. She inhaled sharply. "Actually, I'm leaving the Cape. I'm selling my house and moving to Boston."

"Ah, that makes sense," Maddy said. "Although I can't really picture you anywhere but here."

"I know, same."

"And what about work?"

Jocelyn shrugged. "I guess I'll be a mom for a while, then figure it out."

Maddy laughed. "I've heard that one before."

"Yeah," Jocelyn said. It felt so long ago, Maddy announcing she was moving back home. "Truthfully, I'm scared to leave."

"Because of Junie?"

It was an odd response, but also spot-on. Jocelyn knew that was why she'd stuck around all this time: to keep vigil over her daughter. She nodded.

"She'll stay with you, Joss."

It was true. It didn't matter where Jocelyn went, Juniper lived inside her. When she'd found out she was pregnant again, she was afraid to make room for the new baby, worried it would crowd out her love for Juniper. But her OB showed her a chart of her heart and explained how it was growing to ensure the proper flow of oxygen and nutrients to the fetus. Jocelyn's heart was literally expanding. Her love would grow and grow.

"And you'll still have Kyle's place," Maddy added.

"Yeah, we'll come some weekends. But it won't be the same."

Maddy shrugged. "It'll be something new."

"Speaking of new." Jocelyn felt a kick and drew her sister's hand to her stomach.

Maddy yelped. "Sorry, that creeps me out, even on someone else."

"Me, me!" squealed Rose from the stroller. She spread her palm next to her mother's, just in time for another rat-a-tat-tat of kicks. Her giggle was infectious.

Jocelyn peered out at the vista before them, the marsh lush with lime-green grass, the sky glowing silver with early light. "This has to be one of the prettiest places on Earth."

"The very prettiest," Maddy said.

Jocelyn wished for the sun to hover a little longer at the horizon. She considered the coming turn of seasons, how after summer's hustle, a hush would descend upon the landscape. Cape Cod could be two different places, with two distinct personalities.

The twins flashed each other matching smiles. The two of them had arrived together to this peninsula of salt water and sand, and then parted ways and come back together, and would soon be parting ways again. It had always been that way, and probably always would be: the sisters moving through each other like tides.

"I've got such a day today," said Maddy.

"Me too," said Jocelyn. "But let's just sit here awhile and look out at the sea."

Epilogue

One Year Later, August 2020

You never knew when it was the last beach day of the season. There were usually a handful of warm days in September and, if you were lucky, in October, too. But this year would be different: Today was the season finale for Jocelyn, a big one, and she'd chosen Nauset Light for the occasion. She and Kyle had packed up the last of their bags that morning, and tonight they'd be returning to Boston, so Nina could start hybrid school next week.

When the world twisted into something unrecognizable back in March, the family had banded together to face the uncertain future. Now it was the pod's last hurrah, and Jocelyn saw them in a slideshow of images: Maddy and Justin thwacking a ball back and forth with paddles, Maddy leaping and lunging despite her belly; Jed following a flock of terns overhead, binoculars fixed to his face; Claire and Rose making patterns in the sand with their toes; Nina in the ocean, cutting forceful strokes through the waves; and Kyle and Iris gathered here on the blanket with Jocelyn.

Iris kicked her feet and clung to her dolphin stuffie. She'd had a rocky introduction to the world back in February, screaming upon arrival and keeping it up for weeks, her infant rage obliterating all else. Jocelyn couldn't hold a single thought in her head. She survived those early weeks only because of frequent breaks, handing the infant off to Kyle and slipping on noise-canceling headphones. They were both exhausted, and often irritable with each other, but the muffled sounds of Kyle soothing their daughter at 3:00 or 4:00 a.m. made Jocelyn's chest go warm. Nina pitched in, too, sometimes calming her sister even after the adults failed. Plus, Jocelyn's parents and sister took day trips to come help when they could. Jocelyn had never felt so cared for, even as she was simultaneously a wreck. It was Maddy who suggested that maybe Iris was allergic to cow's milk protein—Rose's pediatrician had mentioned the possibility back when Rose was colicky—and the fix was like magic: They switched Iris to a special formula, and she settled within a day. Jocelyn had thought she could finally relax.

But then the virus started its spread. Jocelyn was still adjusting to life in Boston, and suddenly they were packing up and returning to the Cape. Kyle worked from the alcove in the bedroom, Nina attended remote school from the couch, and Jocelyn modeled tummy time for Iris down on the rug—everyone together under one roof, day and night. When Iris went down for naps, Jocelyn often took to bed, too, curling into a ball and ruminating on all the loss and grief, more than one hundred thousand people now dead. Most afternoons they bundled up and went to the beach, where Jocelyn would try to tune out the wider world, and focus instead on the things in front of her: the seagulls, the lobster boats, a pod of seals, her people. As Nina turned cartwheels, Kyle stayed close, holding Jocelyn's hand and carrying Iris in her puffer suit that made her look like a marshmallow. It was an intimate, unsettling time.

They survived the spring, and the summer, too. Now Iris was a sublime baby, cooing as Jocelyn burrowed her tiny toes in the sand. Jocelyn and Kyle formed a canopy over their daughter and kissed.

A shark flew in the sky, nylon fins fluttering in the wind. Jocelyn followed the string to its source: Betsy clutching the kite, along with Jewel.

The couple positioned their chairs six feet away from the others, offering everyone air hugs, then propping up a table to set out a spread of snacks. "Appetizers before the main event," Betsy announced. Kyle fixed Jocelyn a Triscuit with Brie and fig jam—a perfect bite.

Rose zigzagged up to their blanket, carrying the desiccated shell of a horseshoe crab. She collapsed next to Iris and plunked the shell onto her cousin's tummy. Jocelyn stopped herself from advising caution. A powerhouse of a toddler, Rose got enough scolding already from her mother.

"I'm two," she declared, as she'd been telling anyone and everyone since her birthday last week. She pointed to Nina traipsing up the beach. "She's a teen," she said, proud to know the word. She grabbed Iris's foot. "She's zero."

"Amazing!" said Jewel, echoing Rose's enthusiasm. It *was* amazing, Jocelyn thought; she was a mother to both a baby and a teenager.

Nina idled, dripping wet, and when Kyle wrapped her in a towel, she didn't even flinch. A grin spread across his face, and Jocelyn captured it in her mind like a photograph.

Justin and Maddy jogged up the beach. "Ninety-two volleys," Maddy reported. Her belly looked even bigger up close, a golden mound rising between two strips of navy-blue bikini. Her cheeks had grown rounder this time around, and lately for the first time in the twins' lives, strangers were asking if they were identical. "Should we try for one hundred?"

"Maybe later." Justin was already settled into a chair. "Gimme this Rosie."

Rose plunked into her father's lap, and Maddy eased herself into her own chair. As they munched on crackers and hummus, Maddy didn't seem to notice the crumbs collecting on the shelf of her stomach. She looked happy. Jocelyn memorized the image.

◆ ◆ ◆

Rose pressed her mouth to her mom's belly, crooning, "Hello, baby." Maddy was eager to see her as a big sister.

They'd started talking about a second child around when Rose turned one. Maddy thought two years was the ideal spacing for siblings: close enough in age, but also with some breathing room. Still, she'd felt scarred from her postpartum experience. So she decided to go off birth control, and just wait and see. Three months later, she was pregnant.

She hadn't been sick this time. With each passing week, she'd felt stronger and sturdier. She hoped this would translate into having an easy infant—or at least easier than Rose and Iris had been.

A part of Maddy felt smug when her niece was born so cranky. Jocelyn wasn't the paragon of motherhood anymore; she was a mess. But as it turned out, it felt more satisfying to help. Back when Rose had wailed nonstop as an infant, Maddy had discovered some tricks to soothe her—this one hold, a particular pacifier, James Taylor played on repeat—and she was happy to pass on that hard-won knowledge to her sister. Plus, she'd been the one to hit on the root cause of Iris's crying, and the look of thanks on Jocelyn's face was forever imprinted on Maddy's brain. Naturally, as soon as Jocelyn got some sleep again, she was back to her usual self: a shining star of a mother. Which, thankfully, Maddy had witnessed nearly every day since March, when her sister's family was suddenly back in town.

In those early weeks of the world going to shit, Maddy couldn't look away from the TV. She spent hours watching New York on the news: the eerily empty streets, the constant wail of sirens, the city brought to its knees. The scale of suffering was staggering, and Maddy found herself in mourning not only for the city she loved but also all over again for the fact that she'd left it behind. Still, she was thankful to be where she was, surrounded by wide open space and at least the illusion of safety. Plus, she had a toddler to take care of, and it was a relief to focus on simple tasks, like baths and meal prep. The outside world might've been in crisis, but her daughter still needed her. Not to mention the other child she was growing inside. When Justin appeared at the end of each workday, Maddy was flooded with gratitude. She thought of Krista, alone in her Upper East Side studio, and ached for her friend. Maddy knew how lucky she was.

"So what's the plan, folks?" she asked now. She was excited for Jocelyn and Kyle to be taking this next step, even if Jocelyn claimed it was only so she could legally adopt Nina.

"When do I throw my flowers?" Rose whined.

"Soon, my love." Jocelyn rustled her niece's hair, and Maddy blew a kiss to her impatient daughter.

"Just say the word." Betsy held up a folder. "I've got my notes."

"Thanks, Bets."

Betsy curtsied. "Respectfully, please address me as Madam Minister today." She'd gotten ordained online for the occasion.

Jocelyn lobbed a grape at her. "Not a chance."

"I've been looking forward to this," Kyle said, gazing at his wife-to-be, and Jocelyn beamed back. Maddy had finally gotten used to seeing her sister so in love.

"Everyone should come swimming first," said Nina. "The water's amazing out past the breakers."

Maddy piped up: "I bet Jocelyn wants to start getting ready." Really, she herself was not enthusiastic about ruining her makeup.

"I could go for a dunk," Jocelyn said. "We've waited this long to get hitched; we can wait another half hour."

So Justin helped Maddy up, Claire and Jed took their grandkids, and they all went down to the water. The afternoon light was growing slanted across the beach. The twins hung back a bit from the others. They watched Rose kicking up sand to send sandpipers skittering away, and Claire gently chiding her.

"She can be such a little shit sometimes," Maddy said.

Jocelyn chuckled. "Like mother, like daughter."

"Hey!" Maddy kicked up sand at her sister, further proving her point, she knew. She felt a sudden urge to share what she and Justin had been keeping private for months. "Guess what? I'm having a boy."

"No!" Jocelyn exclaimed, eyes wide, almost as if Maddy had said she was incubating an alien. It sort of felt that way, actually. "I didn't think that was possible in our family."

"I know," Maddy said. "I heard they pee all over the place while you're changing them. I have no clue how to take care of a boy."

"Me neither. But we'll figure it out."

Maddy appreciated that "we," even though in reality Jocelyn wouldn't be around to help figure it out. Maddy missed her already. "So when does your program start?"

"Next week." Jocelyn was going back to school to study psychology—she hoped to become a child therapist. "It's all remote, so I considered deferring. But I thought if I put it off, I might end up chickening out."

"Right," said Maddy. "Better to just go for it."

"You should see my stack of books. I don't know what I'm getting myself into."

"I mean, does anyone ever? You'll be great." Maddy couldn't imagine anyone better suited to help children.

"You ready?" Jocelyn asked.

"Yup."

"Me too."

◆ ◆ ◆

Jocelyn was perched at ocean's edge, little waves lapping up against her ankles, sun warm on her skin. Kyle was out in the surf with Nina, beckoning her in. She wished she could stretch out the day like taffy; she felt nostalgic for it already. She kissed her baby in her mother's arms, she looked out to sea and sent another kiss to her firstborn, and then she grasped her sister's hand and the two of them leaped in together.

Acknowledgments

Joelle Delbourgo, thank you for your continued faith in me and tireless championing of my work for the past dozen years.

Emily Freidenrich, right from the start you understood and believed in this novel, and I'm so grateful. Thank you for bringing me into the Lake Union fold.

Christina Henry de Tessan, it's been a dream to work with you on revisions. Your feedback pushed me to deepen the characters, and your edits elevated the story to another level.

Ariel Djanikian and Alicia Oltuski, every month I look forward to our meetings, to sharing our work, discussing books, and commiserating over and celebrating this writing life. I'm beyond appreciative of your support, not to mention your brilliant notes on this novel. Wise editors and kind friends, the both of you.

Juli Breines, you brought such insight to this novel, in draft after draft, and I'm deeply thankful.

Jessi Breland, Andrew Hart, and Adam Palmer, you are very smart people who offered very smart notes at various stages of this novel, and it's better because of your feedback.

Leslie Mullen, you are a true local who helped this washashore get the Cape details right. It means so much that every time I see you, you say you can't wait to read my next novel. Ashley Mullen, thank you for your helpful notes, too.

Katy Day and Kait Logan, thank you for showing my family more than fifty houses in the most intense housing market, which happily ended in our finding a home, plus friendship, and the inspiration for Jocelyn's job in this novel. Kait, thank you for the Realtor fact-check (and in record time!).

Nick Kuppens, when I asked if you'd fact-check my pages about clamming, you offered something better: to take me out to experience the real thing. Thank you.

Jen Doll, thank you for the debate fact-check. You were a tad overqualified for the job, having written a whole book on the subject.

Suzanne and Kyle Bartholomew, thank you for introducing me to the secret beach that made its way into this story, and for being the best summer people.

Erin Griffith and Matt Siefker, thank you for hosting Old Year's Eve parties so epic that I had to stick one in a book.

Zick Rubin, thank you for your legal advice, once again, which is worth so (so!) much more than what you bill me.

The Eastham Public Library staff, thank you for welcoming me to set up a makeshift office in your space, which happens to have the world's prettiest views. Thanks especially to Corey Farrenkopf, for your enthusiasm for talking shop and for fostering a local community of writers.

Tom DePeter, thank you for giving me the tools, the passion, and the confidence to pursue a writer's life, as I wrote in your memorial years ago. And thank you for inspiring me to follow in your footsteps to teach AP English.

Max Apple, you've been such an important mentor to me, and your writing workshops were my favorite part of college. You once told me my stories reminded you of Philip Roth's "Goodbye, Columbus," which is still maybe the nicest compliment I've ever received.

Jon Feldman, Tamara Fisch, Andrea Alfano, and Sandy Fernández—the BrainPOP editorial team—what a pleasure it's been to work with such talented writer-editors and decent humans for over a decade (!). If I weren't in such a good situation nine to five, I don't think I could commit to the before-hours fiction writing.

Mom and Dad, I couldn't ask for more supportive, loving parents. I know how proud you are of me, and it means the world. Thank you.

Seth and Adam, I wrote a novel about sisters, but I'm so lucky to have you as brothers. Seth, thank you for reading all the books I recommend featuring complex female characters, and for being the best five-minute book club partner. Adam, thank you for answering the phone at any hour, and for hyping me up by claiming this is one of your top-three favorite novels (along with *1984* and *The Shining*, lol).

Emilia, I may shoo you away when you hover over me, asking what I'm writing, but I cherish your curiosity and spirit. I've written hundreds and hundreds of pages about motherhood, but I could never capture the depth of joy and meaning I find in being your mother.

Damian, you always give me the time and space I need to write, you hold down the fort while I hole away with my laptop, and you believe in me even more than I believe in myself. I'm thankful beyond words to have you as my partner through this roller-coaster ride.

You, the reader, I'm so grateful you picked up this book, especially knowing there are countless other ways you could've spent your time. Writing wouldn't be the same without you. Thank you!

Book Club Questions

1. How would you describe Jocelyn and Maddy's relationship? Did your sympathy for one or the other shift over the course of the story?

2. The book explores motherhood in many different forms. How did you respond to these portrayals? Which one resonated most with you?

3. So much of Jocelyn's life is shaped by losing Juniper. How did you see that reflected in her choices and relationships? What is the novel saying about grief?

4. How does life on Cape Cod shape the characters? Could this story have taken place elsewhere, or is the Cape setting essential?

5. Jocelyn and Maddy both have experiences of falling apart and of rebuilding. In what ways do they mirror each other's journeys?

6. What did you think of Kyle and Justin—as partners and as fathers? Did either one surprise you?

7. How does Jocelyn's relationship with Nina evolve over time? Why is each an important yet complicated figure to the other?

8. How do Claire and Jed affect their daughters? Do Claire's optimism and Jed's wish for the sisters to be close help or hinder them?

9. What kinds of friends are Betsy and Kelsey, and how do they influence Jocelyn and Maddy?

10. By the end, do you think the sisters have truly forgiven each other, or simply found a way to coexist?

About the Author

Photo © 2025 Agata Storer

Lindsey J. Palmer is the author of four novels: *Reservations for Six*, *Otherwise Engaged*, *If We Lived Here*, and *Pretty in Ink*. She is the deputy editor of BrainPOP, an animated education site for kids. Previously, she was an editor at *SELF*, *Redbook*, and *Glamour*, and taught high school English. She holds a BA from the University of Pennsylvania and a master's in English education from Teachers College, Columbia University. Lindsey lives on Cape Cod with her family. For more information, visit www.lindseyjpalmer.com.